Roman Holiday

ALSO BY LIONEL WARD

The Shakespeare Thief (The First Elliot Todd Mystery)
Somerset Odyssey (The Third Elliot Todd Mystery)

Roman Holiday is dedicated to our dear friend Madeleine Mcauslan-Crine who sadly died in May 2023. She is the main inspiration for the character of Aggie who appears in this and the first book.

Roman Holiday

An Elliot Todd Mystery
Book 2

Lionel Ward

1 3 5 7 9 8 6 4 2

ISBN 13: 978-0-9532876

Roman Holiday

an occasion on which enjoyment or profit is derived from others' suffering or discomfort.

Oxford Languages

1

For book lovers there are few greater pleasures than the thought of sitting down with a new book. For myself, the owner of Ex Libris bookshop, this was a regular experience. What was particularly exciting for me was the thought I could order and receive new books, almost on a daily basis, that had never before seen the light of day (except, if you want to be pedantic, by the author themselves or their publishers and a few advance reviewers). I may also discover a gem from the past among our second-hand books; perhaps an old travel book with illustrations from a tour of Egypt from centuries ago, a first edition of a much loved classic or even a 'new' author that I had been unfamiliar with before.

'Like Christmas every day,' I said to Esther, my main employee and 'partner in crime' (as I liked to think of her) one late autumn afternoon when we already had our eyes firmly set on the approaching Christmas season. The sales over the last few weeks of the year were critical to the survival of our independent bookshop. Autumn was also when the majority of new titles for the year were published, so in book terms it was a bountiful time.

The book I had in mind to read that day, though, was not a new one. In fact, it was Esther who suggested I read it and was surprised I had not already done so, when it turned up in a box one day.

'Of course I know it,' I said defensively. 'I've sold a number of copies and heard many people sing its praises.'

The book we were talking about was *If On a Winter's Night a Traveller*, written by Italo Calvino. It is post-modernist fiction, a story about the reader trying to read a book. That much I knew. I suppose I may have been put off by that post-modernist tag. I favoured stories with a strong narrative, a beginning, a middle and end such as the books of Robert Louis Stephenson, condemned by 'stream of consciousness' writers like Virginia Woolf and by others as 'just a children's writer', though now, thankfully back in fashion. On the other hand, I did like the crazy, surreal *The Third Policeman* by Flan O'Brien, considered by many to be one of the first post-modernist novels. I digress.

'You have never been tempted to read it? You have to!' Esther had said.

This was one of the things I liked about Esther, whom I had employed the year before. Some might say she was being a little forceful or too insistent but it was her enthusiasm along with what I knew was her great knowledge and experience of literature that was infectious - and I knew that in the area of literature our souls touched.

Anyone who knows my earlier story will know that I wanted Esther's and my souls to meet in areas other than that of literature. By common consent, we got on very well but she had only recently been bereaved and was still grieving. I was not sure if she had had a chance to consider her own feelings towards me. We had, though, developed a very close working relationship and companionship that had been tested earlier in the year with the death of a Shakespeare expert, following one of the book talks we frequently held at our bookshop. This had been an unnerving experience for both of us, which I felt had brought us closer. I was happy enough for now that we were good friends and did not want to jeopardise that relationship.

The fact that I had not read *If On a Winter's Night* was an apparently glaring gap in my book reading experience and I felt an indecent haste to right that wrong. I also knew that she was very likely right about the qualities of the book, which I would no doubt enjoy and feel better for the actual experience of reading, what psychologists call *consummatory pleasure*. However, for the moment, I was still in a state of *anticipatory* pleasure as I walked home with my book later that November evening. It made me wonder which was the more powerful of the two, the anticipation or the real experience; the smell of the coffee or the actual taste? I also reflected that the anticipation of a good book was not always rewarded with a good experience in reading it. After all, despite the fact that I respected Esther's opinion and that the chances were that I would like the book, it did not mean that I would necessarily agree with her about it being a great book. Our friendship was an open and honest one, and neither of us was inclined to temper our critical faculties for the sake of a quiet life.

One thing I already liked about the book, was the title. As with the books *Do Androids Dream of Electric Sheep, The Curious*

Incident of the Dog in the Night-Time and *Love in the Time of Cholera*, the title drew me in and promised much. And, of course, it was perfect reading for the time of year. On cue and as if to set the scene, as I turned into the short drive that led to my house and opened the door, a thin drizzle started and the wind got up, sending a recycling bin clattering and a shiver through me. I was grateful to close the door and shut out the night.

Every room in my house, including my bedroom and the bathroom, was in part a reading room for me where, at a minimum, a clutch of books could be found, new and old favourites – in case of a reading emergency. But I also had a special reading room, a small sitting room with a few bookcases and a small fireplace. It wasn't the grandest fireplace in the world but it drew a good fire. In the dark months of autumn and winter this was my natural habitat. A cup of tea, a small fire of coal and logs just beginning to throw out some heat and I was ready for my reading experience – always a special one when I was starting a new book. It was the case that evening as I opened the book with its cover of chunky letters, underlined and falling against each other at random angles. The book addresses the reader directly. I began reading, *You are about to begin reading Italo Calvino's new novel, 'If On a Winter's Night a Traveller'. Relax. Concentrate. Dispel every other thought.* The author continues in this vein. I had just reached the point where he writes *try to foresee now everything that might make you interrupt your reading...'* when the phone rang.

It was my mother. It always seemed to me that she conspired to ring me at the most inopportune moments, that she had a kind of sixth sense that told her when these were, in this case watching the clock, as it were, until I had set and lit the fire, made my cup of tea and settled down with my new book. Of course, I knew that my feelings towards my mother in this respect were at heart entirely irrational and that Esther, who found my mother much more reasonable and even admirable and inspiring, had influenced me to moderate my attitude towards her, to make myself more amenable and to take more account of her wants and needs. However, I felt I had had some cause for genuine concern in recent times. In my estimation, she had been cavalier in a relationship with an academic assistant at the local university whom she had narrowly avoided marrying. She also had a habit of making me feel bad about the fact that I had not provided her with any grandchildren. Not oblivious to

Esther's criticism of my attitude towards her, I had developed a technique that I believe sales people, especially cold callers are taught: when you talk on the phone, smile as you are speaking. You will make a much better impression at the other end as human beings can differentiate vocal intonation between a smile and a non-smile (the theory goes) and the whole experience feels less challenging. So it was, when I picked up the phone and my mother said:

'Oh, good. Elliot you weren't busy were you?' I smiled and said:

'No, its fine,' even though I really felt it was a wrench to be taken away from my book and the cosy fire.

'I just wanted to ask you about Christmas.'

Ah, that old chestnut and potential can of worms. I sighed within, though outwardly keeping my composure – and my smile.

'I hadn't really thought about it,' I said, though really I had. There was also the question of where my mother would fit into Christmas. Would she stay with my brother or would she come over to me? Would I be expected to visit her? And what about Esther? Would it be a quiet Christmas for her and an opportunity to reflect on her late husband? Would she visit her father who, from Esther's account, seemed indifferent to her fate except when he was showing her off to his golf club chums? We had very few days off at Christmastime, just Christmas Day and Boxing Day. This did restrict my options.

My secret hope was that my mother would go to my brother and Esther would not go to her father, or her sister or brother or one of her girlfriends, or want to be by herself, but just want to have a quiet Christmas with me. We would get snowed in at my house, she would be delighted by my choice of book for her as a Christmas present (not yet chosen) which would go a long way to confirming that we were right for each other... I knew, in reality, that this was not going to happen. What my mother suggested next, though, was not that far removed from my fanciful speculation.

'I wondered if you and Esther wanted to come to me.'

This took me by surprise. My mother had tried, ever since Esther's arrival at the bookshop, to be a matchmaker for the two of us. Whilst becoming closer to her was something I earnestly desired, I respected her position of non commitment and resented what seemed to me was my mother's interference.

4

Besides, it was not as though we would be on our own but with my mother - and Esther frequently took my mother's side. It could work out to be counter-productive...

'Do you want me to ring Esther?' she asked.

Better to scotch any hopes before my mother made any firm plans.

'No,' I said more firmly than I intended, 'I mean, I think she planned to go to her father for Christmas.'

I did not know this at all but it was reasonable guesswork.

'I don't think it would be much fun with just the two of us.'

'No,' I agreed, perhaps too fervently.

'I've had an invitation to go to Dominic and family and I'm sure it will extend to you.'

'I'll check a few things and give him a ring. I'll see if I can catch him now, before it gets too late.'

This enabled me to put the phone down and get away with an uncommonly short exchange. I returned to my book (I could ring Dominic later) but could not help being distracted several times by the thought of what would happen at Christmas. This led me to put my mind over to which days we were closing at the bookshop, late night shopping and Sunday opening for the busy December period which, I realised, if I had been better organised, I would have given greater thought to already.

The next morning when I saw Esther at the bookshop I broached the matter of Christmas arrangements with her.

'My mum rang last night asking about Christmas.'

'I hope Elizabeth's well.'

'Yeah, I think so.'

Of course, I had not asked.

'Going to your dad?' I said.

'I hadn't really thought it through.'

She had just picked up an early illustrated second-hand edition of *Treasure Island* to price.

'This is rather nice.'

I went across and looked at one of the coloured plates.

'Yes, very.'

'You could come with me to my dad's at Christmas if you like,'

'What?'

'There's plenty of room. But then you probably ought to see your mum. Is that what you have arranged?'

'I think there's an invitation to my mother and me to my

brother's, but nothing's set in stone.'

An opportunity to be closer to Esther at Christmas? My Machiavellian side saw this as an opportunity to get to know her father and perhaps receive his approval. He may even become an ally in my quest for a closer relationship with Esther. At the same time I also knew that Esther was independent-minded and that she would not seek his approval if she really wanted to become closer to me or anyone else for that matter. The temptation to get to know her father better, though, was a strong one and I was also a little curious to see what he was like and whether I could spot any of Esther's characteristics in him.

'Of course, your mother could come too.'

Any thoughts I had of taking up Esther's offer suddenly seemed fraught with danger. My mother as chaperone again? Potentially disruptive and counter-productive. And what if my mother did not get on with her father? His golf clubbing, gardening and position on the parish council and, what appeared from Esther's description, aloofness, seemed a world away from my mother's radical chumminess. I could see arguments or, worse, long awkward silences. And what if they did actually get on? I didn't think I could bear a repeat of earlier in the year when my mother nearly became married to Nicholas Pearson – and it would make things even worse if it was with Esther's father.

'Elliot, what do you think?'

'Well, the thing is, I should really take the opportunity to see my brother and, as you know, we are only closed for a couple of days and I wanted to give you a bit of extra time away from work. It would be unfair to call Aggie in and I can easily manage the shop on my own after Christmas.'

'If you're sure? I'm sure my dad would be delighted to meet you. Catriona might be there too, though I don't think Tom will be.' They were Esther's brother and sister.

In the end, my thought was that I needed to act unselfishly and in the best interests of everyone and that this was likely to make Esther respect me more in any case. I was very conscious that if anything did come to pass between Esther and myself, it would be for real and, despite all my faults and sometimes irrational way of behaving, I did not want to mess it up. I was certain that other opportunities for me to meet her father would come along outside the frenetic and compressed period of the Christmas break, flattered as I was to be asked.

'Perhaps another time?'

'Of course.'

'Anyway, what did you think of the book?'

'Well, I only read the first couple of chapters. For a moment I thought I was reading the novel of *Brief Encounter*.'

'Ah, yes, all that stuff in the station at the beginning.'

'I think I need to give it a bit more time but I must admit I am already intrigued by it.'

2

There are Christmas lovers and Christmas haters. The haters despise the crass commercialism, the resulting wanton over-indulgence and the enforced company of family or friends, whose company they would not normally seek, over an intense few days which can sometimes seem more like a month of confinement. I felt particularly sorry for those who had to work in shops where *Jingle Bells* and the familiar collection of Christmas songs rang out from November onwards. We did not inflict this music on ourselves (or our customers) or any music come to that – despite the fact that I received a regular phone call from the Performing Rights Society asking me if I had a music licence.

Though I could accept that there were some negative aspects to Christmas, I had to come down in its favour. Christmas was for ourselves, as for many small High Street traders, the lifeline that ensured our survival for another year. There was something else, less easy to define, a general excitement and buzz that we felt as we became busier and busier. Best of all, there was a great feeling of community and, very often, warmth in our exchanges with our customers, many of whom had become our friends or acquaintances. We knew so many of our customers by their first names and I knew that several of them enjoyed coming in for a chat (sometimes a grumble) as much as for buying a book. There also seemed to be an increasing number of customers who felt as though they were making a stand by coming to us in favour of keeping trade and jobs on the 'High Street' rather than by going online to traders whose profits often went outside the country.

One key way of promoting ourselves and our books during Christmas was an annual Christmas catalogue, that we distributed far and wide through local newspapers and by tramping the streets during October and November evenings, pushing it through the doors of local businesses and residents. I hoped that our catalogue would not be too unwelcome. We received what seemed like weekly mail-outs for Pizza and, whilst piles of so-called junk mail can seem wasteful and irritating, compared to cold calling at the door or by phone, I had always felt pieces of paper were a less intrusive option when informative in some way (at least to book readers), as I believed our catalogue was.

We opened on Sundays in addition to the other days of the week during December and stayed open late on Thursdays. It was an exhausting but an engaging and satisfying time. There was myself and Esther, Aggie and the student employee, Anusha. Aggie had been with me ever since I had opened the shop and had become a firm and close friend. She had contemplated retirement on several occasions. Luckily for us, it had never quite happened. She proved an invaluable part time employee, loved by our customers, able to cover when either of us had to be away, and an extra pair of hands during our busiest time during the approach to Christmas.

Throughout the year we put on a number of book talks from authors and book club or reading events at the bookshop, less so in the busy Christmas period, but we did have one planned for mid December, a reading of Christmas pieces.

While Anusha, whose family was from Kerala and who mainly worked weekends, was propped on top of a ladder hanging up a Christmas bauble I asked her:

'Did you celebrate Christmas in India?' I knew that she and her family had moved here when she was quite small.

'Yes, we call Father Christmas *Christmas Papa*. We make up cribs in our houses and every house has a Christmas star. It's a big thing.'

'I don't suppose you know any Indian Christmas stories – I'm trying to get away from the Dickens thing.'

'I have a book of them at home. There's one I particularly like called *Salem's Christmas*. It's about a boy from Delhi who returns to his parents' home in Kerala for Christmas. He has a hard time to begin with but it all works out in the end.'

'Do you fancy reading it as part of our Christmas reading evening?'

'Yes, why not?'

A couple of days later I went to see my actor friend, Bill, at The Dirty Duck, the nearest thing to a local pub for me and a short walk from the bookshop. Bill had become a friend very soon after I opened the bookshop and ordered plays from me for the productions that he was involved in. I, in turn, made every effort to see any play that he had a part in.

'So nice to see a friend!' announced the rich fruity voice as I came through the door of the pub. He was perched on a stool at the bar, a gin and tonic beside him on the counter.

'Not on the beer tonight?'

'No, I've rehearsals tomorrow and beer has a derogatory effect on my vocal chords.'

He was an actor of the 'old school' - old enough to have taken part in repertory theatre, which meant he was willing and able to take on, more or less, any role.

I ordered a pint of Otter and we retired to a corner table where we chatted about the material.

'The trouble with Dickens is that it has been done so much,' I said. I think people are a little over familiar with it. Though your Dickens readings are always excellent, I have to say.'

'Perhaps just a smidgen of Dickens, then. We could do something from one of the less well-known of the Christmas books, perhaps *The Chimes*?'

'Yes, that's a possibility. There's also a nice jolly bit in *Pickwick Papers* as I remember, when they are all sitting down to lunch.'

'What about other authors? *A Visit from Saint Nicholas*?'

'Well, I think that's a bit overdone too. I was thinking about Tolkien's *Letters from Father Christmas*.'

'That's a good idea. And what about that Mark Twain one to his daughter where he pretends he is Father Christmas?'

'Yes, I can see that working. And there's the tragic story of the early death of his daughter behind it, which is very moving.'

'Well, yes, that's true, I can talk about that. And we have to have *A Child's Christmas in Wales*.'

'Oh yes, you can really go to town with your rich Welsh accent. I've heard it before when you did that play on Dylan Thomas. I think that was the first time I saw you in something. I really thought you were Welsh.'

'I thought you were going to say "I really thought you were Dylan Thomas". Or, at least, Richard Burton.'

'Of course, that too.'

'Your flattery is very welcome. "A little flattery will support a man through great fatigue" – as James Monroe said.'

It was difficult to be bored in Bill's company. He was always coming up with a memorable phrase or aphorism. Over the course of the evening, with a further gin and tonic for Bill and a second beer for me (and a bag each of cheese and onion crisps) we came up with a list of reading material, which I was to put together and Bill would read with possible small contributions from myself, Esther and Anusha.

*

I found a bit of time to catch up with my post first thing the next morning before the shop began to get busy. So much was dealt with by email now it was sometimes easy to forget there was still important information that came through the post. One of the envelopes contained a slim pocket travel guide. At first I thought it was a customer order but I soon realised that it was a gift to the bookshop from the publisher and an invitation to enter a window competition. January is traditionally a busy time for booking holidays. First prize was a week in Rome with runner up prizes of complimentary travel stock. Very often we missed out on competitions, especially at that time of year, as non-urgent pieces of literature had a tendency to get buried and, by the time we discovered them, the closing date had long gone. I mentioned the competition to Esther and passed the details over.

'Perhaps we should give that a go,' I said

'Yes, why not? We could get Anusha involved. What's the theme?'

'*A Roman Holiday.*'

I called across to Anusha.

'How do you fancy putting in a window for a competition after Christmas? We could go really overboard and put a scooter in there. I used to own one but, unfortunately, it's long gone.'

'I'd love to.'

Our large window at the front of the shop was good for this sort of window display as the glass pane went nearly to the floor and you could walk in big pieces as we had done for a military window the previous year.

'I think there's a guy who sells them in town. I could ask him if he wants to take part in a cross promotion.'

'Sounds great.'

'What about the film of the same name?'

'*Roman Holiday* with Audrey Hepburn and – was it Cary Grant?

'Gregory Peck.'

'I suppose everyone will be doing that.'

'Ah, but we could broaden it a bit. We could also feature *La Dolce Vita* and all the resonances about having a good time on holiday.'

'As I remember, *La Dolce Vita* is quite a dark film.'

'Well, yes, I think you're right, but the title conveys the right sentiment.'

'We may not win the main prize but that complimentary stock would be very useful – and, in any case, it may attract a few customers. It's good to create a bit of interest.'

A customer came to the counter with a pile of books and Esther began serving him.

'I'll put it in my new diary now for, January, so we don't forget,' I said.

When the customer had departed I quizzed Esther.

'So, what other Italian films do you know, I mean, apart from *La Dolce Vita* and *Roman Holiday*?'

I was testing her as I had a present in mind for her for Christmas. Perhaps I would not buy her a book after all.

'I love *The Bicycle Thief*.'

'Me too.'

'*Cinema Paridiso*, *Life is Beautiful*. Ah, and *La Strada*. I think that's all I can think of for now unless you count *Godfather and Godfather Two*.'

We had more than fifty people for the Christmas readings event. Esther read a Maya Angelo piece, I read *The Oxen*, Anusha the piece about the boy who travels back to Kerala - while Bill read everything else. There were interludes for mulled wine and mince pies and quite a few bought books from the various authors that we read from, along with several books that were nothing to do with the readings - mainly for presents as we were now so close to Christmas and it was on people's minds. Bill finished with his personal favourite, a reading from the beginning of *A Child's Christmas in Wales*. He began:

One Christmas was so much like another, in those years around the sea-town corner now and out of all sound except the distant speaking of the voices I sometimes hear a moment before sleep, that I can never remember whether it snowed for six days and six nights when I was twelve or whether it snowed for twelve days and twelve nights when I was six...

As he read I looked across at Esther and she smiled back. There was that feeling of friendship and community and I walked home afterwards with a warm glow, ready for the last few mad hectic days of Christmas trading.

3

The time between the Christmas reading and Christmas Eve was the most intense and profitable piece of trading of the whole year. We often found it difficult in the same day to manage receiving in the stock, contacting all the customers who had ordered books and dealing with all the customer sales and enquiries. Often, we had to work well beyond closing time. It was exhausting but there was also a deep feeling of satisfaction. I knew I would not get a day off until Christmas Eve and would have to work late into the night on many occasions. It felt like a mission, but a happy and productive one.

It was something of a relief when we finally reached Christmas Eve. I was looking forward to the few days of rest, though it did mean driving over to my mother and then on to my brother on Christmas morning, followed by a return trip on Boxing Day. Though Christmas Eve was a busy day in the shop, it was a more relaxed day than the preceding ones as most people had organised their main present buying by then. There were no more stock or customer orders to be processed and all the books were out on display. Nothing more was to be done except to serve customers at the till. There were a few customers who had started to celebrate Christmas early and were slightly the worse for wear from drink, but in general, most people were in a relaxed and convivial mood.

Anusha went home at lunchtime. As we moved into the afternoon of Christmas Eve, the gender of the customers became increasingly male. It seemed that they were willing to buy anything at the last minute as a Christmas present. Aggie, who was not working that day, came in to give us our Christmas cards. I was in the embarrassing situation of having forgotten mine to Aggie and spent an awkward moment behind a shelving unit hastily writing one to her.

'Coming to the church later?' she asked.

'Yes, I think I might.'

The waves of customers became less frequent as the light began to fade. The plan was that Esther would leave at three as she had a journey of several hours to her father. Before she went we exchanged a hug and presents and cards.

'You sure it's all right about the extra days?'

'Perfectly sure. As you know, nothing much happens after Christmas and most of the publishers and suppliers are closed for a few days.'

'Well, if you have any problems or get ill don't be afraid to ring. I can always come back early.'

She left smiling and waving and my heart skipped a beat. It would only be just under a fortnight but, at that moment, it felt like a long time to be without her company.

Then she called back, 'I will ring you on Christmas day to wish you a happy Christmas.'

That made me feel better.

I closed a little earlier than usual, at five rather than five-thirty, and then went home for a quick meal. By eight-thirty I was in The Dirty Duck with Aggie and Bill, and saw a number of familiar faces, many of whom were customers. Though it was Christmas Eve, I wanted to avoid having too many drinks before we walked up to the church. The service was termed Midnight Mass but began at eleven-thirty and finished sharpish just after midnight.

Some of those at the pub had been at our Christmas reading event at the bookshop and recognised Bill.

'You were wonderful,' a woman said to Bill.

'Yes, you were brilliant,' said her friend.

'Most kind, dear ladies,' he said in his best Dickens impersonation and kissed both their hands.

I could not decide whether he reminded me most of the actor manager of *Nicholas Nickelby*, Vincent Crummles, or the indomitably cheerful Mark Tapley in *Martin Chuzzlewit*. They giggled and went away happy.

'You were definitely a big hit,' Aggie said to Bill as we departed for the church. He shouted, already making his way up the street:

'Yo ho, my boys! No more work to-night. Christmas Eve! Let's have the shutters up.'

'Hilli-ho!' I shouted back.

Aggie and I walked on towards the church. I was not a practising Christian but I respected Aggie's beliefs and I felt a warm glow as we all gathered together singing carols and celebrating the birth of Christ. Whilst I may not have believed the veracity of the story and the account of the journey of the Magi, it was certainly one that was well told and had stood the test of time, and many of the tenets of the New Testament I found difficult to disagree with.

Aggie had not drunk anything alcoholic as she was driving home. She offered me a lift after Mass but I preferred the walk. This was a moment to wind down after the Christmas rush. Knowing that I had a long journey to pick up my mother and then go on to my brother in the morning, I avoided the temptation of a nightcap when I reached home despite the fact that I spotted a small bottle of brandy in a corner that I had bought in a nod towards Christmas. I went straight to bed with a mug of hot chocolate and set my alarm clock. I read a chapter of my latest book and settled into a virtuous sleep.

4

My two hour journey to collect my mother was soothed by playing *Messiah*. A predictable choice, maybe, though despite the fact that I had heard it a number of times, it did not disappoint and helped while away the hours. My journey was made longer when I encountered a number of traffic hold-ups. I had decided to take the country route rather than the motorway and, though it took longer overall, I felt more relaxed for it. Esther rang as she promised she would.

'Merry Christmas to you. I haven't opened my present yet but I'm sure it will be lovely.'

'Same here.' I said.

That was just about the extent of the conversation as the traffic jam I was in suddenly cleared.

'Drive safely,' she said. I was on my way again and I wished her a hasty goodbye. However, her call, brief as it was, had put me in a good mood and I sang along with the music playing as I was at last able to motor along with few hold-ups.

Once I had picked up my mother and we were on the way to my brother's house, we talked about my dad and how we both still missed him, about Esther and Aggie, and when her next visit might be. I also went fishing a little as to whether she had any further romantic interest.

'Have you heard from Nicholas?'

She showed me a card her erstwhile partner had sent for Christmas, which she had put into her handbag. Predictably, it was of a steam train. He was a technical assistant at the local university. She had threatened to marry him until she finally admitted that he was too boring for her.

'Did he have any other interests except steam trains?'

'Not many. Except for me.'

She giggled like a little girl, which made me feel uncomfortable.

'I'm not sure if there is anyone who can replace your father,' she added.

I remembered how they had argued. My father was much quieter and less outgoing than my mother. However, there was no doubt that their relationship had endured.

'I have been in touch with Sam though,'

My mother had become friends with Sam, who had worked for me in the past and with whom I still kept in contact. Sam was studying at the university where my mother had formed her friendship with Nick Pearson.

'Oh.'

'Yes, she's suggested that I should study as a mature student at the university.'

I could see a situation developing where she would come and live with me while she studied. Much as I told myself I loved my mum, I enjoyed her company in small doses. I had a spare bedroom but that was the way I would prefer to keep it.

'Wouldn't it be better to study at the Open University?'

'While I have great respect for the Open University, there's nothing like the experience of mixing with fellow students – and I already have good contacts at your local university with Sam and some of the other students.

'Do you need qualifications? I know sometimes they require an access course.'

I was pedalling lightly trying to see if there was some obstacle she had not thought of. My mother had left school at fifteen but had gone to what used to be called 'Night School' and taken a number of adult education courses on English, arithmetic and typing. There was no doubting her intelligence and her propensity for further study. I just did not want her to be doing it all in too close proximity to me.

'Sam said that if I go in with a foundation course I probably won't need any formal qualifications, and if I do well, I can make it into a full-time degree.'

Three years of my mother living with me, I thought. I knew I may have to get involved in helping her out as she became older but I had not envisioned this.

'Where are you are going to live?'

It was as though she had divined what I was going to say.

'You needn't worry, I won't be living with you. I want to live on campus for the first year so I can become involved in all that university life has to offer.'

The previous year she had caused quite a stir with her radical views in the student union bar. I could see the headlines in the local paper now. 'Grandmother in University protest fracas.'

'In any case,' she continued, 'if I can't get a place on campus

Esther has said that she will gladly put me up during term time.'

'You've spoken to Esther about it already?'

Before me, her son. I was a bit miffed. But the worst of it was, I feared that whenever she spoke to Esther she was invading the relationship between the two of us, which was a delicate one. She was convinced there was something going on between us. I sincerely hoped that one day there would be, but if my mother blundered in, I was worried that she would irrevocably damage any real prospect of the closer relationship I desired.

'How would you pay for it?'

'There may be a grant or a loan I can get. But, in any case, I do have a bit put by and you did say I should use money as I saw fit while I was alive.'

That I could not deny.

'What would you study?'

'What do you think I went for?'

'I don't know. Politics, I suppose, has to come into it somewhere.'

'Yes, but with philosophy, which I believe includes a dash of theology.'

'Well, if it makes you happy.'

I could not deny her the opportunity but at the same time it made me extremely wary of the consequences – though what they might be I could not exactly put into words.

We were greeted warmly by Dominic and his wife, Andrea. Sam and Celia were now eight and ten and appeared to have grown and matured since I had seen them the year before, but there was still a palpable Christmas air when we arrived and I caught a whiff of that indefinable feeling of excitement that Christmas and children together can engender.

In a wistful moment I could still recall the time when I was seven and found out that Santa did not exist. My best friend, through an older and, to my mind, vindictive sister had found out before me and had delighted in telling me that he did not exist. This resulted in a fight. I jumped on him and pinned him down saying 'he does exist' whilst he smirked and smiled at my ignorance. Even though I maintained I was right after the fight, the doubt had been planted and the spell had been broken. I don't think I have ever again felt so wretched and disappointed.

*

On Christmas afternoon, after a traditional Turkey dinner, we all went out for a walk with their dog, Royster, to a nearby wood. The children were excited and took any opportunity to climb low hanging branches and piles of stacked wood. I joined in, played football with a half size ball they had brought along and then we all played tag. At one point my mother said, 'That could be you Elliot. You are actually quite good with children,' as though it was a huge surprise. This was her usual mantra.

'Well I was one once, after all,' I said as lightly as possible. 'I'm perfectly happy seeing Dominic's once or twice a year. You know there's no law that says you have to have children.'

'There isn't - but it's a shame.'

That there isn't a law or that it was just a shame I did not have them, I wondered.

'Do you think Esther wants children?' she continued.

'I don't know,' I said. And really I didn't and it hadn't occurred to me to think about it. 'If she does, it has nothing to do with me.'

I wanted to make this clear to my mother in case she had any thought that whatever decision Esther made somehow involved me. Every time my mother mentioned her to me I was certain that she was exploring our getting together. She had made this assumption early on, which made me wary of mentioning Esther in case she took it the wrong way. However, the sight of Dominic's children did make me think about her feelings on the subject. I supposed I had assumed that Esther and her late husband David had never wanted children but then I thought, perhaps, it was more complicated than that and David's illness may have prevented it, or it may be that Esther was unable to have children. If so, that was a kind of second tragedy. An ambition unfulfilled.

My mother joined Andrea in an intense conversation leaving Dominic and myself behind while the children ran on ahead.

'You're the lucky one,' said Dominic. 'Not having children.'

'Really?'

'No, I wouldn't be without them. But if we'd never had them? There's a certain freedom you have. Everyone has to work it out for themselves, I suppose.'

'You're right of course but our mother doesn't feel that way.'

'She shouldn't put pressure on you like that. But, do you think you'll ever settle down?'

'Well, I sort of am settled down. It's just that I don't have anyone settled with me. But, I don't know. It's not that I don't want to. I think the problem is that the longer I'm on my own the more independent I become and it makes me less willing to compromise. I suppose the bookshop has taken over everything.'

'It's a shame we don't see more of you.'

'I know. It's that bookshop again. I'm tied to it.'

'I'm tied to the law but, mercifully, I do get some decent holiday.'

'That's the trouble with being self-employed. There is no obligation to give yourself any holiday at all. Not that I regret having the bookshop,' I added quickly. 'In fact, I love it. It's just the way it is – it seems to take up every scrap of my time.'

We went to the *matinee* of the Christmas show at the local theatre the following day. It was a musical adaption of the *Railway Children* by E. Nesbit. The children were full of it. They had been on a steam railway at Pickering in North Yorkshire earlier that year and it was still clear in their memory. We had eaten before going to the theatre, so afterwards I said my goodbyes at the car park and continued on my way home. My mother was staying a few extra days with Dominic.

I played some CDs of *Bleak Expectations*, a Radio 4 comedy series from a few years before – a parody of Dickens - and laughed most of my way home. My Christmas had not been unpleasant. I had enjoyed the warmth of the company of Dominic and family and my mother but I felt a slight nagging ache inside. I was missing Esther.

5

On the days following Christmas and Boxing Day and before the New Year I looked after the shop myself, so that Esther could have her extended leave and Aggie could have a complete break from the shop for a week. I had quite a few customers in the shop exchanging their book tokens and some interesting conversations with people visiting family but, mostly, they were quiet days. There were some books returned, usually because more than one of the same book had been received at Christmas. Generally, customers exchanged their books, often adding to their purchase. There were only a few refunds so I had little to complain about in this respect.

There arose the question of what to do on New Year's Eve. I could go to the Dirty Duck and seek out a few companions, but I was saved from such an anonymous arrangement by a phone call from Aggie who invited me around to her place, to join her and her two sons and daughter, their spouses and a few friends.

'And before you worry about drinking and driving,' she said. 'If you can't get a lift there is a bed in the spare room that you can collapse on.'

I was not a great lover of New Year's Eve. My attitude was that I wanted to hold on to the old year as long as possible as a new year only reminded me that time was passing ever faster, as it seemed to as we got older. I had tried in previous years going to bed at nine and sleeping my way into the New Year, only to wake up depressed as I heard fireworks and the sound of people outside enjoying themselves or making a lot of noise under my window. I resigned myself to the fact that I might as well be up rather than have my sleep disturbed. But neither did I like the idea of a large party where everyone was encouraged to enjoy themselves in a fake attempt at bonhomie. So Aggie's invitation was just about right: supper with a few like-minded people that I already knew. I could cut off early if I wished, or stay the course.

*

I arrived at Aggie's at about eight-thirty. She had a roaring fire going and she was serving up a buffet evening meal of snacks – and of course, plenty of wine, beer and cider, which we all contributed to with our own offerings.

'Be a dear and get some more coal from the shed,' Aggie said to me almost as soon as I arrived through the door.

The shed was an adjunct to the house and rather rickety, half open to the elements and accessed from the back door of the house. A little reluctantly, I admit, I slipped out into the cold night air with the coal bucket in my hand. I scrabbled around looking for the coal in the shed, with just the dim outside light above the doorway to the house to help me find my way around. I stubbed my foot and cursed Aggie. I took out my mobile phone and shone the light so I could better get my bearings. The shed looked eerie and ghostly in the dark. I could see a myriad of dark shapes waiting to trip over the unwary. Eventually, I made out the bag of coal and began filling the coal scuttle. As I became more accustomed to the light, I became distracted by a shape in the corner. I shuffled over, trying to avoid tripping on an unseen obstacle, so that I could get a better look. There was a piece of T-shaped metal peeping out from under a tarpaulin. I pulled the tarpaulin back a bit to reveal a scooter. I noticed the Lambretta insignia. It did not look in bad condition. After a few moments of further examination, I finished off filling the coal bucket and went back in with the coal.

'Remind me to take a torch next time I go rooting around for coal,' I complained to Aggie. 'I stubbed my toe.'

'Didn't you find the light?' she laughed.

'I didn't know there was one.'

'Actually it's tucked away a bit. You have to reach back behind the door frame.'

'I'll try and remember that next time.'

'Come and have a drink. That will help make the pain go away.'

'Actually, I found an old scooter while I was fetching the coal. Is it yours?'

'Ah, my old Lambretta. I used to love whizzing about on it when I was younger.'

'Does it still go?'

'No, it started to become troublesome and then I was told that it would cost more to fix than buy a new one - that's when I got my Citroen Dyane. Though, as you know, I do like using my push-bike when the weather's fine.'

'I don't suppose you would consider loaning it to the bookshop for the window competition?'

'Be my guest. But how are you going to get it to the shop.'

'That could be a problem.'

'I know! Matthew and his van.' Matthew was Aggie's second son, gardener and Jack of all trades.

So it was all hatched that very evening. Matthew would transport the Lambretta to the shop and we would put it in our large window as part of the *Roman Holiday* display.

The scooter, in fact, became one of the talking points of the evening. There seemed to be endless tales of 'the mother' Aggie zooming around on it, of Henry (Aggie's other son) running off with it to the beach with a girlfriend on the back without asking his mother's permission and returning two days later. It seemed that Aggie and the Lambretta were an item for many years and a familiar part of the local landscape. Under the influence, it must be said, of a considerable amount of alcohol, it was decided that the scooter must be restored for Aggie so that she could roll back the years, re-invigorate herself and, by extension, her local community, and once more be witnessed whizzing along the local lanes. Even though this was all being foisted on Aggie by her enthusiastic offspring with very little consultation with her, I could see a twinkle in her eye and, I think, for a moment she was won over and became complicit in the plan.

'You know what the name Lambretta means?' Matthew asked me.

'No idea, though I like the sound. It's the sound of youth.'

'A mythical water-sprite named after the River Lambro which runs through Milan.'

'The preferred machine for mods as I remember.'

'You weren't one were you?'

'I suppose I was a kind of literary mod for about 5 minutes.'

'The heyday of the Lambretta was the fifties and sixties,' he went on. 'They became really popular here as well as in Italy but then people started turning to small cars or Japanese motorcycles. Innocenti sold it to British Leyland and then, later on, when sales went downhill, it was sold to an Indian Company. That seemed to work for a while but it eventually went as well.'

'That's a shame.'

'Yeah, but there's still a lot of interest. There are Lambretta clubs all around the world. Some of the rallies have thousands of people attending.'

'Was it a Lambretta used in *Roman Holiday*, I wonder?'

'What's that, a film?'

'Yeah, with Gregory Peck and Audrey Hepburn. Before your time but in its day... I think Hepburn won an academy award. They used a scooter in the film. 'It would be good if it was a Lambretta for the sake of this window competition.'

'I'll check it out later.'

But Matthew was already tapping away on his phone.

'Here we are,' he said after a moment peering hard into the screen. He came by my side and showed me a still image of Gregory Peck at the front of the scooter and Audrey Hepburn at the back. Gregory Peck had his mouth open so, obviously, was mid speech. I wondered what he was saying at that moment.

'Doesn't look like a Lambretta to me.' Matthew said.

'I'm not sure if I'd know the difference.'

'No, definitely not. Look you can see the Vespa insignia.'

'Well, I suppose that's pretty conclusive.'

We were interrupted by Aggie shouting that it was nearly twelve o'clock.

There were a few fireworks, which Matthew and his friend set off at the stroke of midnight, while we stood outside in the cold. I texted Esther wishing her a Happy New Year and received an almost instant text back with three kisses. There were more drinks and, at about two, people began to drift away. I found my bed in Aggie's small bedroom and swiftly found sleep in the company of one of her cats.

6

After all the hustle and bustle and momentum of the run-up to Christmas I found it difficult to motivate myself and avoided the accounts that I knew I should be preparing for filing the tax return that was due at the end of the month. No matter how I tried I could never get them done in good time and always left them to the last minute.

I made my working days as truncated as possible. As soon as it came to closing time I left the bookshop and walked home, closed out the chilly air and lit the fire. I made myself simple meals of pasta or pizza and retired to my reading room-cum-lounge, poured myself a glass of wine and read for as long as possible before I fell asleep. I left the heating off and relied on the fire and a hot water bottle. I told myself I was saving money but I also experienced a feeling of fortitude as I began to tough out the long nights and the short days of January.

Matthew turned up with the scooter without forewarning on the first Saturday into January. I did not have any spare space in the shop to store it so we put it straight away into a hurriedly cleared window.

'Someone will notice it's not a Vespa. They always do in these sort of situations,' I said to Matthew. 'The other thing I meant to say to you is: the original Vespa used in the film, do you know how much it sold for?'

Of course he didn't. I had looked it up.

'£200,000.'

Once we had positioned the scooter in the window, we carefully covered over the Lambretta insignia with a poster representing one of the holiday guides. The scooter produced quite a bit of comment as we had not put together the overall window display as yet. One person thought we had begun selling scooters, another regular customer was afraid that we were closing down as a bookshop.

When Esther returned after her Christmas break on the Monday, she was delighted to see the scooter and loved the tales of Aggie's adventures on it. She thanked me for the DVD of *Il Postino* that I had given her as a Christmas present. As I had guessed and hoped, it was not a film she had seen.

'I realise now why you quizzed me so much on Italian films. It makes me realise what a devious person you are.'

'I think you will find it is one of the main characteristics of us psychopaths.'

We both laughed.

'Did you manage to watch it over Christmas?'

'I didn't really have time. In any case, I thought it may be nice if we watched it together- unless you have seen it?'

'No, I saw it in a list of top Italian films when I was researching for the window. I'd be delighted to.'

'Well, in that case, I will invite you to *Cinema Wayside Cottage*, for a private viewing.'

Her Christmas present to me had been a leather bound notebook. Her inscription read, 'Please fill it with some wise and interesting words. Merry Christmas, with love Esther.'

'Have you filled your notebook yet?' she continued.

'Thank you. It's a fine notebook. How can I put this? I have given serious consideration to filling it up. The trouble is, it's such a fine book I feel that I may be defiling it by writing anything in it at all.'

'But how on earth are you going to write the next great novel if you never start?'

This was something of a joke between us.

'Honestly, Elliot, that was not just a gift but the incentive for the beginning of a great enterprise so I expect you to use it accordingly.'

Then we began discussing the window project in earnest. We would need posters and Italian literature and would have to make provision to put in lots of travel guides from the publisher who was running the competition.

'Of course, you know there is that other meaning to a *Roman Holiday* – apart from it being a holiday in Rome that is,' she said.

'When someone experiences enjoyment on account of someone else's suffering.'

'Like *schadenfreude*.'

'Exactly.'

'Do you know it comes from Byron's *Childe Harold*? He got the idea from the work-free days that were given when gladiatorial games were held.'

'You're beginning to sound like Cameron,' I said. Cameron was my good friend, a history teacher, who had accompanied me on a bicycle tour during the previous summer.

*

Anusha, our temporary student employee, took the window project on board immediately she arrived the next day from her Christmas break and began researching on the internet. She printed out a copy of the original poster from the film *Roman Holiday* and blew it up as far as she could without losing all its definition. With the poster in place behind the Lambretta we could see the potential for creating an interesting and attractive window display. We added a *La Dolce Vita* poster that Anusha had also tracked down. Then we thought about which Italian literature to include and sought out the relevant books. Volumes by Dante, Petrarch and Boccaccio accompanied more modern texts by Alberto Moravia, Tomasi Di Lampedusa (*The Leopard*), Alessandro Manzoni (*The Betrothed*) and, of course, *If on a Winter's Night a Traveller*. (I was able to contribute my copy now that I had finished it). There was, we thought, a judicious mixture of the old and the new plus, of course, a decent spread of travel guides.

The books, the posters and the Lambretta looked splendid displayed in a group, though, in what was quite a big window, we thought there was room for something else. Anusha came up with the idea of blowing up the busts of statues of Roman heroes to A3 size and adding a short caption telling the name of the subject and their whereabouts in Rome. So we had the bust of Emperor Claudius in the Vatican Museums, Mars in the Capitoline, and also the Capitoline Brutus. There was a representation of a painting by Caravagio, Michelangelo's *Moses* and a Rafael fresco. Anusha worked hard at putting it all together with occasional assistance from Esther and myself. There was an agonising hour or two when we couldn't decide how to finish the window off. I made a radical decision to change the display around, which I was convinced would look amazing. It took an hour but it soon became clear as we stood there trying to admire it that what we had before was much better. We spent another hour trying to retrace our steps and get it back to where it was...

There was a point when Esther said, 'That's it, no more changes.'

'Who's in charge here?' I asked.

Esther and Anusha looked at each other.

Anusha said: 'She is right, though.'

We snapped a photo and sent it off. Esther put it on Facebook and Instagram and attached a photo to our Twitter account.

All in all, in the end, we decided that it was an impressive window that already had been attracting attention from customers.

7

The window display accomplished, Esther and I kept our appointment to watch *Il Postino*. It had turned into a kind of celebration of finishing the window. I joined her at her cottage with some popcorn after duly admiring her hens (from which I received my regular supply of eggs).

'Make sure you don't need to go to the loo too often as I've lost the remote and it's a pain trying to find the right button on the DVD player,' she said as she fiddled around on the floor, loading the DVD and trying to locate the right button to press to get the film started. I wistfully thought that there would probably not be many more occasions when we would be watching a DVD, anyway, as films were becoming widely available online.

We watched together on her sofa as the star Mario (Massimo Troisi) falls in love with Beatrice Russo, a beauty who works in a local café. To woo her he tries to enlist the help of Pablo Neruda, the famous Chilean poet who is in exile on the small Italian island where most of the inhabitants, including Mario's father, work in the fishing industry. Mario, who exclusively delivers the mail to Neruda because, due to his fame, there is so much of it, asks Neruda to write a poem to Beatrice but Neruda protests that 'A poet needs to know the object of his inspiration.' This leads eventually, to Mario, writing his own words with some advice from Neruda. When Mario plucks up the courage to meet Beatrice, and describes her as a butterfly, her mother suspects his motives, saying to Beatrice that 'When a man starts to charm you with his words he is not far off with his hands.' At that moment Esther gave me a pointed look and shifted away from me on the sofa. We both laughed. No doubt she was thinking that my choice of film was another example of my deviousness.

In the film, Beatrice's mother enlists the help of a priest to try to dissuade Beatrice from the match with Mario and then, in desperation, approaches Neruda himself and makes it clear that if Mario does not stay away from her daughter she will shoot him. In fact, Mario and Beatrice do eventually get married and Neruda is the Best Man. During the wedding celebrations

Neruda receives a letter informing him that his warrant for arrest in Chile has been revoked, which leaves him free to return there. Neruda promises that he will write to Mario and asks him if he can look after a few possessions that he will leave at his island home. The only communication that Mario receives, though, once Neruda has returned to Chile, is a formal instruction from Neruda's secretary to return some of his possessions. It upsets Mario greatly that he has had no personal communication from Neruda because he thought they had become friends. Neruda does return to the island five years later to find that Mario and Beatrice have a five year old son but that Mario has died at a Communist rally during a clash with the authorities, when he was due to read out a poem in praise of Neruda. Mario had said several times that he would call his child Pablito after Neruda, though each time he said this Beatrice replied that she was not going to call him by that name. However, in the end, following his death, she relented.

'Do you know another tragedy of that story?' I said to Esther, wiping my eyes a little once the film had finished, 'The actor who played Mario, Massimo Troiso, died the day after the film was finished.'

'Oh. There is a kind of vulnerability about him. I thought that was just his acting style.'

'Apparently, he was so ill when they filmed that most of those scenes where he is shown biking are not him at all. He could barely stand up.'

'That's very tragic and sad.'

The *Roman Holiday* window stayed in for two weeks. There were a number of favourable comments for which we tried to give Anusha due credit as she had spent the most time on it. Matthew arrived to pick up the scooter. His plan I learned was not to return it to the shed but to restore it to its former glory.

'Do you really think we may see Aggie riding it?' I asked him.

'I don't know. But if she doesn't ride it I may have it for myself.'

Mathew loved a project and a challenge; anything that involved a lengthy spell of DIY or reconstruction or mechanical repair. Exactly the opposite of me, I thought.

*

Anusha moved on in February. She was to take a gap year in India, rediscovering her Indian roots and for part of the year working as a volunteer in a school in Kerala. With the way things were going with an expanding and growing Indian economy, with many opportunities presenting themselves for a well – educated young woman, we wondered whether we would see her again.

'You've been absolutely brilliant,' I said to her.

'Brilliant and charming,' said Esther.

We gave her a hug, Esther an especially long one.

'I've so enjoyed working with you both,' she said.

There were tears in her eyes, and ours, as we waved goodbye.

8

In March, the London International Bookfair was held at Olympia and it was decided that both Esther and I would go. I had been to the book fair at Olympia a few times over the years, especially during the first years of opening the bookshop, whereas for Esther it was her first time.

The soaring Victorian iron and glass arches greeted us once we had registered and found our way through the entrance. The Book Fair had taken over, as far as we could tell, just about all the space. Against a palpable continuous mumble we began our journey through the vast network of stalls. Part of me had vowed never to return again after endless slogging around stands but there was also part of me that was excited by the business of it all. All the major publishers and many of the smaller ones had stands. There was advance information on new titles that were to be published that year. A few well-known authors were signing their books and there were talks on various aspects of publishing and bookselling. There was also an event about the best way to approach publishers for author events. This was useful in that it might help us to find some authors for talks that we may not otherwise know about and, perhaps, an introduction so that we may more likely secure an event. Bookshop events, though they required an extra investment of a considerable amount of time, helped attract customers into the shop and the book sales as a result could be quite considerable – and, of course, there was the enjoyable experience of engaging with authors, some of whom were our literary heroes.

The last time I came to the Book Fair I had walked around by myself so Esther and I had a decision to make: whether it would be better to walk around together or whether we would cover more ground by going it alone and then meeting up later. After a brief discussion we decided to begin walking around together and then maybe split up later, according to how things progressed.

Rows and rows of smaller stalls decorated the edge of the arena. As we got further into the centre there was a maze of various sized exhibition spaces with some real monster stands from some of the larger publishers such as Penguin, HarperCollins and Random House. Catalogues were available to take away and there were plenty of complimentary environmentally friendly cloth bags to load them into. Alternatively, it could be arranged for the catalogues to be sent to you later, which gave the sales people the opportunity to make a note of your interest and your contact details that they could follow up later. We thought we may be able to carry a bag around each and be very selective and not overburden ourselves, but after a short while we realised that this was not very practical and resorted to having the information sent on to us.

The first half of the visit was pleasant enough as we sought out some familiar publisher names and encountered one or two publishers' reps whom I was used to seeing two or three times a year.

We had several complimentary cups of coffee as we made our way around. Mostly people were kind to us but we were also aware that we were a small cog in the middle of a huge publishing machine. Sometimes we were met with quite frankly bored indifference. But at the same time we were aware that this was what we had signed up for, a fact finding expedition, and not to be welcomed with open arms at all the stands. The fair itself was as much as anything a fair about book rights and the signing up of big name authors, whereas as booksellers we were at the end of the chain once the books had been written, publishers decided on and distribution rights established.

Eventually, as time moved on and it seemed that we had not progressed very far, we decided that the best bet was to split up so we had time to visit all the stands that we wanted to and still have time to go the sessions on pitching to publishers at 'The High Street Theatre'.

'Thank God for mobile phones!' I said to Esther once we had finally co-ordinated things so that we could meet up later.

'But wise to have a back-up plan.'

'Yes, you're right.'

I had a habit of either not charging my phone properly or doing something inadvertently to make the battery run-down and of course there was always the possibility that I would lose it or it would get stolen.

As it happened, when the time came for us to meet up at the entrance point, we did not need our phones as I spotted Esther waiting there before I had a chance to phone her. We went off to the venue where the presentation was being held about how to pitch to publishers to persuade them to offer authors for events. There was some useful general information on the kinds of things that we should say, the sort of thing that when you thought about it was obvious but may not always be appreciated at the time the pitch was made: a realistic estimate of how big an audience your bookshop can take, whether you are able to pick up from and to take to the station, the format of the talk, whether you can accommodate an interview style event, if travel or accommodation can be provided, whether slides can be shown if required – and so on and so on. There was also the opportunity to question publicists who could sometimes be difficult to make contact with on a day to day basis.

Once we had finished the session, by mutual consent we had had enough for that day and went back to the car park. We had chosen to drive to the Book Fair rather than travel by train or coach because Esther wanted to take the opportunity to visit an old friend who lived near Winchester on the way back. We would break up a long day by sleeping at her friend Chloe's home and then would arrive back home by the end of the following day.

9

The roads out of London were predictably busy and we spent quite a bit of time crawling along the M25 before we made it onto the M3. We switched to the A31 which eventually took us all the way to Winchester. We skirted around the edge of the town following Chloe's directions to her house a few miles away from the centre.

It was dark by the time we arrived, both tired from our day touring the exhibition stands and from the journey. My old Volvo Estate (I needed something big for all the second-hand book collections) was comfortable and I had yawned several times on the journey.

'Perhaps I could make my excuses and go straight to bed when we get there. Do you think Chloe would mind?' I said after one particularly long drawn out yawn.

'She definitely would mind and so would I. You'll be all right once you get some food inside you. The house is in a great spot,' she added. 'There's a lovely old orchard at the back full of ancient apple trees. Perhaps we can have a look at it in the morning.'

'It's so good to see you,' Chloe said once she had opened the door. She gave Esther an enormous hug. 'And you, Elliot, delighted to meet you at last. I've heard so much.'

A small figure appeared as if from nowhere.

'And Max,' said Esther scooping up the child.

We followed Chloe into a kitchen-cum-diner. Max left Esther's arms and retreated into a corner to some toys.

Chloe was an artist and there was evidence of her striking art on the walls around. In fact, there was an easel in the middle of the room, where, she said, she spent a lot of her time.

'That "little bugger",' (she nodded towards Max who was now fighting an imaginary war with Star Wars fighter planes in the corner) 'has been known to eat some of my work or practice his own version of art on top of mine when he feels like it. Once, I did this drawing, one of my best I thought. But it was too boring - he wanted to improve it by adding a bit of colour - and managed to completely obliterate it. Little monster!'

'I suppose it's a dangerous game trying to work with him around,' I said.

'Two and a bit years old and *bold as a pig*,' said Chloe in her best Dublin.

'I do have an art studio at the back that I don't usually let "the terror" into – otherwise there would be carnage - as you can imagine – but I can work in there when he is asleep. I have now learnt my lesson and just use in here to put together ideas and drafts.'

'Are you working on anything in particular now?' asked Esther.

'Just this and that.'

'Go on, show us your studio. I bet it's amazing,' said Esther.

She took us down to the back of the house. Max seemed content to stay with his toys.

'Do you get the sun in here?' I asked, when we had arrived at her studio.

'No, absolutely not. It's north facing.'

'What a shame.'

'No, it's good. It gives you a nice uniform light. What you don't want is light that shifts throughout the day – like bright sunlight then shadow.'

'I suddenly feel very ignorant.'

'Why should you? It's natural to think that south or west facing is good because that's what we all like at the end of the day - with a glass of wine.'

'I'm sorry Chloe, Elliot is more your literary type. He doesn't have one single painting in his house. He isn't big into art. I'm surprised you haven't come across that in one of your literary stories though Elliot, or in a biography of Turner or Constable.'

'Well, I might have done – but I obviously didn't take it in. And you're right, unlike you Esther, I'm ashamed to say, I don't have any art hanging in my house ... and I've just thought, looking at these, don't you have one of them in your house?'

'Yes she does, one of apple trees I think?'

'Yes, in pride of place.'

When I did enthuse about art it was usually about something classic like Turner or Gaugin. However, I found these images of Chloe's very striking. They were mostly of landscapes. Trees featured heavily, though distorted in their focus.

As I looked more closely at one of the pictures I was not sure if I was looking at a tree or a figure bending. Which was it?

'I like the ambiguity,' I said.

'It's for the viewer to make up their own mind. It's not necessarily what I think myself – if I think about it all.'

'That's what many a writer of fiction would argue as well,' I said.

'Give Elliot five minutes and he'll become an art critic,' Esther said.

'It's just what occurred to me.'

'I know.'

She gave me a playful little punch.

There were also a couple of studies that I guessed were of Winchester Cathedral with shadowy figures walking along the corridors and up the stairs, though they could be of any cathedral or large church. The walls were at a seriously wonky angle.

'There's that distortion again,' I said as I peered at the painting.

'Well, you are right and wrong at the same time. Winchester was my inspiration for that particular piece of art and some of those walls, particularly on the right hand side as you go in really do lean at an angle – at a greater angle than the leaning tower of Pisa, apparently. In fact, you'll see when you go there tomorrow that there's an amazing story of devotion by a diver called William Walker who probably saved the cathedral from falling down. He worked in incredibly difficult circumstances to save the foundations - in water that often looked like it was a murky soup. Six hours a day over seven years, often in total darkness, he packed the foundations with thousands of bags of concrete. It was him that I had in mind a lot of the time when I was doing the sketches.'

'What a lonely job. And I guess the reward was that it didn't fall down?'

'That's it, you could not claim his reward was being able to see his work it in all its glory like you could, for example, one of the carved screens because, by its very nature, it was hidden from view.'

'In some ways it makes it an even more heroic act.'

'He was awarded something. Something I'd not heard of before, the Royal Victorian Order.'

'I was about to say he deserves a medal.'

'No pictures of Max,' Esther said.

'Not quite sure how you paint the devil.'

'Chloe!'

'It might happen. I don't know though. To be honest, it's not my usual sort of subject, a portrait. Most of my figures appear in the landscape. I'm not much good at them.'

'Not much experience at portraits may be more accurate,' said Esther.

'But you have to choose the direction that's right for you, I think. It's the landscape that motivates me. The figures come second.'

*

Chloe had cooked up a lasagne, salad and her own bread, 'made just this afternoon.'

'Hand crafted,' said Esther.

'Yes, I can't be doing with those machines. I don't think you get the same result. Also, kneading is a good way of getting rid of all my angst – of which I have a great deal.'

Was it against anyone in particular or the world in general – or that Max again?

We ate late, after Chloe had put the 'mad Max' to bed – but not before he had been read several stories. Esther had had the foresight to bring some picture books with her to add to his already copious collection. She was used to reading to Max from her previous visits and dragged me in. Particular favourites were *Farmer Duck*, a kind of picture book version of *Animal Farm*. ('I need to get his politics sorted out early,' said Chloe) and *Where the Wild Things Are'* by Maurice Sendak - which had been a 1960s cult classic I remembered from my own childhood and had recently been reprinted.

Esther had brought with her *The Highway Rat* by Julia Donaldson and insisted that I read part of it ('as it was somehow appropriate') while Esther read the other parts and the narrator. Max loved it so much that we had to read it again as soon as we had finished. At one point Esther looked across and gave me the broadest smile and I felt a tremendous feeling of warmth which I could only interpret as a fuzzy kind of love.

After many cries of 'Again! Again!' Max was persuaded under the covers, the lights were turned down and Chloe began to sing.

When Irish eyes are smiling, sure 'tis like a morn in spring.
In the lilt of Irish laughter, you can hear the angels sing.
When Irish hearts are happy, all the world seems bright and gay,
And when Irish eyes are smiling, sure, they steal your heart away.

Max looked up at her and smiled. As she continued to sing it was as though he had become transfixed. By the time she had finished three verses his eyes had closed. She gently covered his little frame, gave him a kiss on the head and we all crept out of the room. Chloe left the door slightly ajar and we sneaked down the stairs like burglars. It was just after nine when we sat down to eat our supper.

Esther and Chloe were at university together and had a close and warm relationship, and I enjoyed listening to them telling stories about mutual old friends and acquaintances. Esther had been involved in dancing and singing and I remembered that was how she had met her late husband David. Chloe's husband worked away for weeks at a time in the oil industry so Chloe was used to spending a lot of time on her own with Max.

After the meal I offered to clear the plates and take them into the kitchen. When I returned it was evident that they had started a conversation about David, Esther's late husband.

'I'm getting better – honestly, really', Esther was saying as I re-entered the room, 'and Elliot's such a dear.'

'I can imagine,' said Chloe.

'Not sure about that,' I said approaching the table.

She reached out to me. I gave her my hand and she rubbed it. I was, I admit, a little embarrassed by this sudden public show of affection. Esther had been drinking quite quickly and looked a little flushed.

We had a relatively early night planned. Max would be up at the crack of dawn which would give us the opportunity for an early start. Once we had finished eating, Chloe went to check on Max and suggested that Esther accompany her so that she could show her which room she was having.

I poured myself a glass of wine, which I promised myself would be a night cap. I wandered up and down the room in a distracted sort of way and, inevitably, found a bookcase in the corner. There was a variety of fiction: Helen Dunmore, Haruki Murakami, Zadie Smith, Colson Whitehead, Ian McEwan, Julian Barnes, Aravind Adega, Ali Smith – and then, finally I spotted an art book, *Ways of Seeing* by John Berger – an antidote to Kenneth Clark's *Civilisation*.

I could hear Chloe and Esther giggling. From the scraps of conversation I could make out I gathered they must be discussing sleeping arrangements and whether we would be sleeping in the same room together. I heard Chloe say the word romantic.

'Chance would be a fine thing,' I said – to myself.

There were two spare bedrooms apart from Max's. Mine doubled as a study, so I was saved a night on the sofa. There were several of Chloe's pictures on the wall. I had never been a fan of pictures on walls, I think because I worried about them imposing themselves on the space they occupied or acting as a distraction. I did like Chloe's art though and wondered whether I may change my mind and invest in a picture or two. Perhaps I should change them every few months to get over this idea of them taking over the space? On that thought, I fell asleep.

10

Before we left we had a quick look around the garden and the orchard. It was, as Esther had said, a lovely old orchard. The trees were mostly old varieties, Chloe explained, such as Bramleys, Newgate Wonder, Russet and Laxton Superb.

'Not the dwarf varieties you often see now, bred for ease of picking.'

'Yes, I can see, they are fine big trees,' I said.

'You would need a good long ladder to reach the highest points,' said Esther.

'The great thing about apples,' Chloe said, 'is that you can have apples straight from the tree right from the end of June to the middle of November – if you choose your varieties carefully.'

I picked up a broken piece of wood from the ground.

'That's the broken pin of an easel. I love painting out here too – when the weather's right.'

We were on raised ground. A beautiful vista presented itself before us: a patchwork of fields with hills in the background. The sky was menacing and suggested rain but for the moment it was dry and the sun was peeping through enticingly between the clouds.

'I think I would be tempted to sit here all day and read my book.'

'And drink wine.'

'I might be tempted to do that too.'

'Well, you must come again soon. I would be delighted to see you both.'

Chloe gave me a hug and a kiss and winked at me. I was not sure how to interpret that wink.

As we drove into Winchester, I said, 'I like Chloe, she's a lovely friend to have.'

'Yes, she's very important to me.'

'That Max, though, he's a bit of a handful.'

'But a rewarding little handful?'

She looked at me askance.

'If you like that sort of thing.'

'I think I could learn to live with it.'

I was not sure how to react. There was a silence for a while between us. I seemed to have acquired the habit of saying the wrong thing at a key moment.

'I'm really looking forward to this. You've been to the cathedral before haven't you?'

'Briefly, one time when I visited Chloe, though we didn't stay very long and it was long time ago.'

'Must be difficult with her husband being away?'

'Yes, he returns every few weeks. His work is going to dry up soon by the looks of it. Well, oil doesn't have much of a future does it? And Chloe's quite uncomfortable with it, being of an environmental frame of mind.'

'I suppose it's good in some ways – means they don't get bored with each other and the relationship keeps getting refreshed.'

She looked at me in a curious kind of way.

'You would think so wouldn't you? And to tell the truth Chloe is a bit worried about what it will be like if he returns and gets a regular job. She enjoys her freedom and is used to it – you know, especially with what she does, being an artist and all, having that space to think and create.'

'I know what you're going to say but she says Max is a different kind of interruption that she has learnt to cope with. She's worried about the emotional demands he'll put on her while he's at home. When he comes back for the first few days, she says, it's wonderful. He's very full on and attentive – gives all his attention to Max. But it doesn't last and within a week or so he's getting itchy feet and wanting to be back on the rig. If he's like that now, how's he going to be when he's back all the time? That's what she worries about.'

'That's the trouble when you're used to being on your own. I suppose you start becoming selfish and used to doing your own thing.'

I wasn't sure if I should have said the next thing.

'I feel that. I've been on my own for so long now that I'm not sure if I could cope with a long term relationship.'

'You have me Elliot.'

'I know but we're work colleagues.'

'I hope we're a bit more than that.'

'Well, yes, of course friends. Probably my best friend in many ways...but.'

'Elliot look out...'

I slammed the brake on hard. I missed a badger by a whisker. I had become distracted by the conversation I really wished I had not started. We watched the badger disappear into the undergrowth.

Shortly afterwards we passed the sign announcing that we were entering Winchester.

11

We walked past the statue of King Alfred and through the bustling market area before the long facade of Winchester Cathedral came into view, the longest gothic cathedral in Europe.

One of the reasons Esther was keen to visit was to see the memorials to Jane Austen, a favourite author of hers. It did not take us long to find one inlaid into the floor. The inscription read: *In memory of Jane Austen, youngest daughter of the late Rev George Austen...* It then went on to mention *the benevolence of her heart, the sweetness of her temper* and how much she would be missed.

'No mention of her books,' said Esther.

'That's strange.'

'I don't think she was appreciated much in her lifetime. Her books never carried her name while she was alive. *Sense and Sensibility* was described as "written by a lady" on the cover. All the rest of her books were described as "written by the author of *Sense and Sensibility*."'

'They were successful, though, weren't they?'

'Yes, mostly – but they only took off after she died'

'She was only forty?'

'Forty one, July 1817.'

'Not that much older than you.'

I was standing side by side with Esther and received a painful elbow to the ribs.

'They really came to prominence when Richard Bentley bought the copyright of all the novels in 1832 and published them as a collected edition. They've never been out of print since.'

Then we discovered a shiny brass plaque to her.

'Ah, at least this alludes to it: *Known to many by her writing*.'

'I suppose you have to think that, though we know her as a great writer, for her family it was the personal loss that was more important.'

Esther gazed towards the stained glass window above.

'There was a subscription request by *The Times* for the erection of this.'

'But where's Jane?'

Esther read from a booklet we had picked up.

'Apparently, in the centre you have St Augustine who abbreviated is St Austin, so a kind of pun on the Austen name. At the top in the middle you have King David playing on his harp. Then below him is St John reading *In the beginning was the word*. There is a Latin inscription which asks us to remember Jane Austen and the date of her death. The four remaining windows depict the sons of Korah who have scrolls describing Jane Austen's religious nature.'

'I don't suppose a lot of people even realise it has anything to do with her.'

'There seems to be a reluctance to shout out to the world "This woman was a genius of the written word".

She looked me squarely in the eye as though daring me to challenge her.

We began to explore the rest of the cathedral.

'Cameron would have loved this: The longest medieval cathedral in Europe. He would be salivating at the thought,' I said.

'Unless he's already been?'

'Yes, you're probably right. No doubt he has. Probably visited every cathedral in Britain. I must ask him if he has.'

'Could be another one of your projects?'

'What, visiting all the cathedrals. Yes, well, might be fun.'

'I'm sorry I'm not Cameron.'

'Well, you know, you'll have to do for now.'

I felt that I could have said something then. *You will more than do. I can't think of anyone I would rather be with than you.* I might have said that but I didn't. Everything I thought of sounded corny. So, in the end I thought it was better to return to Jane Austen.

'Why do you like Jane Austen's writing so much?'

'I'm not really sure where to start.'

'Try.'

'Well, you may find this a bit strange but I think one of the best things about her writing is the imperfections of her characters, especially of her heroines.'

'You mean like Emma Woodhouse.'

'Yes, like Emma Woodhouse but then she's probably the most extreme example.'

'You mean with all her meddling.'

'*A heroine whom no-one but myself will much like* – she said.'

'Well, she was wrong there wasn't she.'

'Well, that's sort of my point. It's the imperfections that appeal.'

'Good people are dull?'

'I wouldn't exactly say that. Eleanor Dashwood is loyal and kind-hearted. Elizabeth Bennet is independent and opinionated but she is very complex – and, of course, wants to marry for love.'

'There should be no other reason.'

'Well, it was difficult, I suppose. Sometimes one has to compromise. That sort of happened, or nearly happened, to Jane Austen herself. In fact she was engaged - but only for twelve hours.'

'Twelve hours?'

'Yes, to Harris Bigwither – brother of her great friend.'

'Are you sure you're not making that name up. Wasn't he one of the rabbits in *Watership Down*?'

'I think that was Bigwig.'

'Why only twelve hours?'

'I think he was a bit awkward and liked to tease his sisters. It's difficult to know but it sounds like, though he became heir to the family house when his older brother died, he just was not very attractive to Jane. The truth is we'll probably never know why she accepted him and then, so swiftly rejected him.'

'It's almost like you studied it.'

'I did, at university – but it still didn't put me off.'

We strolled a bit further.

'So which one am I then Elliot?'

'Which one was the most provocative?'

'I suppose that would be Elizabeth Bennet.'

'Come to think of it, you're quite a meddler. There's a few times you have pushed me in a direction I wasn't sure I wanted to go.'

'Nonsense. You need someone to push you sometimes, otherwise you wouldn't ever get anything done.'

'I think you meant to say "otherwise you may never know what you might achieve."'

'Besides,' she continued, there are other times when you don't take a blind bit of notice of what I say and take unnecessary risks. I was thinking that I may be more like Anne Elliot in *Persuasion* whom we haven't mentioned yet, sensitive and attentive to others.'

'Well you can be that, on occasion, I warrant you.'

'That sounds a very Jane Austen type phrase. But mentioning Anne Elliot, that reminds me of another thing about Jane Austen. How revolutionary she was. Think about *Persuasion*. It's all about how unworthy Walter Elliot is of his wealth and position, as is Lady Russell who tries to cheat Anne out of her only chance of happiness when she is given the opportunity the second time around with Captain Wentworth.'

'Seems like I need to re-visit Jane Austen.'

'So, I might be winning you around, Mr Todd? Shall we stroll in the Jane Austen manner? She took my arm.'

We began walking towards the end of the cathedral.

'Now you've mentioned Anne Elliot that has reminded me of George Eliot. Surely she's the greater writer. Now, *Middlemarch*, there's a book. The themes are much wider. She has a grander vision.'

'You have to remember they were writers of different eras. Austen died before Eliot was born. She was a contemporary of Dickens.'

'And Dickens admired her. He was one of the first to guess that she was a woman. Do you know that he sent a signed edition of *A Tale of Two Cities* inscribed to her and it recently fetched a quarter of a million.'

'I didn't,' she said 'but it's quality of the literature that we're talking about not what a collector thinks it's worth. Austen did things that were never done before. *Sense and Sensibility* was a parody of sentimental novels like *Pamela* by Richardson. She's critical *and* humorous. She uses irony to criticise the morals and mores of the day and her use of dialogue is brilliant – much better, I would have to say, than the use of dialogue by Eliot all those years later.'

'Well, I agree, it's all very clever.'

'And there is her use of free indirect speech – you know where she gives a voice to a character in the book as part of the narrative. Clever? It's brilliant!'

'Well, yes you have a point but, you know, Eliot's view of contemporary society was much deeper and broader.'

'And sometimes she was quite out of her depth.'

'But look at the issues she deals with. The 1832 Reform Act, the coming of the railway, the status of women and marriage ...'

'Austen deals with marriage too – and it's not Jane Austen's fault that there was no railway when she started writing.'

'How come we are getting so passionate about Jane Austen?'

'There is much to be passionate about!'

I let Esther walk along ahead of me and followed her into the presbytery where we saw the magnificent screen and the quire. Reading about it being the longest gothic cathedral in Europe and then seeing it and appreciating it were two different things. We looked along the whole length of the building as far as we could see.'

'Of course, the reason why you may subconsciously identify with George Eliot is that you are one yourself.'

'A what?'

'An Elliot.'

'She's one "l" – though, honestly, I hadn't thought of that.'

We continued our journey around the cathedral.

'Marvellous, isn't it?' Esther said

'Yes.'

'I love the sense of space,' said Esther.

We admired the screen. There was a tour wending its way along, free to everyone who had paid an entry fee like ourselves. We had elected not to join it earlier on but as I heard the guide declaiming the origins of the screen, the fact that it was completed as early as 1475 but that the statues that stood there now, good as they are, were added in the 1880s (the original colourful statues were removed during the Reformation), I decided to tag along while Esther continued exploring on her own.

Our guide told us that the quire at the opposite end to the screen was where monks, as required by their founder, St Benedict, performed 'the work of God' and prayed there seven times a day. The oak stalls were the oldest in existence in England dating back to the 1300s, saved it was believed from destruction during the Reformation because the representations were more secular in nature - of the 'green man', mythical beasts, animals, men and foliage. The carvings on the stalls were very intricate and sometimes humorous. I particularly liked the one of a cat with its dinner.

I moved aside as a modern day choir entered. They had evidently assembled to practice and, after a few moments of instruction from the choir master, a glorious pure uplifting sound emanated from them.

I broke off from the tour and wandered the aisles looking for

Esther. Eventually I came across her in the Lady Chapel lighting a candle. I stayed back not wanting to disturb her as I watched from a distance. She retired to one of the stalls and knelt down in prayer. I guessed she was praying for her late husband.

In the Lady Chapel there was a striking image of Mary cradling the body of the dead Jesus. The notice informed me that it was a recent sculpture from 1990 by Peter Eugene Ball, carved in just two weeks following the death of the artist's brother in a car accident. I found it intensely moving. It contrasted sharply with the more traditional saccharine image of Mary on the screen behind the altar.

But it is on this image that I saw Esther concentrating, after she had finished praying. She turned around as I approached her and we discussed the two contrasting pieces of art.

'I agree the sculpture is a much better piece of art,' said Esther, 'but this is interesting in itself as it's in commemoration of Charlotte Younge.'

'Ah, yes, the Oxford Movement and all that. Now that's someone I have never read or, I think, that I've ever wanted to read.'

'You should read *The Heir of Redclyffe*. It's a sweet book.'

'Really!'

'Yes, really! I think you'll be pleasantly surprised – and *The Daisy Chain* is not a bad read either.'

'But isn't it all pious religious nonsense?'

'It may have a particular religious slant but it's not nonsense. You have to take into account the times in which she was living and the influence her father had over her. She was in awe of him. He was very religious and High Church. He educated her at home but was very strict. When her father praised her she was happy, when he criticised her she got upset.'

'I suppose a lot of people can relate to that.'

'There's an irony here, though. It is Jane Austen who was not widely read in her lifetime, or at least not as much as she should have been, who is now revered as one the greatest novelists.'

She put up her hand to my mouth to stay the words about to issue forth.

'Whatever you think, in her day Charlotte Younge was one of the most popular novelists there was. Her first big success, *The Heir of Redclyffe* was so profitable that she was able to fund a missionary ship.'

'I knew there was a reason why I didn't like her.'

'That's the problem, I think, and why she is not read much

today. People have a prejudice against the religious nature of her work when she was so much more than a religious writer.'

'You can't blame people for taking against that – all that nonsense and fairy dust.'

'Elliot, sometimes you are so narrow minded. If I can't convince you, I might as well give up. Look at the people who admired her in her day: Tennyson, Trollope, Lewis Carroll, Kingsley, William Morris – and George Eliot. They all admired her. C.S. Lewis compared her to Homer and Tolstoy. And do you know how arrogant you sound?'

'Of course, I respect other people's beliefs.'

'No you don't, otherwise you wouldn't have spoken like that.'

'OK, what I should have said was, there is no rational basis for believing in God.'

'Why does belief have to be rational?'

'Because if it is not explainable how can it have any real credence. I can understand why it was believed in the past. In the Middle Ages, before scientific theory had developed, when life was nasty brutish and short and when death never seemed very far away, I can understand that religion and a belief in God was one way of explaining the trials of life. But now that we know that we are just a collection of atoms...'

'OK. I can't persuade you – and I don't even want to try. I especially don't want to get into that old causality argument about if there is a God who created him. I don't want to defend religion because a lot of terrible things have been done in its name. I can't tell you what God looks like or exactly what it is, but all I can tell you is that it is a feeling and within it are lots of the moral principles I live by.'

'OK, you've convinced me; I'll read *The Heir of Redclyffe Hall*.'

But I knew that was not enough. She was gone, pacing on ahead of me, incensed, I was sure, at my superior attitude.

12

The first part of the journey back from Winchester was spent in companionable silence despite our earlier vigorous exchanges. Eventually, Esther fell asleep and after a few minutes her head slipped from the side of her seat and rested against my left shoulder. I did not wake her, not wishing to disturb her. It was some time before she woke with a start.

'Sorry, Elliot, have I been asleep very long?'

'A few minutes that's all. Nothing to worry about. In fact, I was quite enjoying the peace.'

She gave my arm a little squeeze but within minutes was asleep again.

The book fair and visit to Winchester had overall been an enjoyable experience, though I wondered about those robust arguments between Esther and myself. There were profound differences of opinion between us that I had not appreciated before. I also knew that a good part of it was my fault. I could have and should have expressed my opinions more carefully and more sensitively. Perhaps this was some kind of warning against our ever being more than just good friends.

I dropped Esther off at her cottage and returned to my house. As I walked through the door, I felt a sudden moment of loneliness and loss.

It seemed like the more I desired a relationship with Esther the more I was prone to saying the wrong thing. Our arguments, albeit often rather stylised and literary ones, kept re-emerging in my head. I was not at all sure if I was able to change my ways enough to accommodate Esther's differing views on a number of subjects (though, at the same time, there was an awful lot we did agree on). I had for so long in my own mind felt that Esther was the right person for me that I had not really asked myself whether that was still the case or, more frighteningly, because I did not really want to admit it, whether she had ever been the right person and whether it had really all been in my head.

A sudden weakness came upon me. All I could think of was to make a hot water bottle and go to bed. I was not physically ill, I was feeling sorry for myself. I lay awake for a long time. A kind of numbness came over me and two hours later I found myself still staring into space. A further unwelcome thought came into my mind. Did my relationship with Esther, which I had always considered to be a force for good and my own well-being, make me feel sadder than I would otherwise have been? The phrase, which I had never really believed, 'familiarity breeds contempt' entered my mind like an unwelcome guest.

I also realised that I had no-one to talk to because the person I usually confided in most was – well, it was Esther. I could speak to Aggie but then, the fact that Aggie saw Esther and me regularly at the bookshop made the idea of that approach uncomfortable. I could not confide in my mother because all she wanted to do was get me and Esther together and lacked objectivity. I could ring Cameron but I already knew what he would say – along the lines of tell her what you think about her or look somewhere else.

There was nothing for it: I would have to turn to the best and wisest resource I had ever known – a book. I did not exactly classify my books in any rigorous way but I did group some books together on an informal basis. In one corner of my reading room were some humorous books. *Three Men in a Boat, The Diary of A Nobody* and my most recent addition to the list of funny books guaranteed to cheer, *The Secret Diary of Adrian Mole.*

I had not read *Three Men in a Boat* for years and had forgotten how funny it was right from the very beginning when the narrator discovers that by reading a medical dictionary in the British Museum Reading Room he has every symptom known to man except housemaid's knee. *I had walked into that reading-room a happy, healthy man. I crawled out a decrepit wreck,* the narrator explained. His friends, George and Harris were in a similar state and, of course, this eventually led to the 'cure' from 'overwork' of a boating holiday.

They were just at the point of making plans for their great adventure when my phone rang.

It was Esther.

'I just wanted to say thank you for the lovely time I had. I forgot to earlier.'

'Oh, that's kind. But you don't need to thank me.'

Though I was pleased she had.

'In fact...' because she had so taken over my mind I thought I would mention it.

'Yes?'

'Well, I was worried that – perhaps we were arguing rather a lot and were not getting on as well as we should...'

'Oh, Elliot do you think so? It's me. I'm sorry. It's my way. But you know I find it so stimulating, the conversations we have. I know we don't always agree – though I think we do a lot of the time, especially about important things.'

'I know. I'm sorry about what I said about your beliefs. You're right, I was being arrogant.'

'Perhaps a bit.'

'But I can't make myself believe.'

'I know. I wouldn't want you to.'

'Sorry, I shouldn't have mentioned it. I'm probably over-sensitive about it.'

Probably! There was no question about it.

She was quiet for a good long moment.

'Do you want me to leave the bookshop?'

'What? No!'

'Look, I know I can sometimes be a bit overbearing ... if you want me to leave... The last thing in the world I want to do is to hurt you or upset you in any way.'

'Please, Esther don't give it a second thought. It's really the other way around. I was worried that you may want to leave.'

'If you're sure.'

'I'm sure.'

'That's good. I'm a bit tired now so I'll say goodnight.'

'Goodnight Esther.'

It was not long after I had put the phone down and was about to go to bed that I received a phone call from Simon Bonneville's wife, Miriam. She was concerned about him. His mother had died recently, she explained. They lived in what was Simon's parents' house. Some years before his mother had moved to a smaller house, a bungalow for practical reasons. Now she had died. Simon, the big bright, breezy, good humoured man that he was - one of those people I always felt the better for encountering and was the kind of person who gave other people assurance - had gone to pieces.

'It's worse than with his father – even though he was a great influence on him. He bore that stoically and I suppose, in a way, had prepared himself for it. But his mother, it's as though he is completely stunned into inaction. I just can't get him out of his...' she searched for an appropriate word, 'stupor.'

'I'm really sorry to hear that. Must be a worry for you.'

'I think part of the problem is that his father died quite a while ago and he's become used to looking after his mother and protecting her. You know, he went and saw her every Sunday almost without fail. In fact, it caused a bit of tension between us. Of course, none of that matters now.'

There was a short silence. I felt I should say something more.

'Do you want me to come over, Miriam?'

'Would you?'

'I'm not quite sure what I'm going to say to him.'

'I know it's difficult. I'm sorry to ask you.'

'No, don't worry about that. If it wasn't difficult it wouldn't be so important. I suppose what I am saying is, are you sure it would help?'

'He likes you, Elliot.'

'When would you like me to come?'

'I don't like to be deceptive but I have thought of a pretext. I have some books of my own that I have been meaning to get rid of for years and I have told Simon so. There aren't that many but I think you'll find some nice stuff there – quite a lot of Folio editions. I'll tell Simon that I'm inviting you over to see them, and of course, I will invite you over to dinner at the same time.'

I hesitated a moment.

'That all right?' she continued.

'Yes, I was just hesitating because I was wondering what would be the best day. You know, whenever I come over and see Simon, however good my intentions, I seem to end up with a hangover. Do you remember that time he invited me over to help with the prize-giving for the charity cricket match?'

She laughed.

'Yes, I do but I had thought of that. Could we make it Saturday evening? You don't open on Sunday do you? You could stay the night and not worry about driving home. The thing is, I'm not sure if he's in much of a drinking mood at the moment. That's how bad things are with him! But it's as well to be prepared.'

Once I had put the phone down, I thought of my own mother and the way I was sometimes irked by her phone calls and her interventions and attempts to make a match between myself and Esther. It made me contemplate, reluctantly, how I would feel when my mother was no longer there. I realised that I would miss her more than I could say. For one of the few times in my life I was the one who initiated contact with my mother. Following the conversation with Miriam, I had convinced myself that my own mother was not well.

'Mum?'

'Yes?'

'I was just ringing to see if you're all right?'

'Of course I am. Why wouldn't I be?'

'I don't know. I seem to remember that you were not too well the last time I spoke to you.'

'I'm as fit as a flea.'

'Wasn't there something, last time we spoke?'

'It was so long ago that I can't remember.'

This was typical of my mother.

'Not that long, surely.'

'It was nothing. It was gone within a day or two.'

'Good, I'm glad to hear it.'

'Elliot, is everything all right with you?'

'Yes, fine.'

'You don't sound quite right.'

'I am, really, I was just a bit concerned.'

'Is Esther OK?'

'Yes, she's fine.'

'Is she with you now?'

'No, she's at her house.'

'You two! I suppose something will resolve itself one day.'

'There's nothing to resolve. We're just friends, that's all.'

What a practised liar I had become to my mother about my true feelings for Esther.

We had been over this ground so often, my mother imagining something that was not there. Of course, on my side I wanted there to be something. The fact that there was an element of truth in my mother's observation made it all the more irritating and I felt the guilt of deception.

'Actually, Mum, I have got to go now, but I'm glad you're all right.'

I put the phone down. Within a few sentences of conversation I had cured myself of my brief excessive concern for my mother. My relationship, though in its own way a close one, was clearly different from Simon's with his mother.

13

When I arrived the following Saturday, Miriam greeted me and took me to the library, which also doubled as a snooker room with a three-quarter size snooker table. The books were arranged into three large boxes and were stacked in one corner.

'Just a few for now. There may be more later,' said Miriam. 'I'll leave you to it. I'll just make sure the dinner is OK.'

'I can smell something delicious,' I said.

'Just a rack of lamb, nothing special. You have your usual room.' In my experience Miriam's dinners were always something special.

'Just like my second home.'

I looked through the books. As Miriam had said, there were a number of Folio editions which were always very saleable as they were so stylishly produced with rich creamy paper and good sized type - and cloth bound, often in their own case. I had no hesitation in deciding to take them all. I found Miriam in the kitchen chopping away at some mint leaves to make up her own mint sauce.

'Some very nice editions, just as you said. I'll take the lot.'

'You will be doing me a favour. I'm so pleased you could come.'

'Where's Simon?'

'I'm not sure. I'll go and find him and then I'm dishing up.'

'Well, it it's OK by you I will put those books in the car now and then join you at the table. I probably won't feel like doing it later.'

'Right ho!'

It did not take me long. I took a few minutes in the fresh air leaning against the car. If I had been a smoker as I had been in my youth, that's when I would have lit up. I wondered if I had done the right thing coming here. The fact that Simon had not greeted me when I arrived at the house made me feel a little uncomfortable and Miriam appeared on edge. Yet, I did earnestly want to help in any way I could. I had to go through with the visit however uncomfortable the situation.

When I returned to the house I found them already sitting at the table in the dining room.

'No starter I'm afraid,' said Miriam.

'That's OK, I'll slum it.'

I shook Simon's hand.

'I didn't know you were coming, Elliot, until just now.'

'Yes you did,' said Miriam. I told you the other day.'

'Must've forgot.'

He had a distracted air, just as Miriam had described. I sat opposite him but I could not catch his eye so it was Miriam I spoke to. We talked some more about the books and about the garden. Simon still did not contribute. When he was looking in my direction it was as though he was looking through me. More than that, he looked very withdrawn. Miriam and I finished our food.

'Delicious as always,' I said.

Simon had, unusually, left some of his food and hardly touched his glass of wine. It was as if he was a stranger in a restaurant at the next table to us, eating on his own. I tried to introduce him into the conversation by addressing him directly but he made incomplete contributions such as 'just so' and 'I should think so indeed' rather than having much to say on every subject under the sun as he usually did.

'I just need to check something,' he said abruptly at one point and rose from the table. 'I might have my dessert a bit later,' he said as he left the room.

'He keeps doing that,' said Miriam. 'I don't know where on earth he is going or what he is doing.'

'Are you sure he wants me to be here?'

She put her hand on mine.

'I'm sure he does. I'm sorry if it's difficult for you. You don't have to stay.'

I tried to make light of it.

'What else would I be doing?'

'Something with that charming Esther no doubt.'

I was more tactful than I was in my responses to my mother.

'Actually, I think she's busy tonight.'

At that moment Simon returned.

'Everything all right dear?'

'Yes, just needed to check something.'

Simon sat down but pushed his unfinished portion of food away.

'I tell you what, let's leave the dessert. We can come back to that later,' said Miriam, echoing what Simon had said earlier. 'Why don't you two go off and play a game of snooker.'

'Yes, I might make a better game of it when I'm sober,' I said, remembering my last poor effort following another grand meal when I had had plenty to drink.

'If you like.' Simon sounded less than enthusiastic.

The snooker room-cum-library, where I had started my visit, was always a joy for me as Simon had a great collection of books. In fact, snooker was not really my thing at all. I could never remember which ball to pot next, was always miscuing and relied on Simon's guidance. Simon, as usual, set up the balls and then sat down for a moment to chalk his cue. But he remained stuck there. Then I witnessed something I was not prepared for, Simon slowly collapsing into tears.

I went up to him and put my arm around his big shoulder.

'I'm so sorry Simon that you are hurting this way.'

'I'm sorry that you have to see me like this,' he said eventually. 'I know it's self indulgent, but I can't help it.'

'But it's such a big thing – your mother. Why on earth shouldn't you cry?'

'We're very close you know – were very close.'

'I know.'

'And now I can't protect her any more. '

Miriam had used that word, 'protect'.

'Why don't you tell me about her?'

'There's nothing to tell really. She was here and now she's gone.'

'You have to remember, I know you and Miriam but not really your mother.'

'I forget that, that you are just a blow-in.'

I laughed. It was so good to see a bit of the old Simon humour emerging.

'How about a drink?' I said to Simon.

This was new territory for me, encouraging Simon to drink. Usually, it was the other way around - me trying to refuse one from Simon.

'If you like.'

This was so unlike Simon. I would not call him an alcoholic but he was the archetypal convivial host who always found an excuse for a good drink when the occasion was right.

He had stopped crying but was still sitting there inactive, as though rooted to the spot. I felt that this was the moment I had to go carefully.

'What do you fancy then?'

'Whatever you like.'

'What have you got?'

'Well, you know: wine, beer, whisky, gin, whatever you like.'

If you are thinking at this moment that this was more like the old Simon, reeling off the great variety of drinks at his disposal, you would be wrong. Simon would just not say I have got wine, whisky or whatever. He would be on his feet saying he had a natty little red brewed by some monks or a special infused gin from a tiny family distillery in the Esk Valley, or a whisky flavoured with peat from the bottom of Loch Ness. He would not be offering me a drink but the unique drink that he had recently procured and was determined to enjoy in my company. It was as though he had had the stuffing knocked out of him.

'Like *Toad of Toad Hall* when he was locked in his room by Badger, Ratty and Mole after his motoring escapades,' I was thinking.

I could not help laughing at the comparison and gave out an involuntary giggle.

'What is it, what's funny?'

He wiped away a tear, like a schoolboy in the playground.

'I'm sorry, it was nothing.'

But for some reason this had animated him a little.

'It must've been something. You don't just blurt out laughing like a lunatic for no reason at all.'

This was more like the old Simon. I laughed again. I am not sure if it was because of relief or because of what he had just said.

'I'm not really sure if I can tell you.'

'Ah, I see! Something funny about me. Funny sort of cove you are sometimes Elliot Todd.'

This made me laugh again.

'We had a boy like you at school, would laugh at every damn thing. I swear he would have laughed if his mother...'

He stopped abruptly.

'I nearly said it...if his mother had died. And, of course my mother has.'

He had momentarily sunk back into his gloom. It was one of those things: we trip ourselves up saying exactly the opposite of what we mean to.

'Look, I tell you what,' I said, desperate to retrieve the more engaged version of Simon. 'If we have a few drinks you might just be able to get it out of me. You must have a decent whisky somewhere.'

'Probably.'

There was a pause. Some devil inside was driving me. I had to find a way of drawing him out of himself.

'Surely you have something distilled by a rare sect of hitherto unknown Irish Monks?'

He looked at me a little queerly and I wondered if I had gone too far, taking the Micky out of someone in such obvious distress. Luckily, I had never had to experience it but I was pretty sure that Simon could throw a good punch.

'Now you mention it', he said with more enthusiasm, 'I have a bottle of 16 year old Bushmills single malt.'

'That must have cost a fortune. You sure you don't want to save it for a special occasion?'

He stood up and looked me straight in the eye.

'This is a special occasion.'

He did not quite stride off as he would have formerly, but it was a spirited shuffle.

I heard him shouting.

'Mim, seen that special Bushmills?'

Though I thought this may have been a good move in order to bring out the old Simon, it was not in my own best interests as I had avoided all spirits since my last visit which had ended in a brutal hangover the next day. This was not, though, the time to be half-hearted. When he returned, he poured out two large glasses.

'I think we should raise a glass to your mum - but do you know, I don't even know her Christian name,' I said.

'Catherine.'

'Well here's to Catherine – Catherine the Great, as I am sure she was,' I said, leading the charge into I knew not where.

He raised his glass in return.

'Tell me, what was she like? You said there wasn't much to tell.'

'That's not quite right. What I meant, I suppose, is that there is no point because she is not here any longer.'

'With great respect, I don't think that's true. It's important that you keep remembering her. She's part of who you are.'

He turned for a moment, I suspect to wipe away another tear. Then he turned back to me.

'You're right, of course. I'm feeling sorry for myself, I know.

But it's painful. I can't just pretend everything's OK.'

'I know.'

'She was a remarkable woman in many ways.'

'She brought you up. She has to be.'

'Me and Sandy and my rogue brother John.'

'A saint then!'

'She shared a lot with me in these last few months. She had terrible nightmares.'

He took a gulp of whisky before continuing.

'She was very independent and said that she found it very difficult to get emotionally close to anyone and that this affected her marriage. My father was not always forgiving. Twice he let out his rage and pushed her. He did have a bit of a temper on him. I witnessed it the second time and I said if he ever did that again I would kill him.'

This was news to me. Surprising news. I had expected some stories about him and his brothers when they were younger and the larks they got up to – especially that 'rogue brother'. He was cutting to the chase. I thought it was best to let him continue.

'I don't think he was a bad man. He was frustrated. My mother didn't blame him. The fact was, he never did it again. And, in case you're thinking, that I didn't care about my dad, I did. But he should never have done that to her. She had suffered enough. I have to admit, after that, my relationship with my father was never quite the same. I suppose I had lost some of my respect for him.'

He finished his drink and poured himself another.

'And I suppose, when he died I didn't grieve for him as much as I should have because I knew I had to be there for my mother.'

He came across to me and topped up my glass.

'We developed this special bond, I suppose. I was always there to protect her. And, now...'

Rather than repeat himself he waved his glass and slumped in his chair again with unsaid words hanging in the air.

'Do you think that a part of it is that it is only now that you can grieve for your father as well?' I said.

'I think so. I think you're probably right – but it's difficult to get my head around it.'

We both took another swig.

'She was lucky enough to be on the *Kindertransport*. However, though she was always grateful for the opportunity to come to Britain, life was not easy to begin with, especially at school. She used to get made fun of and bullied as an alien because of her German accent, even though she was the real victim.'

'I'm sorry. I had no idea...'

'That she was Jewish? That's not surprising. I don't talk about it and neither did she. The family changed the surname. She lost her accent and put all that behind her. She became a practising Christian. But I think it bothered her in later years. She wasn't ashamed of everything German. Things just went bad under Hitler. She loved the food that they used to have that they did not have here. In fact, there was much that she loved about Germany.'

'She sounds like she was a very strong, stoical woman.'

'She was, and very intelligent. She loved her Greek and Roman classics. And, talking of stoicism, she was a great fan of Marcus Aurelius.'

There was a further top up. He was now holding the neck of the bottle in his hand as though ready to fill our glasses again at a moment's notice.

'The worst thing at the end was the nightmares. It was as if it all came back to her. I kept telling her there was nothing to feel guilty about.'

'The guilt of the survivor?'

'It was not just the surviving. It was the denial of her past.'

'But she is at peace now.'

'Yes, you're right, I hope so.'

I spent a moment taking all this in. There was so much here – more than I had ever contemplated.

'I don't suppose... well, we're having a memorial service. I wondered if you wanted to come along. I know you didn't really know her but as a friend to me – and now that you know some of her story.'

'Of course, just let me know the date. I'd be honoured.'

We drank another glass of whisky – and then another one. We talked about other things: cricket and the prospect of the England team, latest books and so on. Then, at the point that we had shared the final glass from that bottle of whisky, Simon said.

'Is Esther Jewish - or her parents?'

'Oh, I don't know. She's a Christian as far as I know – but, then, your mother became Christian as well. I don't know about her parents.'

'Of course, lots of people who carry the name Esther weren't

Jewish – I think, especially in the north. But then she qualifies in one important respect like the Esther described in the Bible, she is a beauty.'

I tried to ignore the last remark as in my eyes that was certainly true but I did not want to go down that route.

'I'll have to ask her. Do you know, it's a subject that has never come up?'

He then went very quiet again and held his head. I was worried he was going to collapse into tears again. This was not a normal day.

'What is it Simon?'

'It's nothing. Something at the back of my mind. Something important I needed to ask you but it's gone.'

'It will wait.'

'It's terrible how things seem to slip from your mind as you get older.'

'It happens to me too and I'm just a spring chicken.'

'So you are. Ah, that's it. It's about you. I wanted to know what you were laughing at me for. You said I might be able to drag it out of you after a few drinks. So here we are, tell me.'

So I did.

14

It took me a full day to recover from my hangover. Though Miriam cooked me a reviving full English breakfast, I did not feel that I was in a proper state to drive the next morning. On previous occasions when we had had a lot to drink and I had stayed, Simon had been up before me and appeared to suffer far less than me but this time he did not join me for breakfast. Whether it was the alcohol or whether his melancholy mood had returned, he was nowhere to be seen. Miriam drove me back in my own car and took the opportunity to visit an acquaintance of hers who did not live far from where I lived and would drive her back later. I suspected that she already had this plan in mind as it was arranged with the shortest of conversations on the phone to her friend.

'How did you get on?' she said as we travelled in the car. 'I haven't spoken to him this morning.'

'Well, as you know, we drank a lot and we did eventually get chatting – but, to be honest, you know I'm not sure.'

'I'm sure it did him some good. Anything to get him out of this melancholy mindset of his. You know one of the worst things is that he has become a stranger to our grandchild.'

I remembered that his grandson sometimes accompanied Simon when his daughter was busy. In fact he had been with Simon on the fateful night of Harry Nielson's demise at the bookshop and had discovered his impaled body.

I was still feeling a bit ropey when I went into work on the Monday morning. There was a pile of mail and small parcels that I thought I could not ignore. One of the special aspects of most bookshops is the willingness (if you are to be taken seriously as a bookshop) to order any book in print. This is an important source of income, even in the age of the internet, especially if orders can be expedited efficiently with many books available within one or two days. There are other orders, which may take longer and sometimes bring little or no profit when carriage charges are taken into account, but it is a badge of honour for many booksellers to offer a complete service. Because orders come from a multiplicity of sources, usually on 30 day terms, the bills very often come flying in from all directions, and, if not kept on top of, can come as an unpleasant surprise. Some of the mail that morning I guessed would be invoices chasing money and I felt I could not face them in my delicate state. The letters that looked most potentially troubling I put to the bottom of the pile and tried to deal with the more straightforward ones first.

The post would sometimes contain promotional material for books, or, best of all (when they were any good), complimentary copies sent to the bookseller by a publisher eager to let the bookseller know about their latest published work. I dealt with these less 'threatening' items first. A complimentary book was in the mail that morning, though rather than the usual novel it was a travel guide to Rome. It was the enclosed letter, though, that caught my attention. It said, 'We thought you would like the accompanying guide for your imminent trip to Rome. Congratulations, you have won this year's Travel Window Competition and a complimentary week in Rome for two at a luxury bijou hotel...'

'Esther,' I called. 'We've won the window competition.'

'What?'

She came up to the counter where I had been opening the post and took the letter from me.

'That's marvellous,' she said after a moment's reading. We high-fived each other and gave each other a hug.

'A week in Rome, shouldn't be too hard to cover.'

'Well, no, we do it for our annual holidays.'

I thought for a moment that perhaps Esther and I could go together and that maybe that was what she was thinking, but how could we possibly cover a week with both of us away and only Aggie to hold the fort?

'Were you thinking...?' I explored.

'You must go, of course.'

'But you were more involved with the window.'

'Anusha was if you're going down that route, but no, it's your shop, you must go.'

'It's for two.'

'A double room,' said Esther, 'so probably a double bed apartment or, at least, two singles.'

'Besides,' she continued, 'I've been before.'

'So have I, come to that – though a good long time ago.'

'I know! Why don't you take your mother?'

I broke into a cold sweat, made worse by my residual hangover. She was not even joking.

'Go on, it would be a real treat for her.'

My tongue became tied as I tried to separate emotion and logic and come up with a convincing answer as to why it was not a good idea.

'I don't think it would work,' I was able to say eventually without conviction.

'Why not?'

'If it was a double bed or even two singles…'

What I was really thinking up to that moment was a romantic notion that I may be sharing a room – or even a bed – with Esther, and now, somehow my mother had come between us, which was a completely unnerving thought.

'Why don't you go with one of your girlfriends?' I said.

'I suppose that's a possibility,' she mused.

I was resigned to losing the holiday now, though I had to admit, part of me would regret the missed opportunity. Rome was such a great place, so much to see. And I had watched those Italian films recently...

'Anyway,' she said, 'we don't have to decide now. How long have we got before we need to get it sorted?'

I looked at the letter.

'A week, by the look of it.'

I forgot about the holiday for the rest of the day and became distracted sorting out a load of nineteenth century fiction, mostly improving books with a religious theme and bright attractive covers. It made me think of the books of Charlotte Yonge. I did not come across *The Heir of Redclyffe* and we did not have one in stock in the bookshop, so I ordered it there and then as I had now become curious about what it was like, following Esther's recommendation.

Later that evening, Esther phoned me at home.

'Cameron!' Esther exclaimed, 'You can take Cameron.' Cameron had accompanied me the year before on our bicycling holiday. He was a good friend, even though we saw each other infrequently, and we had an instant rapport whenever we met, despite the fact that we were quite different. Above all, I was comfortable in his company.

'That might work.'

'Of course it would.'

'If he's free.'

'Go on, ring him now!'

I rang but there was no reply. I did not feel like leaving a message and felt that I would rather talk in person.

I rang an hour later and this time got his wife Rachael.

'Hi Rachael, it's Elliot.'

'Oh, Elliot. Cameron's not here at the moment. He's at one of his historical meetings.'

'How do you know it's Cameron I'm after?'

She chuckled.

'I suppose I should be talking to you about it, anyway. I need permission to take Cameron away on a trip again.'

'Off on your push-bikes again – you borrowed mine last time I seem to remember.'

'No, this time a bit more exciting - abroad. Not that our cycling holiday wasn't exciting, of course!'

'Well, I'm all in favour. He came back in a really happy mood after last time. Maybe you are the secret of our long marriage. You can do it as often as you like as far as I'm concerned - but I guess it may come down to when it is. You know Cameron, he may have planned attending an historical conference in Harrogate that week and forgotten to mention it to me – so best to check with him.'

I gave her the dates and she promised to get Cameron to ring back that night.

In fact, Cameron rang me less than an hour later. He was delighted by the prospect of visiting Rome and the dates worked for him.

'I only visited for 48 hours last time I was there and didn't get a chance to see anything much,' he said. 'But I feel I should pay something towards this.'

'Look, its free I told you. We just pay for the food and wine, tickets for the museums and so on.'

'Well, it's very good of you to think of me.'

'You weren't necessarily my first choice,' I said, perhaps a little unwisely.

'You mean Esther?'

'I'm not telling you who or what I mean. Anyway, as you know, we can't really be out of the shop at the same time.'

'Ha!' he said in triumph, knowing he was right. 'I warn you, though,' he continued, 'I may be even more enthusiastic about history than during the last trip. There's so much to see.'

'I have already mentally prepared myself for that.'

'Are we staying in a little *Pensione*?'

'An apartment, I believe. The only problem is that we may have to share a room, perhaps even a bed – though I wouldn't be surprised if there was a comfy sofa.'

'I can cope with that if you can.'

'It's a date then.'

The next morning I told Esther that Cameron was able to come with me.

'Are you sure you can manage?' I said. 'I could see if Cameron can go with his wife.'

'I doubt if she would be able to get the time off work. Besides, you and Cameron get on so well. It's almost like you're married.'

'I'm not sure if I'm good enough for him. He does have some very particular habits.'

'As do you.'

What on earth could she mean? Rather than take too much obvious offence I tried to say as lightly as possible.

'And what would those be?'

'Snoring, for a start.'

'How could you possibly know if I snore?'

'That time you stayed at mine when you drove to Aggie's and forgot not to drink and stayed on my sofa.'

'But I had been drinking. Everyone snores when they've had a bit too much.'

'And when I stayed with you that time I was attacked. I could hear you through the bedroom wall. I wonder the neighbours don't complain.'

'You know, I didn't know that I actually snored.'

'Next time I'll record it and play it back to you.'

'And what other bad habits do I have?'

A customer came through the door at that moment so the conversation about my failings was put on hold and, for a while, they were forgotten.

15

I received a phone call from Miriam on the landline when I arrived home that evening.

'Sorry for bothering you, Elliot. I wanted to thank you for coming round to see Simon.'

'All I did was get him drunk.'

'You brought him out of himself. He said you helped him get things in perspective. I know that too because he took the time to discuss it with me and he was hardly speaking to me before.'

'I don't know if it was particularly anything to do with me. He just needed to talk to someone.'

'Well, whatever it was, it worked. And he's still very keen for you to come to the memorial service. And do you know, he can't stop laughing about you comparing him to Toad.'

'I wondered if I had gone too far, joking like that when he was so....'

'It's gone to his head. He's been preparing what he's going to say at the memorial service and, as you may expect, he has quite a lot to say about his mother. He's been chuckling to himself saying things like: 'Introduction to memorial service by Simon-Toad, hymns chosen for memorial by Simon-Toad, Thank you by Simon-Toad, Refreshments by Simon-Toad... It's done him the world of good.'

That evening at home my eyes drifted towards my bookshelf in my small sitting room. There, accusingly, sat Primo Levi's book *If This Is a Man*. It was a book I had started but not finished. The bookmark stood out from the volume. I was less than a third of the way through. I remembered reading it and having a nightmare. I had put it to one side to read at another time. It had been there for a year or two. After Simon's story about his mother, I now felt a kind of obligation to finish it.

Primo Levi was a Jewish Italian chemist from Turin captured by the Fascist militia and then, via a detention centre, transported to Auschwitz. He was one of only three of 125 people who returned to Italy. *If This Is a Man* are his recollections of his time at the camp, of how he survived. I began reading the chapter *The Drowned and the Saved*, an attempt to explain why some survived and some did not. I did not stop reading until I had finished more than an hour later.

The story was quite different from that of Simon's mum. She had not been in a concentration camp but there was a common connection. She escaped and suffered her own privations, guilt and bullying. Primo Levi's story was no doubt like her mother and father's story. I would be surprised if she had not read it. Some of the most telling moments are the most depressing ones linked to survival: The fact that it paid to become acquisitive and a thief, that Jewish supervisors were often stricter or worse than the non Jewish ones who were there as criminals, because they feared the loss of their privileges, and ultimately, their ability to survive. Prisoners became dehumanised and the usual moral codes of decency and fair play and honesty were no longer of any value. Sadly, Levi was believed to have committed suicide when he fell from his third story apartment many years after. Another holocaust survivor and Nobel Laureate, Elie Wiesel wrote that *Primo Levi died at Auschwitz forty years later.*

It is a remarkable story told honestly and without rancour, one of the books you feel you have a duty to read even though the subject may often be disturbing or even distasteful. It helped me put the life of Simon's mother in context.

When the memorial service for Catherine Bonneville was held the following week at his local church, St Peters, it was well attended and Simon made a very moving speech. Miriam and his son and daughter were at his side.

He told the story of her early life and the *Kindertransport*. He spoke of her kindness and understanding and tolerance and how, though his father was the dominant one – and he did allude to how he had not always been the kindest to her – it was her example that had had the most impact on him and it was her morals and ways of behaving that he tried to act on in life. He would never forget, he said, her gentleness and dignity and her caring for others. He thanked everyone who knew his mother and those that had come to support him and Miriam.

Miriam's speech was, in its own way, just as moving. It was a kind of moral parable, explaining how we must not let prejudice influence how we think; that Catherine, Simon's mother, was conflicted and loved many of the things about her life in Germany and that we should think about her life with humility, especially when prejudice existed in our own society. She concluded:

'She taught us that we must learn that our freedoms are precious and have to be fought for, that we should always be on our guard against ignorance and prejudice, and that tolerance and understanding are the key.'

I felt like clapping at the end of her speech.

At the house afterwards, I met a number of people who knew Catherine. A few of them were our customers but many were strangers. I proved useful as I knew the house pretty well by now and could direct people to the bathroom or take their coats and hang them on the pegs in the hallway, or show them into the garden if they needed to smoke or to get some fresh air.

Usually in these situations I would have a cup of tea and a sandwich and then make my excuses but that day I had the feeling that I was expected to stay and, of course, the food as usual was superb as it was all provided by Miriam. I did, in fact, start with a cup of tea but Simon soon found me and handed me a glass of brandy.

'Thank you for coming he said – and for being such a good friend.'

'It works both ways,' I said.

Miriam joined us at that moment.

'You have both made me feel so welcome ever since I have been here. I remember you,' I turned to Simon, 'coming into the shop and introducing yourself and saying how pleased you were that we were opening a bookshop.'

'I think I actually said that we needed a good bookshop in the town and that we were so pleased that you were providing one – and we still are.'

'I think there has hardly ever been a week when you haven't come in and bought something or ordered something on the phone. I think I'd have to close down if you weren't around.'

I escaped lightly with the one brandy as I had a lift back with Aggie who had dropped me at the church for the service at two and was now making her return visit.

The funeral of Simon's mother had reminded me that being a second hand bookseller often brought me close to 'death'. Many requests from those wanting to sell or donate second hand books were as a result of a parent or other relation dying. A book could reveal much about a person; their love of literature or otherwise, their special interests, whether it be fiction, politics, railways or gardening - and I was always interested in hearing their story.

So it was, when I was collecting some books a few weeks after the funeral, I chatted with the son of my book benefactor and learnt that his mother had been involved in code breaking at Bletchley Park. As seemed to be the case with so many of those involved, she did not reveal to her son any of the details. I could not help making a comparison with Simon's mum. Simon had eventually, near the end of her life, learnt some of her story and the pain and the guilt it had caused her, which I am sure she found therapeutic. But for most of her life she too had kept her story secret, suffering in silence.

On entering the house and learning the story of the mother's role at Bletchley Park at the beginning of my visit, I wondered as I began to empty the shelves whether I would be able to discern her occupation from her choice of books. I expected, I suppose, books on the war, political biographies and one of the recent spate of books on Bletchley Park. Instead I found a wide range of gardening books, travel guides and a mixture of romantic fiction and detective novels – the last, I supposed, the only clue to what I guessed would be a mind attuned to helping with the cracking of codes. From the point of view of the bookshop, the detective novels were always good sales fodder. There were also some nice volumes of old travel writing.

I returned to the bookshop late that afternoon and Esther greeted me with news of a mutual invitation.

'We've both been invited to a party.'

'Whose party?'

'It's a Lambretta party.'

' Ah, I see.'

She showed me the invitation.

There was a line drawing of a motor scooter, lots of stars, a balloon and a bottle of wine.

You are invited to a Lambretta party. Take tea with Aggie and then witness her ride her newly refurbished Lambretta once again. Not to be missed!

'I wonder if Aggie knows about it herself yet?' I said.

The party was to take place the following Sunday afternoon.

'Apparently the Lambretta is refurbished and in working order.

They have worked really hard on it.'

'Is she really going to ride it? I find it a bit hard to imagine.'

'She's being a bit coy. She just keeps laughing it off when I try to pin her down.'

'Well, it's a perfect way to get in the mood for Italy.'

My trip to Rome with Cameron was now only a week away.

That evening I rang Cameron.

'Have you got everything?'

'Yes, I've done loads of research. Shame we only have a week.'

'I was thinking of more practical things, like your passport.'

'It does only have a year to run but it will be OK for this summer. I'll have to remember to renew it when we get back.'

'I realise that for you this is an extension of your history studies but I would like a little time to relax as well.'

'Of course, a few Peroni's at the end of the day and all that.'

I hoped for a bit more than that. Maybe, rising late once or twice and sipping coffee on the balcony while reading a book. But then, I could always let him wander off on his own a time or two, I thought.

When the great day arrived – *The Lambretta Party* – I collected Esther from her cottage and took her over to Aggie's. Matthew greeted us as we entered the house.

'So did you have to do much?' I asked him after we had gratefully accepted a mug of tea.

I was a total ignoramus as far as cars and motorbikes and scooters were concerned. I knew where the petrol and oil went and that was about it – but I thought I should ask.

'We had to replace a lot of the parts which meant visiting car and motor bike wreckers. It's good for getting things like kick-start levers, mirrors, crash bars and so on. But other stuff I had to get from a specialist, you know, like the right size oil seals. You need to judge whether you need the large magneto flange or the small magneto flange – and an inlet manifold can knock you back over £20. Of course, lots of them come from India.'

I nodded sagely though I had very little idea what he was talking about and began to regret that I had raised the matter with him. I did not know what an inlet manifold was, how big it was and definitely had no idea whether £20 represented good value –

though I guessed from his tone that it was probably small and expensive. Unfortunately, Matthew was just beginning to warm to the subject. I noticed that Esther had disappeared from my side. Matthew and I were isolated in a corner.

'You have to check everything to make sure it's roadworthy,' he continued. ' To be honest there are probably plenty of places that would have given us an MOT without too much work being put in but we wanted it to be safe for Mum. So we had to take it completely apart, frame, forks, fuel tank, hubs, wheels and so on. We repaired everything that needed repairing – replaced quite a lot of it and had a few serious paint job sessions. After that there was the not insignificant matter of stripping the engine and cleaning and repairing it. We needed a new crankshaft, a piston, a clutch and a chain, new bearings and nuts – it was endless.'

'Sounds like it,' I said. It did sound horrendous to me. At that moment I was so pleased that I was a bookseller and not forced to repair motorcycles for a living – though I believed he was doing it for fun. I was rescued – or so I thought - by the arrival of a friend of his.

'Hi H,' said Matthew. 'This is Elliot, I was just telling him about the things we have been getting up to with that Lambretta.'

'Tell him about the twisted crank?'

'Oh, yeah, nightmare.'

He turned back towards me while H made his way towards us gesturing with his hands

'That's when one of the crank webs moves on to the crank pin, which causes the webs to go out of line.'

Matthew nodded his head vigorously.

'When it is a violent twist it can cause the engine to stop. We reckon that's what happened to Aggie all those years ago when it went *kaput*. We've had to strip the top end to sort it out.'

If I was out of my depth before, now I was drowning. I had loved hearing about Aggie whizzing back and forth down country lanes, but the mechanics of the engine were completely alien to me.

'Good to meet you H,' I leant forward and shook his hand. 'All that sounds very interesting – but I do, I'm afraid, need a quick pee.'

I made my escape. While I was in the toilet, though, I had to admit to myself the excitement of the idea that Aggie would once again be riding her beloved Lambretta. Whether she would actually do so in reality did not really matter. It was the idea and the project which was the thing that had Quixotic undertones. I could well see that it would be her son riding the Lambretta or even that it would be sold, as I understood that well-restored ones were quite sought after.

When I returned I bumped into Aggie's two daughters, Sylvia and Rebecca. Sylvia explained that she was a gardener.

'Like your mum.'

'Yes, except I'm a bit tidier than her.'

'She does have the knack though. I think she calls it benign neglect.'

'Actually, she says the same thing about bringing up children,' said Rebecca. 'But it's one thing not watering or feeding plants, it's another thing letting children dehydrate or starve. I can't believe that she was ever a teacher.'

'Probably before you needed qualifications,' Rebecca said unkindly. They both laughed conspiratorially.

Aggie's sister Celia appeared, on a visit from Scotland. She backed up what Rebecca had been saying about Aggie.

'When they cried she used to wheel them out of sight in the pram until she couldn't hear them screaming any more.

'Aren't you being a bit hard? It hasn't done you two any harm, has it?' I directed this at Sylvia and Rebecca.

Before they could respond, Aggie appeared around the corner.

'So where's your magnificent machine?' I said.

'Matthew and his friend are bringing it round in a moment.'

'Can we have a ride on it Granny?'

That was Belle, one of Sylvia's daughters.

'You're too young. Don't be silly,' said Rebecca.

'Please Grandma.'

'I'm not sure if I'm riding it myself yet.'

'Oh, go on, Grandma!'

I had to admit, when it came around the corner a few minutes later, propelled by Mathew, it looked absolutely magnificent. Everything about it was new-looking and shiny.

'It looks almost too good to ride.'

'Yes I think I may just leave it on display in the garden.'

'Like a garden sculpture.'

'Yes, we can make it a feature.'

We gravitated towards the magnificent machine at the centre of the courtyard. Henry, Aggie's other son joined us, along with the children who lent a party atmosphere to the situation as they chased each other around the scooter.

'Grandma's gonna ride the scooter,' shouted the older one.

'Granny's gonna ride the hooter,' shouted the younger one.

'You realise you have to have a helmet, Mother?' said Henry.

'I never used to bother.'

'Yes, but that was in the days before they changed the law and common sense prevailed.'

'They're too much of an encumbrance. I can't be doing with them. Besides, I haven't got one.'

'Yes you have.' jumped in Sylvia. 'And more besides. Come with us.'

Sylvia and Rebecca propelled her away.

Five minutes later, Aggie, or someone looking like her, appeared in a helmet and a smart looking pink and black leather jacket.'

'Sylvia and Rebecca bought them for her as a surprise,' said Celia.

'Very smart,' said Esther.

We broke into applause.

Matthew said:

'Do you remember how to ride this thing, Mother?'

There was no reply.

'Take your helmet off for a minute!' he shouted at her, while at the same time making gestures with his hands.

With her helmet off she looked a little sheepish.

'Quick put it back on!' someone said unkindly.

'I said "Do you remember how to ride it?"' said Matthew, over enunciating.

'I suppose it will all come back when I sit on it. But it was a long time ago. Perhaps we can leave it for today.'

'No!' came the shouts.

'Do you want to come on the back with me first to get used to it?'

'Certainly not,'

Aggie pushed him out of the way and climbed onto the seat.

'You have to kick-start it first.'

'I know that. I was just getting used to the feel of it again.'

We all laughed. It was as though they were performing on stage.

'Are you sure this is a good idea?' Esther said anxiously. 'Do you think she'll be safe?'

'Shall I get it going for you?' said Matthew

'Go on, then.'

Aggie removed herself from the seat and stood aside as her son gave a short sharp downward thrust and the engine fired up into life.

There was a round of applause.

He held the Lambretta by the forks while Aggie got back on.

'Your helmet,' said Sylvia, grabbing it from the top of the head of one of the children.

There was quite a lot of revving and a shouting conversation between Matthew and Aggie. Aggie put on her helmet and then suddenly, with a jerk, she was off. We expected her to stop at the end of the drive but she kept going.

'I wonder if we'll ever see her again,' Matthew said.

16

The party at Aggie's had been a perfect way to get into the mood for the trip to Rome. As we sat on the runway waiting to take off the following week, I felt the childish excitement that often accompanies the beginning of a holiday. There was also the guilty pleasure that I was on holiday while others were at work. Though it was a holiday for Cameron too, it may as well have been a study module at university the way he launched into his extended reading schedule. His hand luggage consisted almost entirely of books. He had resorted to carrying two in his hand as he boarded the plane - once he had run out of space in his own bag and had requisitioned the small amount of space I had left in mine.

Wedded to the printed word as I am, I nonetheless found myself saying:

'Have you thought of electronic books for your holiday?'

'I have my notebook. Besides, I need real books that I can see and touch – though I grant you I may be using Guttenberg a bit while I'm in Rome.'

'I hope you've found room for a few changes of clothes. Could get a bit whiffy after a few days if not.'

'I have at least one change of clothes. I presume this establishment has washing facilities.'

'Well, yes I think so. And I guess our clothes will dry in five minutes - if the forecast for the next week is anything to go by.'

'You do see the irony,' he said, returning to my earlier remark. 'You are the bookseller and you are chiding me for taking too many books.'

'Suppose you fill me in on the history of Rome,' I said to placate him as we accelerated along the runway. 'The potted version if you don't mind.'

'What do you want to know?'

'Well I know it was founded by the twins Romulus and Remus.'

'Well, whether it's true or not, it's a great story. They were the sons of Rhea Silvia who was condemned to prison whilst the twins were to be drowned in the Tiber. They were supposed to be descended from two Trojan heroes, Aeneas and Latinus. The servants, so the story goes, could not bear to throw them in the Tiber and left them on the bank of the river by a fig tree to be brought up by a she-wolf...'

'A bit like Mowgli in the *Jungle Books*...'

'Yes, I suppose, though they were later raised by a shepherd, Faustilus and his wife. When they grew up they threw out Amulius who had condemned them to death and set out to establish the city around the Palatine. According to legend, there was an argument between Romulus and Remus – there are several different versions even of this - but the upshot was that Remus was supposedly killed by Romulus or one of his followers and Romulus became King. Romulus founded Rome and some people say he gave it his name. But some historians claim that rather than giving his name to Rome, Rome gave the name to Romulus and a kind of back-story was created.

'Sounds like you're a bit dubious.'

'Well, you know, myth and legend, gods and goddesses, they are entwined with early Roman history. The Greeks, for example, like to claim that they were the true founders of Rome – but then many Romans like to claim that they had their origins in Greece. The great success of the Romans was that they didn't just conquer people, they were experts at absorbing them and making them into Romans and taking the best bits of the culture of the people they invaded. They admired the Greek culture and established links to it - like in the *Aenid*. The Romans were very good at reinventing history. You wanted the short version,' he continued, 'so...the republic was established in about 509 BC and lasted until about 27 BC, when Augustus came to power.'

'SPQR,' was all I could think to say.

'Exactly, the Senate and People of Rome. Then came the Roman Empire – 200 years of *Pax Romana* or Roman Peace. It lasted around 1500 years whereas the Republic lasted about 500. At its height Rome had well over a million people, an enormous number for that time.'

So he continued, though as he brought the history of Italy more up to date he explained in greater detail. By the time the plane had landed I felt I had a thorough background knowledge of the rise and fall of the republican towns and regions in Central and Northern Italy as opposed to foreign rule of the south by the Normans (and, eventually, the Austrians), the struggle between the Papacy and the Holy Roman Empire and all manner of intrigue by the Borgias and other powerful families.

'What do you know about Garibaldi?' he said to me at one point.

'Ah, those biscuits. Squashed fly biscuits we used to call them. You don't see them about as you used to, do you?'

As usual, he ignored my attempt at humour.

'But you do know they really were named after him?'

'Yes, well, I sort of assumed they were. Didn't he visit Britain?'

'Yes, after his visit to South Shields in 1854, Jonathan Carr, one of the great biscuit makers of the time, came up with the idea. He was admired in Britain as he was throughout the world. He was the great hope for democracy following the failure of the revolutions of 1848. As well as biscuits there were all sorts of Garibaldi souvenirs.'

This was typically Cameron. You may have thought he was reading from a book but this was just how he sounded. He could not help himself. And, of course, he had more to say.

'Not only did he unify Italy but both sides of the American Civil War wanted him to be a general for them. In many ways he was ahead of his time. He believed in God but hated the corrupting influence of the Catholic Church.'

'You'd better not say that too loudly when we visit the Vatican,' I told him.

For my part, I had studied, many years before, Italian Renaissance literature and knew about the importance of the 'Three crowns' of Italian Literature, Dante, Petrarch and Boccaccio and how their use of the vernacular language based around Tuscany was important in the development of the Italian language. I said as much to Cameron.

'Yes, you're right, of course. Unlike Britain and France it did not have one dominating capital city like London or Paris that influenced the language of the entire nation.

'What I am always amazed about,' I said, determined to make a contribution, 'is how much travel went on across Europe, when you think of all the difficulties of travel in those days and the length of time it took. Chaucer went to Europe many times for the King.'

'Ah, the *Froissart Chronicles*. I know about him because they are an important source for the Hundred Years' War.'

'That's the Hundred Years' War that wasn't a hundred years.'

'Quite right. There's disagreement about when it started and finished but there is some sort of consensus around 1337-1453.'

'Anyway, getting back to Chaucer, some people even think he met Boccaccio – which is very significant because there is no doubt that Chaucer was influenced by the *Decameron*. Others argue that he went to Padua and may even have met Petrarch there. I'm not sure if any of this has been proved, though.'

Cameron gave a sigh. I thought he was bored by my small contribution, which I thought was a little unfair given that this had been one of the few things I had said to interrupt his long monologue.

'What is it Cameron?' I asked as he let out a further sigh.

'Oh, it's just I think I have forgotten my *Blue Guide to Rome*,' said Cameron. 'I can't think how I managed to leave it behind.'

'You can always borrow something of my literature if you get short of reading material.'

'I'm not really into made-up literature.' This was his phrase for fiction. 'I prefer the real thing.'

'Ah, well, as Tabucchi says...' I turned to the relevant part of *Pereira Maintains*, the book I was enjoying reading at the moment and the phrase I had marked in pencil. *Philosophy appears to concern itself only with the truth but perhaps expresses only fantasies, while literature appears to concern itself only with fantasies, but perhaps it expresses the truth.'*

I felt like I had neatly punctured his non-fiction defence with a significant blow but I should have known better.

'Sounds exactly like something a novelist would say,' he said with his most dismissive air.

After clearing customs, we took a bus from the airport in Rome to Piazza Venezia. Dominating the square was the monolithic white marble building, the Victor Emmanuel Monument, often known colloquially as *The Wedding Cake* or *The Typewriter*.

'What a monstrosity,' said Cameron as we descended the steps from the coach.

'There's a good view from the top as I remember.'

'But it just hides the really good stuff. It shouldn't have been allowed.'

'I suppose it was thought that something impressive was needed to mark the first king of a united Italy.'

'I'm not against that, but it didn't have to be such an eyesore.'

17

Not surprisingly, given Cameron's vehement criticism, we did not stop to explore the Victor Emmanuel II monument. I did, though, hope to persuade Cameron to return so that we could look at the view from the top. A lift to the top was a relatively recent innovation so should not inconvenience us unduly in terms of time and Cameron's search for authentic Roman archaeological monuments.

There was no concierge at the apartments but, as is the modern way, it was arranged that someone would meet us to hand over the keys and explain the workings of the apartment. I had texted our contact, Alice Franzoni who had said she would be there from four. We were running a few minutes late so I texted her again. She came back, 'No problem.'

The fact that she had an English first name I hoped meant that she had good English as we were sadly lacking in anything but the most basic Italian.

Our accommodation was twenty minutes walk from the centre. Cameron and I were both keen walkers and would rather walk than take a bus or tube if we could possibly avoid it. But our first problem was crossing the road.

As we stood on the kerb at the zebra crossing at Piazza Venezia the cars raced past, it seemed without a thought of stopping. I had forgotten how it was. The cars would not stop unless you showed some intent. You had to earn your crossing in a game of bravado, bluff and bluster. I followed in the shadow of an Italian couple stepping out, confidently but not aggressively. As we did so, cars passed in front of us and behind us even as we walked. Miraculously, though, the ground we walked on remained free of traffic and we made it safely to the other side.

Despite his dislike of electronic books, where direction finding was concerned Cameron used electronic navigation. I kept my street map firmly in my pocket and followed in his wake while he paid close attention to a little dot on his phone. I was already enjoying the experience of being in Rome. I loved the feeling that there was a piece of history, an old church, monument or building, just waiting around nearly every corner.

We found the apartments easily enough. A young woman I guessed to be in her early twenties was sitting on a bench outside the closed courtyard area in front of them, reading a book. She stood up as we approached.

'Alice?' I said.

'You must be Elliot and Cameron. Welcome to the Apartments Popolo.'

She shook both our hands.

'I show you.'

She went towards a gate set into a low wall topped by tall railings.

'The small silver key for this lock.'

She held it up to us but had a bit trouble opening the gate with it.

'Ah, I turn to the left. You must turn to the right.'

She led us diagonally across a terrazzo courtyard. We entered a foyer through a glass panelled door and then turned right to a lift in the far corner.

'Press *presente* to make the lift come,' she instructed us.

While we waited for the lift to appear, I asked.

'Do you do this all the time?'

'Ah, no, my main job is artist.'

'Oh, what sort of art?'

'I make illustrations for books.'

Of course, I then had to tell her that I owned a bookshop and would look out for her illustrated books in the future.

We took the lift to the fourth floor, without Alice, as the lift was too small for the three of us and our small suitcases and rucksacks. There was the inevitable delay that seems peculiar to lifts where, just as you think that nothing is happening and you will be stuck inside forever, the lift suddenly launches into life.

'We should do a bit of basic shopping,' said Cameron as we passed between floors. 'I'm happy to do it on my own if you like.'

'Well, I was thinking of ringing Esther to let her know we've arrived safely and to check everything is OK with the shop. I know it will be but – you know?'

'OK. What do we need? Milk, coffee, bread, etc.'

'Yeah, fine, whatever you think. Don't forget some sugar.' I was one of what seemed to be a dying breed that could not give up sugar in my coffee.

'Now, this is important,' Alice said when she greeted us from the stair landing as we began to make our way out of the lift. You have to make sure this internal door is pulled all the way when you exit or the lift gets stuck.'

She gave us a quick demonstration of securing the door firmly into its closed position.

A gold key opened the door to the apartment.

'There are two sets of keys but if you lose one I am afraid you will have to pay.'

'OK, we will try not to,' I said.

She showed us the single bedroom and the sofa, which could be turned into a bed, in the lounge-cum-diner. I elected there and then to take the sofa. Apart from anything else I wanted to give Cameron plenty of space to store his books.

I paid particular attention to her instructions for operating the cooker as I had had frustrating moments on a past holiday when I had been unable to work out how the oven worked. Cameron asked about the nearest shops. She showed us a local map and a book of useful local information and important contact numbers and then announced she was leaving.

'Enjoy your holiday, ciao!'

We would, we assured her. With a cheery smile, she was gone.

Cameron left for the shops. I heard the clank of the lift moving into action once more, this time on its downward journey. I opened the sliding doors onto the wide balcony. There was a wooden table and chairs and, tucked away around the corner, a washing machine and clothes airer. I went over to the railings of the balcony and looked down into the street. There was Cameron emerging from the courtyard below. He began walking in one direction then, suddenly, changing his mind began walking in the other. It was quiet enough with just the occasional vehicle passing through. Every kerbside, though, was crowded with parked cars. In the distance was the faint hum of activity across Rome, the sound of traffic, one or two isolated excited voices and the inevitable sound of sirens - an ambulance, police car or fire engine. I imagined us sitting outside with our food and wine and a whole week of exploring, eating and drinking. Not a bad way to spend a week, I thought.

I rang Esther.

'*Come Stai*?' I said.

'*Sto bene, Elliot, grazie.*'

'I should know better than try to catch you out. Is everything OK in the shop?'

'*Certo.* More importantly, how are things going with you?'

'Well, we have just got here and Cameron has gone shopping. He did have a little tirade about the monstrous Victorio Emmanuel Monument so I hope he's not going to be like this about everything. '

'He does have a point. How's the apartment?'

'It's great. I'm just standing here on the balcony, in the warmth of the Rome sunshine, experiencing what I think they call *dolce far niente* – pleasant idleness.'

'That's great, exactly what you need.'

'And I intend to keep it that way. We're going to a restaurant we have vouchers for this evening - another perk of winning this holiday - the *Fortunato*, I think it's called. It's quite posh. I would like to explore one or two of the piazzas on the way - if we can squeeze it in.'

'You must, but keep that in your head, pleasant idleness, I like that expression. Just take it easy. I don't want to find out that you've been involved in a version of *The Italian Job.*'

'For once I will take your advice without question.'

'Well that's refreshing in itself. I'm afraid I'll have to go – something cooking, or burning rather – but I will catch up with you later.'

I put the phone down, smiling to myself, and I imagined Esther doing the same. I had a sudden great feeling of well-being. Esther was not with me in person but she was with me in spirit, and I was with my close friend Cameron, with whom I always got on well and was comfortable with.

I unpacked and had a quick shower (after spending a few minutes working out how it worked). I had finished by the time Cameron returned. It was still quite early in the evening and Cameron believed we had time to visit the Pantheon before going onto the restaurant, which was close by. I spent a blissful twenty minutes in a calm reading oasis with *Pereira Maintains* while Cameron put the shopping away and made himself ready for our trip out.

18

'The biggest unreinforced concrete dome in the world,' Cameron informed me as we approached the imposing edifice of the Pantheon.

'But not the original.' I had been reading my *Eyewitness Guide to Rome*.

'No quite right. In fact, it says it was built by Agrippa on the front of the building even though his version was destroyed. It hasn't been the luckiest building in history. It was destroyed by fire in 80 AD, then rebuilt by emperor Domitian. Struck by lightning in 110 AD. This is the third incarnation - started by Trajan and finished by Hadrian around 125 AD.'

'However did they build it?' I said as we looked up to the hole at the top (or *oculus* as Cameron informed me it should be called.)

'Amazing isn't it. 142 ft high and 142 ft wide.'

'They sound like remarkably similar numbers to me.'

He looked at me in a despairing sort of way but I was in a good mood. I could not help making corny and obvious jokes and was not about to moderate my behaviour.

'The walls are 20ft thick,' he continued. 'It's a kind of honeycomb structure with voids in the walls. What they did was use increasingly lighter materials as they got to the top.'

'So clever, weren't they?'

'There's a ring of stones at the oculus that distributes the weight of the dome. Can you believe it's 2,000 years old?

'*Of Angelic and not human design*, as Michelangelo said.'

He continued. 'It's the free space - that's the most remarkable thing. Most temples of the time had columns in the middle to hold the structure up.'

'Silencio,' announced a voice over the loudspeaker, followed by a request to respect the sacred building by keeping quiet, repeated in several languages. At first I thought this may be aimed at Cameron. His voice did carry when he was in lecture mode. The same announcement, though, was made several times while we were exploring the interior and it did not always coincide with Cameron speaking. It seemed to me that as a new wave of people entered and were awed by the spectacle of the interior, just as we had been, there was an excited buzz. I did not feel that the visitors were being intentionally disrespectful in any way, merely appreciative. That, though, was the way it seemed to be perceived by those in charge. We continued the rest of our viewing in silence or in whispers. We had both been well brought up and only needed to be told once.

'Pantheon meant "honour to all gods",' Cameron whispered to me. 'It was converted to a church in 609 AD when Pope Boniface IV consecrated the Pantheon as the Church of Santa Maria and Martyres.'

'How did you know that I didn't know that?' I whispered back.

'Just a lucky guess. The marble floor was restored in 1873 using the original Roman design.'

We still had about thirty minutes to spare when we left the Pantheon. We looked around the Piazza della Rotunda - in which the Pantheon stood.

'Used to be full of bird sellers in the nineteenth century you know,' Cameron pointed out to me. We made our way to the centre of the Piazza and the fountain with a red marble obelisk on top, brought over from Egypt, I guessed, not with the consent of the Egyptians.

'It was originally built under Ramses II for the Temple of Ra in Heliopolis,' he continued.

'How nice to have a temple named after you. I suppose "Ra" was Ramses nickname like saying "Ga" for Gary. The Temple of Ga sounds quite good actually – better than Gary.'

'Ra means sun, you idiot. It's The Temple of the Sun.'

'OK, I see I have overstepped the mark.'

Cameron could sometimes be a little harsh when I revealed my lack of historical knowledge.

'Anyway, when it was first brought over it was actually put inside the Pantheon. Eventually, it made its way to the Piazza di San Macuto before finding its way here. In fact, it's still called the *Obelisco Macutè.*'

A little further on we found the impressive columns that survive of the Temple of Hadrian, incorporated into the 17th century papal palace by Carlo Fontana, now occupied by the Borsa Italiana, the chief stock exchange in Italy.

19

A visit to the Pantheon followed by the prospect of a paid for meal at a posh restaurant felt like the perfect way to start our holiday. We had dressed as best as we could for the occasion, given the limited amount of space we had in our luggage. We were hoping that there was no fussy dress code as our options were distinctly limited. We both wore our only jackets with ill matching chinos (mine blue and Cameron's brown). We did not have ties with us.

The restaurant was half full, though it was still early in the evening. We were shown to a table in one corner. Just along from us, next to an ornamental fireplace, was a man sitting by himself. He nodded his head and smiled as we walked past him to take our seats.

'I think we should make the most of this,' said Cameron.

'Quite right!'

It was a bit different from the pub fare we usually had on our holidays, where a steak pie or chicken Kiev were common options. We took our time discussing every permutation on the menu.

The man at the adjacent table looked across at us and met our eyes. He was an elegant man, perhaps in his early fifties, in an expensive looking shiny suit. He caught my eye.

'Are you visiting from the UK?' he enquired.

'Yes, we're here for a week,' I said.

'Ah, I love the UK and its people. A very civilised country.'

'Well, maybe, not all the time. We have our own problems.'

'We are very much looking forward to the splendours of Rome,' added Cameron.

'Well, I can't deny that there is much to see in Rome and the food is very good if you know where to look for it. I eat here quite regularly,' he continued 'and really the food is superb. The fish dishes are particularly fine with fresh fish brought in three or four times a week.'

His English was excellent with a barely discernible Italian accent.

'Thank you, that's good to know.'

'*Enchanté.*'

'How friendly the Italians are,' said Cameron.

We returned to the serious business of choosing our food. I was not sure whether Cameron was influenced by our new acquaintance or not but he decided on *Spaghetti alle Vongole*, spaghetti with clams, for his first course. I had had a bad experience with mussels a few years before and I did not want to repeat it. Instead, for my starter, I had *Cacio e Pepe*, a combination of pasta, *Pecorino Romano* cheese and black pepper corns.

Our new acquaintance nodded his approval when our first courses arrived.

'Ah, you are choosing like two natives. Good choices. You know, *Cacio e Pepe* was not on most menus until a few years ago, considered too routine or more like a home snack. But when it is cooked like they do it here, with just the right *Pecorino Romano Cheese* and ground and roasted peppercorns, it is ...' he kissed his hand, 'fantastic.'

'Great!'

'Sometimes what is simplest is best, no? Well, do not let me disturb you any further. It is good to make your acquaintance. I hope you enjoy the meal and the rest of your stay. *Buon appetito*!' He seemed to know several of the staff intimately. They nodded and smiled as they walked past his table. Shortly after, he was joined by an older man sporting a moustache. He was wearing a mackintosh despite the heat and carrying a large battered leather suitcase from which he extracted a large old book. He placed it on the table in front of him. The other man immediately picked it up and began leafing through it enthusiastically. The newcomer took off his mackintosh, sat down opposite, and they began ordering.

When we had finished our first course, it seemed all too quickly, we looked across to the table and, in a typically English gesture, both put out thumbs up to the shiny suit. He smiled and said something to his colleague who nodded to us in a friendly manner.

We continued the seafood theme for the main course with Cameron choosing lobster while I opted for turbot poached in white wine. We did have to pay for the wine to accompany the meal and it was expensive but we had decided to restrict ourselves to one bottle between us, a *Pecorino*. The label promised citrus fruits, hawthorn and orange blossom. I am not sure if I was quite able to identify them but we had a pleasant time trying. We did not want a hangover as the next day, our first full day, we wanted to visit the Colosseum.

Though this restaurant was not the sort of place we would ordinarily have picked as it was simply too expensive for our meagre pockets, it was perhaps all the more enjoyable for that. We savoured the evening and took our time, revelling in this moment of luxury. I could not help glancing around at some of the other diners, mostly well-heeled and dressed for the occasion, unlike ourselves in our crumpled jackets. I mentioned this to Cameron.

'They probably think we're eccentric English millionaires. You know, there's a theory that people with real money don't care how they dress.'

'Well, in that case, we must be loaded.'

We both laughed like naughty schoolboys.

With the variety of dishes it proved to be a long evening. Despite our good intentions, the one bottle between us proved not to be enough and half-way through the meal, enhanced by our new self-imposed status of pretend eccentric English millionaires, we ordered a second bottle, this time of the house red.

Though I would count Cameron as one of my best and closest friends, in typical male fashion, we did not make much contact with each other outside Christmas, birthdays and holidays like this one, so there was always much to catch up on. Cameron and Rachael had two children, both at secondary school. His children's endeavours to play the clarinet and the guitar, Cameron's history projects and Rachael's experience as a counsellor took up quite a bit of our conversation time. Cameron was at last going to put all his knowledge into a book, cutting back on his teaching time by one day a week, which I applauded.

'You must tell me when it's published so I can make sure I have it in stock.'

'I expect a full window display no less.'

'You must have a launch with us and come and give a talk.'

'I would like that.'

Cameron scooped up a morsel of aubergine and cheese.'

'That's enough about me. How's Esther and, in particular, how are you and Esther?'

This was not an area of conversation I was too comfortable with, but during our holiday the previous year I had confided in Cameron my feelings for Esther so I could not really blame him for asking. However, it was not a topic I wished to dwell on.

'Esther is fine and I'm fine about Esther.'

'Meaning what.'

'Meaning we just rub along together.'

'That sounds promising.'

Cameron gave a very un-Cameron-like laugh.

'Cameron, that's not worthy of you.'

'Sorry.'

'The truth is, nothing has changed. We're just good friends, as we were this time last year, and I am very happy with that.'

He looked at me, I thought, a little pityingly.

'Well, quite happy with that. As you know, I wish it was otherwise but that's how it is.'

'There's no one else in her life?'

'As far as I know, no-one except her chickens.'

'I wonder if she really knows how you feel.'

'I don't understand what you're getting at.'

'Well, you know, have you ever told her how you feel about her?'

'Not in so many words. Not in any words actually – but, you know, she's happy as she is.'

'You surmise?'

'I surmise. But I am in a pretty good surmising position. I see her nearly every day.'

'Does that mean you have given up?'

'No, well, the truth is I don't know.'

'Perhaps you should look elsewhere. I'm sure you will like my Italian friend Laura who you will shortly meet – and I believe she's unattached at the moment.'

'I've never really seen you as a matchmaker. I came to look at old buildings, learn some history and relax a bit, not to find a wife.'

'I wasn't necessarily meaning that you marry her.'

'Neither am I interested in a holiday fling.'

'I'm sure she's not either.'

'Sorry, I'm just a bit sensitive about it. I'm sure she's very nice.'

'Very nice and very clever – and I'm sure you will have much to talk about.'

'Well, I look forward to it.'

'I'll send her a text and see if she's free tomorrow.'

I marvelled at how adeptly he tapped out a text and sent it within seconds.

'You do that like a man half your age,' I said.

As we progressed through the menu and the second bottle of wine, Cameron's conversation became more expansive. For all his knowledge and experience of teaching, and lecturing on various subjects, he was, generally, in normal conversation quite shy and diffident. The alcohol, though, had loosened his tongue. This time we were back on the familiar subject of books and we had strayed onto my involvement the previous year with the theft of a *First Folio* of the works of Shakespeare from the local university. It was worth more than a million pounds. Esther and I were instrumental in bringing the perpetrator to justice. Cameron was extolling our virtues.

'How many did you say there are in existence?' asked Cameron.

'About 200 – but the amazing thing is that because of the way they were produced – with human intervention - each one is slightly different. It's this rarity value alongside the fact that they are each unique that makes them so valuable.'

'You should become knighted booksellers...' exclaimed Cameron.

I put up my hand to try and stop him engaging in his flattery, though deep down, there was a little bit of pride in the recognition that my good and respected friend was giving me.

The man across from us once more glanced in our direction. After a few moments, he rose from his table and walked over to us.

'Excuse me interrupting you again. I could not help overhearing some of your conversation. You obviously have a great interest in books. No doubt you deal in them?'

'A little,' I said.

'Nonsense,' said Cameron, who continued in his ebullient un-Cameron-like manner, 'He thinks about little else and has a marvellous bookshop to match.'

'Really?' He lifted his right eyebrow and put out his hand, 'Let me introduce myself. I am Antonio Cantalbrini. I am in that trade myself. I adore antiquarian books. You know, the moment you came in I could see that you were gentlemen of culture. I would love to show you some of my books.'

This no doubt explained the appearance of his dining companion. How nice to come to dinner with a book in hand to discuss while eating.

'Well, I don't really class myself...'

I was trying to tell him that I was a new and second-hand

bookseller rather than a specialist antiquarian one. Most of our books cost just a few pounds and I had never sold anything worth more than a few hundred.

'I'm sure we would love to see them,' Cameron said, before I could finish getting my words out.

'Are you in Rome for very long?'

'Just the week and today is our first day.'

'Well we must strike, as you English say, while the metal is hot.'

I was worried that Cameron was going to pull him up in the slight error in his choice of words for the phrase but instead he said:

'How about tomorrow?'

'I'm sure that will be fine.' said Cantalbrini. 'How about we say 5.00 pm? I can pick you up if you give me your address.'

'Number 4, Apartments Popolo.'

'I will just make a note.'

He patted his jacket.

'I seemed to have mislaid my pen.'

His dining companion shouted from behind him.

'I have one here, Mr Cantalbrini'

'Ah, Mr Abruzzio. Write it down for me will you.' He repeated the address.

'I know the building. That's not too far. Till tomorrow then.'

Cantalbrini smiled and shook hands with Cameron and then me, bowed and proceeded to follow his companion. When he reached the door he turned towards us and gave a little wave and a smile.

'*A domani,*' he said. We smiled and waved back. My smile I realised was totally artificial for what I really had in mind at that moment was admonishing Cameron.

'Why on earth did you say that? I will be totally out of my depth.'

'Nonsense, you know a lot about books.'

'About literature and the content of books. I'm not so hot in the area of antiquarian books. Very little of our stock is worth more than a few pounds.'

'You underestimate yourself. And, just think, if you did go into antiquarian bookselling, it would open up new avenues for you. You could just sell a few books a week, work less hours and come on more holidays like this.'

'But the cost of the stock and the opportunities to get it wrong and pay over the odds – it's a risky business.'

'And he seems to like you,' Cameron continued, appearing not to hear me.

'Like me. How can he? He doesn't know me.'

'Well, he probably respects what you have done. You know, That *First Folio* business – if that *is* what he overheard.'

'No wonder he's interested in us. He probably thinks that we're used to dealing in items of that worth after hearing our conversation. Don't you see, he probably thinks I'm a high value dealer because of it?'

'I'm sorry, but it can't hurt can it? You must admit Antonio seems a very nice man. We are not committed to anything. You can explain the real nature of your business when we see him.'

'I suppose you're right,' I conceded but without any inner conviction.

20

Cameron was up early the next morning eager to explore Rome. I forgot about any idea of a lie-in. As I had not been to the local shops yet I offered to take my turn to buy some fresh bread for breakfast. The smell of coffee as I passed several cafés on the way to the shop was enticing. I resisted the urge to indulge, hurriedly bought some bread and made my way back to the apartment.

When I returned I was about to call the lift when I noticed it said *occupie*. I waited a little while, but nothing seemed to happen. Then I remembered what Alice had said about closing the door properly. I rattled the door in front. That was certainly closed. I waited two or three minutes but the lift still did not appear. Perhaps a door left open at any of the floors was enough to stop the lift working on all floors? I had not considered this when she had said it. I started to ascend the stairs checking the door of the lift on each floor to see that it was securely fastened. Sweat trickled down my back. Even though it was still early the temperature had already climbed beyond 30 degrees. On the third floor, a little out of breath, I found the culprit – a door only partially closed. I closed the door and called the lift. Almost immediately I saw the sign saying *presente*. It was only one more floor but I was grateful even for that small saving of energy. I related my experience to Cameron once I had made it into the flat.

'Oh, yes, that happened to me as well,' said Cameron. 'You have to be careful to make sure that the inner door is pulled across before you exit the lift, otherwise we all suffer, whichever floor it is.'

I put some rolls on a plate and made some coffee. I took it over to the breakfast table. Cameron came bustling in with a map, a guidebook and a large academic looking tome. I understood that my state of *dolce far niente* was probably now over.

'I was thinking the Colosseum, the Forum and the Palatine Hill for starters. There's quite a lot of other stuff we can pick up on the way if we want,' said Cameron.

'I was speaking to Esther last night and she advised me to take it easy. I don't want to cram too much in without appreciating what I am looking at. Also, if you remember, you have arranged for us to meet with that book collector.'

'Oh, yes, well, you can get a ticket that lasts two days so we can take our time over it.'

'That sounds good.'

He sat down with his history book and removed a book mark.

'Of course, we don't have to stick together all the time if we have our mobiles with us,' I said. 'If you want to go and explore a bit more while I read a book or something – that's fine.'

Though I greatly appreciated his knowledge and guidance, sometimes I just wanted to absorb things at my own pace.

'Of course,' he said with a distracted air, 'Whatever you say.' I realised, though, I had lost him, at that moment, to some Roman God or Emperor or ancient monument as he became engrossed in his book.

An hour later we were strolling along the Via dei Fori Imperiali towards the Colosseum.

'Quite a grand approach,' I ventured.

'Another barbaric act by Il Duce. He destroyed loads of churches, a monastery and a convent and a whole neighbourhood of houses. It was an archaeological disaster. The only good thing they have done in recent years is to pedestrianise the bit near the Colosseum. At least now you can get across to the museum without risking life and limb as before.'

'I hope you're not going to be like this all the time. I thought you were looking forward to coming to Rome.'

'Yes, of course, I'm very pleased to be here – but certain things need to be said.'

As recommended in our guide, we picked up our ticket from the ticket office at the Forum entrance where the queues were shorter and then walked back to the Colosseum to queue for the entrance. As we walked from the Forum to the Colosseum Cameron's phone made a noise.

'Ah, that's Laura. Looks like she has sent a text. She said she's free tomorrow about 7.00 pm. She will contact me later about where to meet. Shall I say it is OK?'

'Yes, do. What is it exactly that she does?'

'She has a role with the library service. I think it's quite a high powered job.'

'Sounds interesting.'

He fiddled around with his phone and sent a message.

'Before we go in we should look at the outside,' said Cameron. 'That way you can get an appreciation of how it all fits together.' Cameron talked as he waved his arms in the direction of the walls while we strolled along.

'As you can see, a lot of the outer wall is missing, roughly half. Byron called it *a noble wreck in ruinous perfection.*'

'That sounds like Byron all right. It's a shame but, even so, the size of it is still pretty impressive. No wonder it's called the *Colosseum.*'

He gave a wry smile. I had often seen that look when he had been explaining some point of history to me and I had made a crass incorrect historical statement.

'I know that look: the teacher pitying the poor ignorant pupil. What have I said?'

'Well, what you have said does not sound unreasonable except it is more likely that the name emanated from the Colossus statue of Nero nearby. It originally stood in Nero's Imperial Villa on the north of the Palatine Hill. It was modified later and then moved closer to what we now know as the Colosseum – because the other thing is that it wasn't known as the Colosseum when it was built. The name Colosseum wasn't really used until medieval times.'

'So, what was it called?'

'The Amphitheatre or Hunting Theatre.'

Once we had finished our walk around the circumference, we strolled towards the entrance.

'The other thing that you have to remember,' said Cameron, 'is that this was not necessarily considered the most important building in Rome. The Circus Maximus, which we will see later from the Palatine Hill, was thought to hold 250,000 when there was a large event such as a chariot race. And many people marvelled more at Trajan's Forum next door. The forum had a vast piazza, 300 metres long by 185 metres wide.'

'Well, it still looks quite impressive to me – though you do have to use your imagination quite a lot, I agree.'

'The building that was often considered the most impressive is the Temple of Jupiter on the Capitoline Hill, the most important temple in Ancient Rome. Unfortunately, it was destroyed by fire in 83 BC. And this was not the last time. The fourth version built by Domitian was thought to have lasted over 300 years until it was closed down by Emperor Theodosius. By the sixteenth century, with people using it for building materials, the temple had practically disappeared.'

'What a sad state of affairs. But going back to what you said earlier. Are you saying the Colosseum wasn't that important?'

'No, I'm definitely not saying that. I just think you have to put it into perspective. The Colosseum was important in its own right. What was really important about it was that it was a kind of gift to the people providing for their entertainment, built on the back of the spoils of the *Sack of Jerusalem* under Vespasian. It was also a means of the Emperor communicating with the people. Though the republic was gone by the time it was opened in AD 80 there was a kind of perceived need to be accessible to the populous and sometimes to be held accountable. It was important for an emperor to make a good impression at the Colosseum. At a big event, for example, he would distribute small gifts or food to the audience.'

As Cameron talked we made our way through the entrance up some steps and towards the centre. I looked across at some seats, trying to imagine people sitting there while a gladiatorial contest was taking place. It was as though Cameron had divined my thoughts.

'Those seats, believe it or not, were not built until the 1930s and, apparently are not even a very good representation of what they would have been like originally.'

We walked further and came by a large Cross.

'You're going to tell me next that the Christians were not thrown to the lions.'

'There is actually very little evidence of that but the Christian Church would have you believe that it was happening all the time. They were very adept at creating martyrs to the Colosseum even if they were born before it was built. For a time you could say they appropriated the Colosseum with the Stations of the Cross. In fact, it wasn't until the late nineteenth century when there was serious archaeological work carried out that the Stations of the Cross and all other Christian remnants were cleared away.'

He pointed.

'That Cross was, ironically, introduced by Mussolini in 1926 as the original Cross had been torn down much earlier.'

'I thought you were a lay preacher.'

'I am, but that does not mean I believe in all the Christian propaganda. To be fair to them, they were persecuted quite dramatically before it was built, if accounts are to be believed, most notably by Emperor Nero.'

'He's the one who fiddled while Rome burnt, right?'

'It's true that he played the fiddle – or, more accurately, the lyre. There is a theory, though it has never been proved, that Nero started the fire himself and that he persecuted Christians to detract from it. If you believe Tacitus, Christians were torn apart by dogs and others were burnt alive as human torches.'

'Makes you wonder why they bothered – being Christians, I mean.'

'A lot of persecutions of Christians happened in the third century when there was a succession of emperors. The Christians were scapegoats in the same way that Jews were.'

'But gladiators – there must have been gladiators.'

'Oh, yes gladiators there most certainly were – though again the actual descriptions of gladiatorial fights are few and far between. They definitely happened but were perhaps not quite as regular a feature as you would think. Apart from anything else, the cost of putting on an event was enormous and gladiators were expensive – so it was not in their interests to get rid of their asset too quickly.'

'So all this stuff about the bloody arena is not true?'

'It probably was but not with the frequency we imagine. What was definitely true was the amount of animals that were killed. Sometimes they were hunted in the Colosseum. Different animals were encouraged to fight each other or kill convicted criminals. It was all pretty barbaric. You know when it was opened in AD 80 over 9,000 animals were killed – if Dio Cassius is to be believed. There are also reports that it was flooded and there was a sea battle – though quite how they contained the water I don't know.'

'But nevertheless it has stood the test of time.'

'Well, yes you're right in a way, but what you have to remember is that much of what you see is reconstruction of the nineteenth century when there was a renewed interest after years of decline.

'Nowadays, rather than be seen as a site of human and animal killing, it celebrates the repeal of the death penalty anywhere in the world by having its arches lit up at night.'

'I think I'm more comfortable with that.'

21

Having finished our visit to the Colosseum, and in order to be ready for Antonio Cantalbrini, we rushed back to the apartment and had the quickest of showers. I was quite pleased with the time constraint as it made Cameron focus more on the essential aspects of things. He did have a tendency to go into a kind of historical revelry from which I was afraid he would one day never return.

We went onto the balcony where we had a good view of the street while we awaited Cantalbrini's arrival. In fact, it was he who spotted us. He pulled up and closed the door on his car in one easy motion, looked up as though by instinct, waved and shouted 'Ciao'. A minute or two later we joined him and slipped into his sleek black Audi. He pulled smoothly away.

'You are in one of the apartments upstairs?'

'Yes, on the fourth floor.'

'I am so pleased you could come. I have some nice things to show you – I think and hope you will agree.'

I was in the front seat so the burden naturally fell to me to make the conversation.

'Whereabouts do you live?' I asked.

'Just off the Via Veneto, or Via Vittorio Veneto if we were to give it its full name - after the *Battle of Vittorio Veneto.*'

'A victorious battle,' chipped in Cameron. 'It helped bring the First World War to an end.'

'And the setting for *La Dolce Vita,*' I added.

That was my cue to tell him about the window competition and how we came to be here.

'Fortuitous, is it not? Perhaps all this was meant to be,' said Cantalbrini. 'The Via Veneto, I'm afraid, is a bit of a disgrace now.'

'Really?' It was not obvious to me. As we began to drive down it I thought it looked rather smart.

'Rubbish on the streets, rats everywhere. There have been rats among the tables of the Hotel Excelsior - one of the smartest hotels in Rome.'

'That's a shame.'

He took his arms off the wheel and raised them momentarily 'The Via Veneto Association has its arms up.'

'You mean it is *up in arms*?' said Cameron.

'Sorry, my English is not always as good as it should be.'

'On the contrary,' I said, 'it's excellent.' I felt annoyed with Cameron for correcting him as we knew perfectly well what he meant. 'I only wish we had a few more words of Italian.'

Cantalbrini parked his car and we took the lift to his apartment. Once through the entrance we entered a large room with a concave brick ceiling, a brick arch and stylish brown doors inlaid with white panels. There were two leather sofas at right angles to each other, a polished wooden floor and patterned rug. Most impressive of all, though (as far as I was concerned), the walls were lined with shelving and a wide array of books.

'My library,' said Cantalbrini.

'Very impressive,' said Cameron.

I nodded in agreement.

'Feel free to have a look. And if there is anything you particularly like, just let me know and perhaps we can arrange a price.'

'That's very kind of you but, unfortunately, I am not here on a buying expedition. I think you may have got the wrong idea about my bookselling activities. Most of my books just sell for a few pounds.'

'Just have a look anyway. There is, as you say, no charge for looking.'

I wondered if he thought that my reticence was a bit of pre-negotiation bluster. Cameron was already deeply immersed in one of the volumes.

'They're not *all* in Italian. The ones in this section,' he strode over to the right hand side wall, 'are all in English.'

This was an extraordinarily well presented library with the books beautifully displayed in elegant natural wood bookcases. On three of the four sides the walls were covered from floor to ceiling with shelves. On the fourth side there were more shelves to the outer edge of each wall and, in the centre, a large window overlooking the street, with a low table in front.

I naturally moved towards the books written in English and saw a tremendous variety of editions and authors. Nearly all of them were in very good condition, mostly hardbacks with their original dust jackets, even though they were old and, in many cases, probably the majority, first editions. I noticed Tennessee Williams, Allen Ginsberg, Agatha Christie, Dashiel Hammett, Hardy and Dickens.

'It truly is a wonderful library,' I said. I probably had nearly as many books in my own house on a variety of bookcases of different designs and quite a few piles on the floor - but they were for the most part poor specimens by comparison.

I could easily have spent the whole day there but I was afraid of looking too interested in particular volumes in case Cantalbrini assumed I wanted to buy any of them. All the same, it was difficult not to become engrossed.

Cameron, of course, had found a volume on Roman history, had taken a seat and was intently reading.

'Can I offer you some refreshments? A glass of wine or a whisky?'

'I think it's a bit early for me,' I said.

'Me too. But I wouldn't mind a cup of tea or coffee,' said Cameron.

Cantalbrini disappeared and, after a few minutes, brought in two cups of coffee on a tray along with a book. We took our coffees and he handed the book over to me. It was an early copy of *Pickwick Papers*.

'A very nice copy,' I said.

'Ah, yes you are probably used to seeing many copies of Dickens work.'

'Yes, people come in all excited because they have an old Dickens book but they don't realise that so many of them were mass produced. Just because it's old does not necessarily make a book valuable.'

'You are correct, of course. But this, as you may be aware, is a fine first edition. What we term a mixed first, early issue. With extra illustrations by Seymour and Phiz. The price on the open market is over £3,000.'

I leafed through.

'Yes, I seem to remember there was quite a lot of controversy over whether Seymour or Dickens was responsible for the idea of the *Pickwick Papers*.'

'I think it's fair to say that Seymour was the illustrator who produced the sketches on which *Pickwick Papers* was based,' Cantalbrini continued. 'It was originally supposed to be his sporting plates with Dickens supplying the text for a kind of picture novel. When Dickens became involved he made it clear that he had no particular sporting knowledge and the way it developed was that the plates accompanied the text rather than the other way around.'

'This is *very* nice,' I said, examining it closely.

'Seymour was a sad soul in many ways. He ended up committing suicide before the second part of the book was published,' said Cantalbrini.

'Then they hired another illustrator, didn't they?'

'Yes, they hired Buss but Dickens did not get on with him.'

'Then they settled on Phiz – Hablot Knight Browne that is.' I was remembering this from a module I studied on nineteenth century English Literature in university days.

'That's right. But you know, that the first two plates were not signed Phiz?'

'No, I didn't know that,' I said.

'He had acquired a pseudonym by then but it was "Nemo" rather than Phiz. They changed it because they thought Phiz was a better fit with Boz – Dickens' pseudonym.'

'Really, I didn't know that. That's very interesting.'

'To hear you two talk is a joy,' said Cameron.

I did not spoil the moment by reminding him that we were discussing 'made up stuff' which he usually held in contempt.

'You know, I like you two,' said Cantalbrini. 'I knew as soon as I saw you and then spoke to you. I thought, these are men I can trust. I would be happy to sell this edition of *Pickwick Papers* to you for just £2,000. You may think that is a little crazy but for me, you understand, this way I can save some money. If you take it I will not have to bother with auction houses and promoting it in a catalogue and all the bother of book fairs. Then I can make room for something else while you take your time selling it and coming up with a really good profit. As you say in English I think, mutually beneficial.'

He saw my reluctance.

'Of course, you need to satisfy yourself that it is a genuine copy. Have a good look, take all the details you want and check it out for yourself.'

'It can't hurt can it to just check it out?' said Cameron who was already jotting down details in the little notebook that he carried around with him.'

I wanted to say 'Where did you get all these?' but did not want to sound impertinent. However, Cameron, in his sometimes innocent and guileless way said:

'How did you acquire such a good collection. I expect you attend a lot of auctions?'

'Auctions, sometimes yes, but you know, there are also contacts and acquaintances within the book trade. Much of my business is done like this. You know, conversations with good people. It is often easier and simpler. As you say, *less hassle*.'

We continued our perusal of the books. The coffee was excellent. After twenty minutes or so of browsing and drinking our coffee I said:

'It's all very interesting but I'm afraid we need to go.'

'I understand. Have a think about the *Pickwick Papers* and, when you have more time come back. I also have a few editions that are *extra special*. I have to be careful, though,' he continued, 'because of their value. So I keep them hidden away, for security purposes. But I would be very happy to show them to you.'

'That's kind,' I said. 'We'll have a think about it.'

'We'll definitely come back,' said Cameron. 'I can't wait to see what they're like.'

'You have an expression in Inglese which is quite,' he searched for the word and then found it (though he mis-pronounced it by not managing to pronounce the 't' sound), 'quite apt. *It is not what you know but who you know*.'

He smiled at us both conspiratorially.

'Ah, yes contacts. Communication is so important,' said Cameron. For a moment I thought Cameron was going to give us a lesson in history where communication was found wanting. I sensed, though, that his interpretation was not quite that which Antonio Cantalbrini intended and I felt just a slight sense of unease.

'You know, I like dealing with clients from abroad, especially the UK. It simplifies things. People don't ask as many questions.'

'Oh, yes?'

'Well, you know, people get the wrong idea about ownership. There is so much distrust about where things have come from. Unfortunately, there is so much of a history of corruption in Italy. Even when it is not there, people think it is.'

'There's a perception of corruption?'

'That's it, exactly as you say, there is the perception of corruption. People are inclined not to trust you even when there is nothing to be suspicious about. I prefer to deal with those that do not ask unnecessary questions. Do you understand what I am saying?'

'I think so,' I said, though I was not at all sure that I did.

'The trouble is culture and politics are inextricably…' he made a revolving motion with his hands, 'entwined.'

22

'Makes you think, doesn't it?' said Cameron after we had returned to our apartment.

'Makes me think what?'

'You know, if you could just find a couple of thousand for that Pickwick book?'

'How likely is that?'

'Well, you know, perhaps a small loan. You could start small, perhaps with the *Pickwick Papers*, and then when you have more than got your money back – go on to something a little bit more expensive. If you did not want to go it alone, I could perhaps help you find the money and we could share the profits. I can see it now, regular visits to Rome financed by just one or two purchases of books a month. Much better than slogging it out the way you do in your bookshop.'

'I understand what you're saying but, you know, one of the few things my mother says that I entirely agree with, is that if something looks too good to be true, it often really is. And the other thing, which I do know about, is that just because something has a high value on the internet, it doesn't mean you are guaranteed to sell it for that sort of price – or at all.'

We looked up the *Pickwick Papers* on a couple of dealers' websites. If anything, he had understated the price of the book. We would be effectively buying something at nearly half price.

'What about eating?' I said to Cameron. I wanted to change the subject. I wasn't comfortable with Cameron the entrepreneur. It was not his normal territory and was all a bit unsettling.

'It's still quite early.'

'We could rustle up some pasta.'

'Well, I was wondering, you know, we still have quite a lot of crusty bread.'

'It'll be a bit hard now.'

'Ah, yes, but there is this trick that I learnt from Rachael. You sprinkle it with water and put it in the oven for ten minutes and it comes out as good as new. We have salami, grapes, tomatoes and all sorts – a veritable feast – and we could visit one or two of the wonderful piazzas we haven't had a chance to visit yet and eat it along the way.'

'Sounds like a good plan. And we would save a bit of money after being a bit profligate on the wine last night when we were supposed to be having a free meal.'

'Exactly!'

After Cameron had made our supper we loaded our rucksacks, left the apartments and began our meandering tour. Cameron was in an uncharacteristically relaxed mood. He usually had a distinct purpose in mind, which generally involved a bewildering number of sites to visit, take in and comment on - but this time his ambitions were quite modest.

'We don't need to go to Piazza della Rotunda as we saw that when we went to the Pantheon but I wondered if this may be the moment to visit the Piazza Trevi where the Fountain is. The piazza itself isn't up to much but the fountain is really something.'

I was also keen to visit it myself. I had been there before but it was so long ago and such a fleeting visit, that I only had a vague memory of it.

'Yes, why not?'

Cameron looked into his phone, pointed to the right and abruptly took off in that direction while I followed in his wake.

'It's quite recent by Rome standards you know,' Cameron said as we bumbled along, 'only completed in 1762.'

'But magnificent.'

'Quite so.'

We had hoped that most tourists would have gone off for their evening meals and that the fountain may not be too busy. However, once we rounded a small street that led on to the fountain, taking us, as it were, almost unaware, we found crowds of people.

'The end points of the aqueducts are called *mostra*,' said Cameron, 'and the Trevi Fountain is one of the most magnificent. There is another one in the Piazza del Popolo if we get a chance to visit it.'

'There's something about all that rushing water.'

'They say it's good for you, all those positive ions. It's one of the things you really have to admire about the Romans, those aqueducts bringing water into the city from the surrounding hills to fountains all over Rome. What a brilliant piece of engineering!'

We eventually made our way to the front of the fountain and took our turn at throwing coins into it. I was about to throw my 50 cent Euro coin in when Cameron stopped me.

'No, this way: right hand over left shoulder.'

'I didn't think you were superstitious.'

'I'm not. I'm just following Roman protocol. And, if there is anything in this superstition, it means we will return to Rome again, which, I must admit, I would rather like to do. I don't think we're going to have a chance to see everything this trip. I'd love, for example, to get the chance to explore underground.'

'Isn't there something about "three coins in the fountain"?'

'Yes, the inspiration behind the film. The first is supposed to ensure your return to Rome – we have already done that – the second, a new romance, and the third marriage. Here we go!' He handed me two 50 sent Euros. 'I don't have any need for the other two as I have my Rachael but you might.'

'I'm not sure about the marriage bit.'

'I don't think you can get away with just two – it's all or nothing.' I humoured him and threw the two coins in to join my earlier one – with my right hand and from the left shoulder as he had instructed.

'You know, over a million Euro gets thrown into the fountain over the year. They scoop it out each day and put it into some sort of charity for the poor.'

'How on earth did they manage to film that scene in *La Dolce Vita* with Anita Ekberg without any tourists around?'

'It was shot in midwinter. Apparently, Anita Ekberg had no trouble standing in there in her skimpy black dress but Mastrionni, who joined her, had to wear a wetsuit beneath his clothes and could only be persuaded to join her after he got drunk as a lord on a bottle of Vodka.'

'Might say more about the fact that Ekberg is from Sweden than anything else.' I said. 'She'd be used to the cold.'

Having left the fountain and after several interesting diversions along narrow streets, we found our way into the Piazza Farnese, fronted by the elegant facade of the Palazzo Farnese and the Church and Convent of Santa Brigida, dedicated to St Bridget of

Sweden and the Swedish national church in Rome. I wondered if Anita Ekberg had visited it while she was here. Then we entered into the Piazza Campo dei' Fiori next door.

'The Field of Flowers. What a beautiful name,' I said.

'Yes, it *sounds* very romantic. But, as so often, there is a dark side. The Field of Flowers was exactly what it was originally but then it became a public square for executions. That statue over there...' He pointed to a hooded statue on top of a tall plinth. 'That's Giordano Bruno who was burned at the stake here in 1600.'

'Did he do something terrible?'

'Yes, he had the temerity to agree with Copernicus that the Earth goes around the sun and suggest that there may be other worlds in the universe than ours. Cosmic pluralism I think they call it.'

'Sounds like he was way ahead of his time.'

'Far too much for the Catholic Church, I'm afraid. He was tried in Rome over seven years, and then executed here – hung upside down naked and burned at the stake.'

'Charming.'

'His ashes were thrown into the Tiber and all his works were placed in the *Index Librorum Prohibitorum - The List of Prohibited Books*, books that were considered heretical and that Catholics should not read. They didn't get rid of the list until 1966. Apparently there was just too much for them to keep up with in the end.'

By now the square was busy and bustling with crowds of mainly young people.

'It has gained a reputation in recent years for a being a bit lively, football supporters and tourist stag parties and the like.'

Though it was noisy, I liked the electric, energetic air and there seemed to be plenty of good humour and tolerance around. There was a busker playing his greatest hits on one side of the square and on another a couple of violinists, a young woman and an old man playing their hearts out in the style of Django Reinhardt and Stephane Grappelli at the Hot Club of Paris. For a moment I thought I noticed some very un-Cameron like moves to the rhythm - and then decided I must be mistaken.

'Doesn't seem to be anywhere much to sit down to eat, though, all the benches are taken up. I must admit I'm getting a little hungry now. '

'We'd be better off in the Piazza Navona for that, I think, as it's a bit crowded here. It's only a few hundred yards, that way, I believe.'

Cameron pointed straight ahead and bounded forward. I trotted after him feeling a bit like his lapdog.

Piazza Navona is a magnificent large oblong square with three fountains. At the heart of the square we found the Fontana dei Quattro Fiumi (Fountain of the Four Rivers). There were four river gods represented and, above them, another Egyptian obelisk thought to have been brought there from the Circus of Maxentius. The four rivers represented the four rivers of the main continents over which the Pope had authority: The Nile (Africa), The Danube (Europe), The Ganges (Asia) and the Rio de la Plata (The Americas).

'It used to be "The Stadium of Domitian" you know and was used as an athletics stadium,' said Cameron.

'Yes, I can easily see how that could be. It's the right shape and size.'

'It was used for gladiatorial fights too and it was the city market for a long time until that was moved up the road to the Campo dei' Fiori in the second half of the 19th century.'

We sat in silence for a while taking in the magnificence of it all.

'It's a much better spot for supper. A lot quieter as you suggested,' I said.

'Perhaps we can finish off with a beer in one of the bars in the *Campo dei' Fioro* - before we go home.'

'Good idea. We don't want to drink too much before our epic trip to the Forum and the Palatine tomorrow.'

'We even have somewhere to wash our hands,' said Cameron.

He went across to the fountain just a few feet away and began his ablutions. When he had finished I did the same before sitting back beside him on the stone steps.'

'Salami, crusty bread, Ricotta and tomatoes. What can beat it?' I nodded in agreement as Cameron chomped away but just as I was about to do the same I heard a whistle and a uniformed policeman ran in our direction gesticulating wildly.

'*No manger…*'

I turned my head around, looking for the source of the trouble. It was a few moments before I realised that we were the offenders and that he was shouting at us. Eating in public, however modestly, it seems, was not allowed. The square was full of restaurants. No doubt they wanted us to visit one of them rather than bring our own snack.

We were embarrassed. We quickly packed our food away into our rucksacks and moved on.'

'I can't see that we were doing any harm. It's not as though we were swigging a bottle of wine,' Cameron said. 'I can see there are still elements of Mussolini's Fascist Italy operating here.'

'That's going a bit far,' I said but I could see that Cameron felt strongly about his liberty being infringed.

Embarrassed, and quietly outraged at the same time, we continued on our way looking around the square. We found the other two fountains, Fontana del Nettuno at the Northern end featuring Neptune fighting with an octopus and the Fontana del Moro at the southern end featuring a Moor wrestling with a dolphin, the Church of Sant' Angese, the Palazzo Torres and the Palazzo Braschi, which houses the Museo de Roma – all the while sneaking pieces of bread and salami and grapes from our rucksacks, in surreptitious defiance of the street police. We decided not to enter the museum in the square as we did not have enough time to fully appreciate it at that moment. We would come back another time, we promised ourselves.

Once we thought we had had our fill of the square and feeling a little less welcome than formerly, we went back to the energetic atmosphere of the Campo dei' Fiori and found a bar where we ordered two bottles of Peroni.

Our little contretemps for now forgotten, we took in the atmosphere observing the comings and goings, the music and the conversation that drifted our way. It was the most relaxed I had felt in ages. The atmosphere, the energy, the music - we soaked it up like sponges and ordered a second beer. Inevitably, we came back to our visit to Cantalbrini and his vast and interesting collection of books.

'So, what do you really think about Antonio Cantalbrini?' I asked Cameron.

'He's very pleasant. Very Italian, I suppose.'

'I think he inhabits a much more rarefied bookselling atmosphere than the one I inhabit.'

'He's very voluble – as many Italians are. And very knowledgeable. Isn't that a British thing, we are distrustful of those who are too clever? Don't they say, "Intellectuals begin at Calais"?'

'It's not the intellectual bit I'm wary about. It was something about the way he talked about people being mistrustful about how books are acquired. I wasn't exactly sure what he meant but one interpretation could be that he is not averse to a little sharp practice where books were concerned.

'I must admit, it didn't strike me like that.'

We returned to our beer and the sight of a fire-eater swallowing a sword in front of us in the square, the spectacle of which was spoilt for me by the anxiety I felt that this might be the time when it went wrong and that I would witness a tragedy. I would rather a juggler and the embarrassment of a few dropped balls than someone with their throat on fire. How exactly would you help someone in that situation? The First Aid course I had taken many years before did not cover that sort of thing.

'Which police were they do you think – the ones who stopped us eating?' I said.

'I suspect the *Municipal Police* or the *Provincial Police*, but you can take your pick. Do you know there are more police in Italy than any other European country? There are five national police forces.'

'I know there is the *Carabinieri* and the *State Police*.'

'Well, there is also the *Finance Police* and the *Prison Police*. There's even, believe it or not, the *Forestry Police*.'

'You mean the Special Branch?' I ventured, expecting the usual disdainful response from Cameron at my attempt at a joke. But, at last one of my jokes had made its mark. He collapsed in his chair with uncontrollable laughter and began choking. We became the centre of attention and such was his distress a waiter brought him a glass of water and I patted him on the back.

'I'm so sorry he said; It caught me off guard. I'm not used to your jokes actually *being funny*.'

'I suppose we had better be getting back,' I said after we had finished our second beer.'

'Would you mind if we made one slight diversion on the way back via the Theatre of Marcellus? It's just a few minutes down the road and you can see a lot of it from the main road.'

The diversion (as was usual, I had to admit) was worthwhile. The Theatre of Marcellus, Cameron explained, was originally begun by Julius Caesar and finished by Augustus, dedicated to his nephew Marcus Claudius Marcellus. It was the largest and most important theatre in ancient Rome and, in its day, held cultural events such as plays, musical contests and poetry recitals – before the rise of the popularity of circuses and gladiator games when they needed bigger venues, so the Circus Maximus and Colosseum were built.

'I think I would be more suited to living in ancient Rome.' I said. 'I'd much rather go to a poetry evening than watch someone being run through with a sword.'

'And look you can,' he said, 'well at least an opera.' He pointed to a poster. They were going to put on a performance of *Tosca* over the next few days. 'Not really my sort of thing, all those nonsensical stories.'

'Esther would love it, I bet,' I said. 'Her late husband was an opera singer and she did some singing herself. And Puccini. Even I can appreciate that he could knock out a good opera tune.'

There were many alterations to the Theatre of Marcellus building over the years, Cameron explained. During the eleventh and twelfth centuries it had been turned into a fortress by the Pierleone family and then in the sixteenth and eighteenth centuries alterations were made by the Savelli and Orsini families. The upper floors were divided into apartments but many of the columns and arches remained and the influence on later projects like the Colosseum was obvious.

On the way back, I received a text from Esther asking how we were.

'All fine,' I texted back. 'Will it be too late to give you a quick call when I get back to the apartment – probably about 10.30?'

She came back:

'No problem, please do.'

When we arrived back we were a little tired but in good spirits. Cameron made us both coffees while I rang Esther.

I explained about our meeting with Cantalbrini. I wanted to know what her thoughts were.

'Sounds like an interesting character. Do you know anything about him?'

'Nothing – except that he is a bookdealer, has excellent English and is very convincing. I have to say he is really quite charming.'

'I have known second-hand car salesmen like that.'

'At last the voice of reason.'

'Not something I can remember you saying to me too often.'

'Well, you know, Cameron is becoming all gung-ho about it and keeps saying what a great idea it is. It's like he's suddenly changed character. I guess it's because he's on holiday. I think what's behind it is that he wants more trips to Rome and believes that we can become rich by doing high class book deals.'

'It makes you wonder why we're not doing it over here if it is such a good idea. I guess it's OK if you have a bit of cash behind you.'

'That's probably the big difference in the end. If you have a bit of a war chest, you don't mind a bit of speculation. But I feel that if I borrowed like Cameron suggested, it would be more like gambling than bookselling.'

'I think you have got to do what you are comfortable with. For what it's worth, I think I would feel the same way.'

'Thanks, Esther. I needed this conversation and I think you have confirmed what I really feel. Anyway, how are things at the bookshop?'

'Not too bad. Quiet really, but only to be expected at this time of year.'

'Yeah.'

'A few tourists on their way to somewhere else.'

'Ah, yes, that's us - always the staging post never the destination.'

23

The following day we had breakfasted by seven-thirty. We wanted to make an early start so that we had plenty of time to use up the other part of our ticket to visit the Forum and the Palatine. There was so much to see and I knew, with Cameron's desire to experience everything in great detail, that we would struggle to get round it all in one day - and we were due to meet Cameron's friend Laura in the evening.

Once again we made our way along the Via dei Fori Imperiali via Piazza Venezia, past Trajan's Market on the left and turned right before the Colosseum, which we had visited the day before. The Via dei Fori Imperiali, Cameron explained, had been built by Mussolini who saw himself as a modern day Augustus restoring Italy to its glorious imperial past.

The Forum itself adjoins the Palatine at the point at which you begin to ascend the hill. We decided we would leave The Palatine until last – after we had tackled the Forum.

Turning right as we entered the Forum we came across the Temple of the Deified Caesar, the site as Cameron explained to me, where the corpse of Caesar was cremated. It had originally been intended that Caesar should be buried at the Capitoline Hill among the other 'gods' but the priests would not allow it. There was a quarrel and in the end the people of Rome, the family and Caesar's close associates decided to build his funeral pyre in the Forum. Mark Antony delivered his famous speech over the corpse. There was a wax image of Caesar on display with the 23 wounds of his assassinators.

'I remember studying the play Julius Caesar at school,' I said to Cameron. '*O, pardon me, thou bleeding piece of earth, I come to bury Caesar not to praise him* and all that'.

'One bit of history Shakespeare got more or less right,' said Cameron. 'Caesar had a lot to do with development of the Forum and many other buildings of Rome. It's difficult to think now, but Rome was not considered as great a city as Alexandria. He created more space for law courts and for voting and a new senate house. He also wanted to create a theatre that would rival Pompey's and, this will interest you, a library to rival Alexandria's. But, as he was assassinated in 44 BC none of that ever happened.

'So he had in mind a sort of public works building scheme.'

'Well, in a sense it was what was needed. His biggest problem was lack of money. There was widespread debt, lenders were demanding repayment of loans and house values had plummeted. Sound familiar? There was a shortage of coins in circulation as people began to hoard money. Caesar made it illegal to keep more than a certain amount of cash and declared that property must be sold at pre-civil war value. It was the war that helped precipitate the crisis that led to widespread unemployment. The erection of public buildings helped deal with this and he also offered the poorest a new life in an overseas Roman colony. When he died he left 300,000 Sesterces to the citizens of Rome and left his villa, gardens and art gallery to the public.'

'Sounds very Keynesian. No wonder they wanted to build a temple to him.'

'Then, of course, there was his calendar.'

'The Julian Calendar. Isn't it great to have the calendar named after yourself? Just imagine the Elliot or Cameron calendar. What would you do? Probably introduce an extra day each week where everyone was made to study more history.'

He ignored my silliness.

'Well, the old Roman calendar was a bit of a mess. Romulus introduced a calendar that only had ten months. March was the first month of the year. Winter was not given any month so the year only lasted 304 days with 61 days unaccounted for. The Republican calendar came later and two extra months, January and February were introduced but it was a bit confusing. For example, September whose name means seventh month now became the ninth month. Anyway, it got a bit closer to what we have now with 4 months of 31 days, 7 of 29 days and one of 28. The trouble is the year only lasted 355 days. To try and keep the calendar in keeping with the seasons they introduced a leap month every two or three years after February 23 or 24. They usually added 22 or 23 days to the year.'

'Talk about complicated.'

'Crazy, isn't it?'

'Why didn't they just add an extra 10 days each year?'

'Politics came into it.'

'Doesn't it always?'

'The trouble was that the leap month was initiated by the Pontifex Maximus, the chief high priest of the College of Pontiffs. It was the most important position in the ancient Roman religion. The decision of when to introduce the extra time meant an official could stay in office longer. It was when Julius Caesar became the Pontifex Maximus that he put in place the Julian Calendar – in 45 BC. He introduced the 365 day year and every four years a leap day to adjust the extra quarter day, in February. The first problem though, was to address the misalignment that had occurred between the natural seasons and the calendar at that point. In order to do this 46 BC was made 445 days long.'

'When people say it's been a long year they really meant it then.'

'It's often termed the *last year of confusion*.'

'I'm not sure if that's true. I still find most years confusing.'

'They incorporated the phases of the moon - the Ides which were the day of the full moon were the 13th or 15th of the month depending on the length of the month...'

'Beware the Ides of March and all that... but hadn't we better get on,' I said, 'if we keep talking like this we will never get round to seeing anything.'

All this talk of the Julian Calendar was sending my head into a spin.

'Yes, of course, you're right. We can discuss the Gregorian Calendar later.'

Cameron was full of childish excitement and intent as we moved from area to area, walking among the ruins of the Forum. It was already hot at this early hour and 32 degrees centigrade was predicted as the day progressed. However, I don't think Cameron noticed it. I made a mental note to keep an eye on him as he was liable to be oblivious to anything else when he had so much history to contemplate in front of him.

As we wandered along he began to issue forth in his accustomed way, drawing on his recently acquired knowledge from his extensive reading. On occasions he would refer to one of the half dozen texts he was carrying in his large bag – though not that often, as so much of the information seemed already to have been absorbed into that inordinately large brain of his. I am afraid I was not always as dutiful a student as I should have been and sometimes found my mind wandering. Every now and then, though, something he said would attract my attention as it did at that moment.

'Where we are walking now,' he said, 'was the Argiletum. This was the route of the *Cloaca Maxima*, the amazing sewer system built in the sixth century. It drained the local marshes and carried the effluent away to the Tiber. It still drains some of the rainwater away even today.'

'What a grand name for a sewer.'

'It does literally mean *The Greatest Sewer*. Tarquin Superbus is supposed to have been responsible for a lot of it.'

'I'm sure I travelled on the Tarquin Superbus last time I went to London. They do these amazing deals on day returns.'

As usual he did not give due recognition to what I thought was my extremely witty comment.

'*Superbus* means lofty or proud. He was the last king before the republic. I think he fell out of favour with the people because he was forever building things.'

'How ungrateful. You would think they would be pleased to have all that waste taken away?'

'You're right, even though many see it as just a sewer, it was rightly renowned and even had a temple in its honour, The Temple Venus Cloacina. You can still see the base of it over there...' He pointed vaguely as though I would somehow be able to recognise the remains. 'It was begun by the Etruscans as an open air canal but the Romans gradually covered it over and developed it.'

He should have one of those laser pointer things, I thought to myself, so he could give me a more accurate idea of where I was supposed to be looking.

Eventually, we came to the impressive Arch of Septimus Severus built in AD 203 to commemorate victory over the Parthians. Until the 18th century most of it was buried.

'There's a palace built by him on the Palatine, which is supposed to be mighty impressive. Can't wait to see it – but there's quite a bit more still to see here.'

Beyond, were the eight surviving columns of the Temple of Saturn.

'That's another Superbus project but this is the third reincarnation. The second one was destroyed by fire.'

We came across another great arch, the Arch of Titus built, as

Cameron explained, in about AD 82 by the emperor Domitian (again) in memory of his older brother Titus and his victories in battle, including the *Siege of Jerusalem* which Cameron had mentioned before. According to Josephus, the Jewish historian, over a million people were killed, the majority of whom were Jewish.

'The destruction of the first and second temples is still mourned at the Jewish fast *Tisha B'Av*,' said Cameron. The arch has become a model for many others since, including the Arc de Triomphe.' We looked at the inscription which Cameron read in translation from one of his books: *The Roman Senate and People dedicate this to the divine Titus Vespasianus Augustus, Son of the divine Vespasian.*

There were many other fascinating sites including the House of the Vestal Virgins, once a complex of 50 or more rooms, full now of decapitated statues but overlooking ponds of water lilies and goldfish. It was oddly evocative and gave me a strange and slightly eerie feeling of contact with this vanished world. One of the pedestals had the inscription removed, it was speculated, because the disgraced Vestal Virgin (Claudia) betrayed the cult by converting to Christianity. Further on were the elegant Temple of Vesta and the Temple of Romulus

But in terms of scale, the Basilica of Constantine and Maxentius was difficult to match. Looking at the remaining massive three barrel-vaulted aisles, which were used as law courts, it felt as though they were built for a race of giants or gods rather than mere mortals.

Cameron in his meticulous way, examined every piece of ground and masonry in great detail, seemingly immune to the heat that became more oppressive as the day progressed. Though I had truly enjoyed the experience, I was relieved when he said, 'I think we can now move onto the Palatine.'

At the Arch of Titus we began a slightly weary ascent of the hill before turning right into the long underground tunnel of the Cryptoporticus, built, I was informed, by Emperor Nero. On the walls of the House of Livia were mythological scenes. The God Mercury is seen rescuing the mortal woman Lo, who had been transformed into a white heifer in order to hide his affair with her.

'What a lot of trouble to go to,' I said.

The picture on the back wall of the central room showed the monster Polyphemus in water with a young cupid riding on its shoulders, chasing the nymph Galatea as she rides a sea-horse.

We then moved on to the House of Augusta and further frescoes before a visit to the Iron Age Huts and the Hut of Romulus.

We decided to have lunch in the Farnese Gardens. There was a landscaped area in which we found some shade. We had a magnificent view of the Forum and beyond. Before we ate, we explored a tomb in the centre of the rose garden. It was dedicated to archaeologist Giacomo Boni, who took part in the excavation of the Forum and the Palatine Hill, and lived here between 1907 and 1925. We had our customary fare of crusty bread, cheese and grapes on a shady bench among the ruins. This time we were not interrupted by a whistle and the waving arms of an outraged policeman. With the panoramic view over Rome as our background, we felt as if we were on top of the world. I felt a kind of peace here and hoped for a good long break. However, after only a few minutes, once we had finished our lunch, Cameron said:

'Must be getting on. Don't want to be running out of time when we have so much to see.'

24

From the Farnese Gardens we made our way to the ruins of the palace Domus Flavia. Cameron, as usual, was waxing lyrical, using his recently acquired knowledge, explaining how Domus Flavia was conceived by the third of the Flavian Emperors, Domitian in AD 81 and how, in order to achieve what he wanted, he flattened a number of houses in the process. I have to admit that at that moment I was feeling the need to be solitary and was not as receptive as usual. It was then that I noticed a small group of Japanese tourists listening attentively to Cameron just a few feet away from us. At that moment he was explaining that Domitian had the walls of the courtyard covered with shiny slabs of marble to act as mirrors so that he could spy anyone trying to stab him in the back.

'As it was,' he went on to explain, 'it didn't save him. Some say that his assassination was organised by his wife. Suetonius, though, put it down to a conspiracy of court officials.'

'It seems to me that he had a reason to be paranoid, with all those mirrors', I said. 'He probably went around saying to himself, *I used to be paranoid but now I know they are watching me.*'

I didn't even get a smile out of Cameron following my comments.

One of the Japanese tourists put up a hand. I hoped he didn't want me to explain the joke. I tend to think they rather lose their force when you have to go into explanations. But it was to Cameron that he directed the question.

'Why not they don't like him?'

Cameron flinched slightly as he realised that the question had not come from me but the little group that had formed behind him. But, after only momentary unease, he began to take it in his stride and addressed his reply to the group, now in teacher mode. I was thankful that Cameron did not admonish the tourist who had asked the question for using a double negative. It was the sort of thing he was perfectly capable of.

'Well, he had lots of enemies in the Senate.'

'But this was not a republic now?'

'No, it was what is known as a *Principate*. It was, in fact a kind of monarchical dictatorship but the trappings of the Senate and the idea of a democracy were still there. A lot of the emperors were sensitive to this and kept some of the decision making in the Senate. Domitian was not like that. He didn't like the senators. He took away every bit of their powers and ruled along with a small set of his friends.'

He's the one who was responsible for building so many things. Perhaps dictatorships were not so bad after all, I thought to myself.

'He also spent long periods of time away from Rome,' Cameron continued. 'It's fair to say that he was loathed by the Senate. He didn't try to appease them in any way and began executing them in large numbers. After he was slain himself his name was erased from memory, which indicates just how much he was hated.'

I had suddenly changed my mind again about the positive aspects of a dictatorship.

'Did he never do any good not at all?' asked another of the tourists.

It must be double negative day, I thought. I felt it was time for me to make my escape.

'Sorry to interrupt your lecture but I think I may just wander a bit and find some shade. I'll meet you at the exit at six.'

Cameron waved his hand in a peremptory gesture of acknowledgement. He would have made quite a good emperor I decided - if he had better fashion sense. He appeared to be enjoying the status of informal guide and I did not want to cramp his style – eccentric as he looked in his cheese-cloth shirt, long ill-fitting shorts and odd-looking hat. Perhaps this is what attracted the Japanese tourists to think of him as a bona fide tourist guide – a kind of uniform of the British academic. He didn't need to walk along carrying a flag.

I slipped away as Cameron explained that it was difficult to appreciate Domitian's true standing as Emperor because of the fact that his memory was wiped from history, but that he was probably a sound financial manager, had rebuilt the Temple of Jupiter on the Capitoline Hill and spent plenty of time invading England. I was not sure why Cameron considered the last point a positive one.

Probably his Scottish ancestry, I thought.

After a few minutes wandering, and I have to admit I was enjoying this less intense way of touring the Palatine, I found myself in The Stadium, which looked like a kind of Roman circus for chariot racing but, I discovered as I read my guide, was too small to accommodate chariot racing. It was, in fact, believed to be a sunken garden.

Once I had rounded the corner I saw below me a large grassy space that I realised represented the former grandeur of the Circus Maximus. I consulted my guide once more. In its time it had been the largest venue in Rome and the site of many famous events including chariot racing. It had reputedly held 200,000 people, as Cameron had said, dwarfing the capacity of the Colosseum. It was particularly popular in the early days for the *Ludi*, or public games, connected to religious festivals - including chariot races and beast hunts. Some of these festivals lasted several days – like an Irish wedding I once went to. It found its ideal form under Trajan who rebuilt the Circus entirely in stone – though it was not without its disasters: 13,000 people were killed when a section of seating collapsed. After the sixth century the Circus fell into disuse and it was quarried for building materials. The area had always been prone to flooding and over the years the original track and much of the seating had been covered by soil. There have been archaeological digs to uncover some parts of it but it has proved to be a mammoth task and most of it remains covered. In recent times it has been used for large concerts. In 2007 Genesis performed in front of an estimated 500,000 people (apparently it was free) and the Stones to 71,000 people on their tour in 2014. I wondered if Cameron knew, or whether this information was far too modern for his tastes. Perhaps I would test him out later, I thought.

I turned back towards the centre of the Palatine Hill and found my way to the Museo Palatino, built in 1936. Inside were reconstructions and artefacts ranging from the Iron Age to Roman times. On the first floor were fragments of architecture and sculptures from the Augustus era and later, and some artefacts from the Temple of Apollo.

I spent a little more time there than I had intended and when I emerged from the museum it was after 5.30 pm. I needed to cover everything else that I wished to see within the next thirty minutes. I had already visited the Stadium but not seen the ruins on the other side of it, which are part of the Domus Severiana, the palace extension conceived by Septimus Severus in the 3rd century AD – so I hurried in that direction.

I descended a staircase and turned right and, after ten minutes or so of further exploration, I eventually found my way to a platform where there was a further view of the Circus Maximus. I returned up the staircase and, conscious of the time, made my way quickly back towards the exit. I gave Cameron a quick ring to let him know my whereabouts. There was no reply but I imagined that he was too busy and had a vivid image of him pursued by the Japanese tourists, still being plied with questions. Or, perhaps, the group has swelled to ten or twenty or more and they were following him around like the Pied Piper – not to their own death but to their own enlightenment through the exposition of his knowledge. I chuckled to myself at the thought and sent him a text instead.

I gave him until 6.15 before I tried phoning him again. Once again the call went straight to the messaging service. Now the museum attendants were in full cry in that insistent way they have – broking no compromise. I imagined they were hungry and keen to have their evening meal rather than indulge lackadaisical tourists. I hoped Cameron would not accuse them of being *Fascists* as he had thought the police who had stopped us eating our picnic were.

'The museum attendants will flush him out,' I thought as I was myself propelled towards the exit so that I had to wait on the other side. It was now nearly 6.20. I decided to sit down and read a book for a while rather than agitating after there was no reply from a further phone call. I sent Cameron another text saying that I was now outside the exit in case there was any misunderstanding. I read some more of the book on the Palatine. When it reached 6.25 I heard the sound of a text arriving (the sound of a bottle opener).

Ah, I thought, at last.

But it was not Cameron. It was Esther hoping I had had a great time in the Palatine.

I was having a great time, I thought, but now I was feeling distinctly grumpy with Cameron. I would reply to her later.

'Where are you?????' I launched off a text to Cameron.

By the time it reached 6.35 the area around the exit had gone quiet. There were no more gatekeepers around so I was not even able to ask if they had seen a lost Englishman. I started to walk away from the exit towards the Arch of Constantine, which stands between the Colosseum and the Palatine Hill, and rang again. I became distracted for a moment by the monument which, like the one to Titus in the Forum, was also very impressive. In fact, it is the largest of the triumphal arches.

With no reply from Cameron I sent another message without too much hope. I was now beginning to think that perhaps his phone was at fault. Perhaps it had run out of battery or he could not get a signal? I tried ringing rather than texting. The call went straight to answer-phone, an indication, I guessed, that the battery had run down. I looked at the map inside my guidebook again. It was then that I saw that there was more than one exit. I had exited at the Palatine but you could also exit at the Forum entrance where we came in with our tickets at the beginning of the day. I could see it all now. Cameron, I suspected, had gone back to the Forum entrance/exit. Probably, he remembered something that he needed desperately to see on the way. There was a logic to it I had to agree – to exit from the way you came in. I had been herded along with a number of other tourists to the Palatine exit, by the Italian gatekeepers, expecting the same thing would happen to Cameron. I hurried round to the Forum entrance. There was no one there at all. I stood for five minutes slap bang in front of the entrance so that I could easily be seen, but there was no sign of Cameron.

I was not sure what to do. I walked back to the Palatine exit and waited five minutes. Then I returned to the Forum entrance, hoping that he had had the same thought and I would meet him on the way. There was an ominous lack of activity and no official to ask. Time was marching on.

Well, no matter, I'm sure he has done the sensible thing and gone back to the apartment, I thought to myself. I guessed this is what I might have done in his place.

I sighed, partly at my own incomprehension, and the fact that some of our precious holiday time had been frittered away. No doubt he would be back at the apartment when I arrived and we could have a good laugh about it with Laura, have a nice evening meal and share a bottle of wine between us.

As I walked the twenty minutes or so back to the apartment, I had a vision that he would greet me at the doorway, arms folded and slightly grumpy, which at this stage I would not have minded at all. I put the key in the lock, opened the door and called his name. There was a profound silence. I looked around the flat and called again. He sometimes would listen to a history podcast with his earphones in, which meant he could not hear a thing. I searched for him in the bathroom, the bedroom, the toilet and the sitting-room-cum-dining-room. I went out onto the balcony. No Cameron.

I felt I needed to share this with someone.

25

I sent Esther a delayed reply to the text message she had sent me when I was at the Palatine and asked her if I could Skype her. She came back to me within five minutes.

'I seem to have lost Cameron,' I said and explained the circumstances.

'Well, it's a big city, I'm sure he'll turn up soon. Maybe he stopped to see something on the way back to the apartment.'

'Yeah, I'm sure you're right. That's the sort of thing he would do.'

'You're worried though aren't you? I can see that.'

For a moment I had forgotten that she could see me. I remembered a film some years ago, set in the future, where seeing each other on a screen as you talked to each other on a device had been shown as an everyday concept – and now here it was. It was as though we were living in a science fiction film. Of course, this was my take on it. Most people, I realised, especially those a few years younger than me, took it in their stride without any sense of awe or wonder.

'It's unlike him, though. He's been missing for two hours,' I said. 'He's quite careful as a rule. I'm usually the more reckless one.'

'Don't I know it!'

'Even if his phone is dead, you would have thought he would have found a public phone and contacted me by now.'

'He may not have your number, especially if his battery has run down or he may have lost his phone.'

This was where science fiction came face to face with reality; technology did not mean anything unless it was working.

'That's true.'

'Perhaps he met someone.'

'As far as I know the only person he knows in Rome is Laura and surely she would have contacted me if they had met. It's possible that he bumped into someone from home, though. It happened to me once in Paris, in the *Champs-Elysees*. But I'm sure he would still have tried to contact me.'

'Perhaps he got the time wrong – you know, he may have remembered seven when you said six.'

'I suppose that's possible. But, then, the Palatine definitely began closing at six – though it was effectively nearly six-thirty by the time they got everybody out. Do you think I should go back and have another look? It's just gone seven now.'

'How long does it take to get there?'

'About twenty minutes walking – fifteen if I hurry.'

'It may be worth it. You never know, you might meet him on the way. At least it will feel like you are doing something.'

'OK, I'll do that then.'

'I know it's a worry but usually these things work out. It's usually some silly misunderstanding.'

'I know.'

I left the apartment but not before leaving a note for him in big letters, ending it 'Do not go anywhere. I will be back'. I left it on the carpet in front of the doorway entrance so he could not possibly miss it. I made my way slowly back along the streets, all the while keeping my eyes peeled in case I spotted him. The entrance, the kiosk and the area around it was, as I suspected it would be, devoid of all life except a lone pigeon contentedly cooing and picking away at some discarded food.

I waited there self-consciously for ten minutes making myself as visible as possible just in case Cameron was keeping an eye on the entrance too. I tried his phone a couple more times and still got the message service. I then walked to the other entrance and waited another five minutes before deciding to go back to the apartment. It now seemed like a foolish enterprise. Had I not already tried this when I could not find him when the Forum and Palatine closed at six? I was killing time as much as anything, hoping that in the meantime the situation would be resolved. Perhaps that was why Esther had suggested it, to keep me busy rather than moping around the apartment in the hope that he would turn up in the meantime.

The one person who may be able to help me, I realised, was Rachael, Cameron's wife. He may have contacted her, perhaps to ask if she had my mobile number. And if he had contacted her, well, at least I would know if he was all right. The trouble was, if he hadn't, Rachael would be worried - even though he had only been missing two hours or so.

I had Cameron's landline on my phone. It was just after eight thirty when I rang.

'Hello.'

'Rachael, it's Elliot.'

'Is something wrong?'

It was clear that Cameron had not contacted her.

'Yes, actually, I have lost Cameron,' I gave an unconvincing laugh.

I explained.

'So it's only a couple of hours or so since you have seen him?'

'I suppose, technically, it is only about four or five hours, if you count when I went off on my own at the Palatine.' I explained about the Japanese tourists. She laughed at this.

'I must say, that's typically Cameron.'

'But it feels longer,' I continued. 'But you're right, I'm probably worrying over nothing.'

But then, why did you ring me if it is nothing, was the obvious reply?

'He's usually pretty sensible,' she said.

'I know.'

'What do you think?'

'Well, I think he's either lost his mobile or it has lost its charge or got broken or something.'

'Didn't he know the address?'

'I'm pretty sure he did. It's not a difficult one to remember. But you know it's easy to get confused in a big city. It's possible that he could have got lost, but then he would probably ring you wouldn't he – unless he didn't want to worry you.'

There was an uncomfortable silence. I was rambling and probably making her more worried rather than reassuring her.

'He has this friend, Laura,' I said.

'Ah, yes, you don't think he is with her – or he could have rung her if he had her phone number rather than yours?'

'I don't know even if he knows where she lives but we were due to meet her this evening. I don't have her number I'm afraid.'

'I suppose if he did know where she lives and he did get lost he may have made his way to hers.'

'Well, that's logical. But then wouldn't they have contacted one of us?'

'But if they didn't have your number – if Cameron has lost his phone or can't get it working?'

'Yeah, but they could have come to the apartment – but then I am not there at the moment and if he really can't remember where it is... I think I had best get back there - then at least that takes one of the variables out.'

'I don't know if I have any details but I could do a bit of snooping through Cameron's office. I will see if I can find a number for Laura and come back to you.'

'I suppose I might be able to find something at this end – in the apartment. But then he probably took his contact details with him. But I'll have a snoop around as well. You never know.'

She rang off.

I returned to the apartment. After another quick round of shouting out Cameron's name in the forlorn hope that he may have turned up without me noticing, I went into the bedroom and started to look through Cameron's things. It was a strange feeling being given permission to snoop. In truth there was not that much stuff as we had restricted ourselves to the one small case we were allowed and our hand luggage, despite the fact that Cameron had gone a bit overboard with books. In fact, his belongings were dominated by books. There were three or four history books and one guide book on the kitchen table but there were six more in the bedroom, some open, all marked with bookmarks in some way suggesting that reading was in progress. I opened his case, which contained a light jumper (probably not needed), a couple of T-shirts and underpants. In the flap of the suitcase lid were some more personal looking items, some corn plasters, adhesive plaster tape and some paracetamol. What I was really looking for was a note with Laura's phone number. If I could contact her, not only would I be able to apologise for not meeting her but she may, being a local, have some good suggestions about finding Cameron or reporting him missing.

I returned to his books and began examining the bookmarks and pieces of paper. Whilst I found several interesting looking notes relating to Cameron's world of history, (Was Caligula mad? Roman warships not rowed by slaves?), none of them was a phone number. I did get into a mild panic when I realised that I had taken one of the pieces of paper that he was using for a bookmark and had forgotten which page it had come from. I guiltily shoved it back about a third way through the book hoping it was in about the right place and that he would not remember. I knew I was clutching at straws about finding phone numbers as he had in all probability stored them on his phone.

I went back to the lounge and I tried to make myself read one of the guide books. I opened it at the pages covering the Palatine. Maybe the book would give me an answer. But all it did was confirm that there were two entrances. My mind kept wandering. My appetite had gone and I wondered whether, wherever Cameron was, he had an opportunity to find something to eat. He did have quite a healthy appetite. It was difficult waiting and not doing. By the time nine-thirty came around my thoughts had turned to whether I should report that Cameron was missing to the police. I remembered something about waiting 24 hours before the police would take your missing persons enquiry seriously.

Then my phone rang again. I was hoping it was Cameron or, if not, Laura or Esther. In fact, it was my mother.

'Ah, I'm glad I caught you,' she said.

'Actually, Mum, I'm really sorry but I am in a bit of a fix at the moment.'

'What sort of fix?'

'I've lost my friend Cameron and I am waiting for an urgent phone...'

'That's a bit careless.'

'When I say lost, I mean he got separated from me.'

'Hasn't he got his mobile?'

'Yes, but I think his battery must have run down.'

'Perhaps he could do with a new battery.'

As usual, under my mother's influence, our conversation was meandering in all sorts of directions.

'Are you sure he hasn't just gone home?'

Then I realised that she probably did not realise that I was in Italy. It had not come up in our recent conversations. Esther's suggestion, at one stage, that I might take my mother to Rome had made me wary of bringing up the subject when talking to her.

'Mum, you do realise that I'm in Rome?'

'Italy? I thought you were at home – not Rome.'

I was not sure if she meant it as a joke.

'I wondered why you weren't answering your landline.'

At one time my mother only had my landline. Esther had helpfully passed my mobile number on to her to make it easier for her to get in touch with me.

'It's probably costing me a fortune.'

The phone went dead shortly after. I smiled. Perhaps I could use the ruse of saying I was abroad another time – even if I wasn't, I thought wickedly.

*

Then my conscience got the better of me. It was only recently that I had spent time with Simon who had been in a real state after his mother had died. I rang back.

'I'm sorry, I forgot to ask why you were ringing. Was it just a catch up or was there something specific?'

'I was just wondering about a summer visit. You know, sometimes I come down for a few days in the summer. But, of course, now you're on holiday.'

'Well, there will still be time when I get back. If you can give me a few days to catch up with things.'

'I suppose I could ring Esther. She may appreciate some help. Unless you're with Esther are you?'

I knew this is what she was hoping for.

'No, she is looking after the shop - with Aggie. They should be able to manage all right. I speak to her most days. It's up to you but she's probably quite busy.'

It always worried me when my mother spent time talking with Esther.

A few minutes after we had finished our phone call, my phone rang again.

'Hi, is that Elliot? It's Laura.'

'Oh, Laura, good to hear from you. I'm so sorry we didn't meet you this evening. No doubt you heard from Rachael?'

'Well, in fact I rang her and luckily you had just rung so she gave me your number. Yes, I think she's a little worried. I'm afraid Cameron's not been in touch with me.'

Like Cantalbrini, she had excellent English.

'I know it's not been that long but I admit I'm beginning to worry a bit.'

'It could be that he can't find his way back and if his phone is not working – what I would hope is that he goes to the nearest police station and asks. They should be able to find the street from the name of the apartment but, of course, he may have spent a lot of time looking and getting lost before he thought of going to the police...'

'You know us British, we hate having to ask directions.'

'Yes, and especially you men don't like to admit to getting lost.'

'How long should I give it do you think? Isn't there a rule about 24 hours before you can report a missing person to the police?'

'I think that's a bit of a myth. If you have a good reason to think he's in trouble you should contact them. Of course, they're always so busy, but that's another matter. If he doesn't turn up by midnight give me a ring and I'll help you. I presume you don't speak Italian?'

'Only the odd word.'

'Well, there are plenty of policeman who speak English in Rome but I think it will probably be easier if I help you.'

'I'd be really grateful for that.'

'There is one thing you can do in the meantime, though, and that's to use social media.'

'Ah, yes, but I don't think Cameron had a Facebook or Twitter account.'

'That shouldn't really matter. Do you have an account?'

'Yes, mainly because of the bookshop, though it's Esther, my main employee, who does most of the postings.'

'If you could get a photo out there that would be all the better.'

'I could see if I can get one from Rachael.'

'I'll give you my Facebook details and Twitter handle and then you can include me and I can spread it around.'

'Thank you, Laura. At least that's doing something positive. Now I've got your phone number I'll let you know when he turns up, or if not, we'll speak at midnight. Oh, and I will ring Rachael to let her know and get that photo.'

I felt better for Laura's phone call. Her thoughts about getting lost struck a chord with me. Forty minutes walking in the wrong direction meant another forty retracing your steps. It did seem a long time, but was it really?

I rang Rachael and told her about Laura's call.

'I was wondering, 'she said, 'whether perhaps he got ill or had an accident. Do you think he may have sunstroke?'

'He had his hat on most of the time as far as I remember – though it was very hot. It's not impossible by any means.'

'And if not sunstroke, perhaps an accident? I've heard there are some crazy drivers over there.'

'I hope not but I suppose that's possible too. Laura is going to contact the police if he does not return by midnight. She also suggested that we try social media. I wondered if you have a recent photo?'

'Ah, yes, I'm sure I could find one. Oh, Elliot, he was so looking forward to this holiday.'

'I know, I'm sorry. I should have kept a closer eye on him.'

'It's not your fault. These things happen.'

'I know but…you know…'

'We have to be positive.'

'Yes. He will probably walk in at any moment,' I said, more in hope than conviction. 'In the meantime, though, I think we should go ahead with the social media thing. Then I will contact the police and the hospitals. Do you agree?'

'Yes. Better to be doing something.'

'OK, if you could send me a photo I will try to compose something to go with it and get it out onto social media. Did he use Facebook much?'

'A bit. Off and on. Only where history was involved, I think.'

'And Twitter?'

'No, not at all. But I do a bit. Anything is worth it, I suppose. Let me know the moment you hear anything – I don't care how late it is.'

'Yes, I will.'

Within a few minutes I had the email from Rachael together with a photo and Cameron's barely used Facebook account details.

I wasn't sure, though, how to proceed. What information should I put out there? I rang Esther to get her help.

'Send it to me and give me the password and I will get it out there on our Facebook and Twitter account.'

Facebook was how Esther kept in touch with many of her friends who lived away.

'It'll probably be better if it comes from you but I'll respond to it and pass it around my friends as well.'

I hesitated for a moment worrying about the fact that this may be a bit humiliating for Cameron and myself, though quickly realised that this was pure self-indulgence and that the situation was potentially far too serious to worry about anything like that.

'We need a good description,' she said. 'What was he wearing?'

'I don't know. The usual Cameron clothes.'

'Elliot! Think! You have to describe them accurately – and what he looks like.'

'OK, so he's tall, about six foot two.'

'Hair colour.'

'Well, you know.'

'He's *your* friend.'

'OK, so, brown with flecks of red.'

'Distinctive features?'

'A pain in the arse, especially when he goes missing.'

'Elliot, are you drunk?'

'No, I'm just worried that's all.'

There was a pause.

'OK, He was wearing one of those hats.'

'A baseball cap?'

'No, though he does sometimes wear one of those. More like a *Fedora* or *Panama*.'

'Which?'

'Well, it was white like a *Panama* but not straw.'

'So, a white *Fedora*.'

'Actually, it was more creamy. A cream coloured *Fedora* type hat.'

'Shirt?'

'Cheesecloth.'

'Nobody wears cheesecloth anymore.'

'Cameron does! I think it was white with yellow or maybe light green stripes.'

'Trousers?'

'Yes, he was wearing trousers. Sorry. Actually, he was wearing baggy shorts, khaki, down to his knees – or nearly down to his knees – he has long legs.'

'Footwear?'

'This is the really embarrassing part. Sandals with *socks*. He looks so English. We don't ever have a hope of passing off as natives. No one would hurt Cameron would they? He just looks too much like a tourist.'

'That may make him vulnerable. But it also makes him look distinctive, which is good. Look, I have typed this all up. I am going to copy it into an email and send it to you for you to check and see if there is anything wrong or if you want to add to it. What we really need, though, is a photo.'

'Ah, that's OK, Rachael's sent me one. I will forward it on.'

Within a few minutes Esther had something on social media.

'Missing tourist Cameron Fall. Have you seen this man? Let us know as we are just beginning to get a little worried...' There was a description and a photo and contact details.

I opened my tablet at the Facebook page and kept it open in case there was any news of sightings of Cameron. I made another cup of coffee.

By the time I returned there had been quite a lot of activity though mostly along the lines of 'poor guy' and 'that must be such a worry for you.' There were several suggestions of contacting the police and checking all the hospitals. I was well aware that these were options that I would probably have to take up.

For now, I would stick with Laura's idea of waiting until midnight. I sat down for a moment keeping the tablet on my lap hoping for the response that told me that Cameron had been found safe and sound.

I suddenly felt very tired and closed my eyes for a moment. The next thing I knew I was back in the Palatine again looking down on Circus Maxima but this time there was a bustling crowded arena with stone walls and seating intact.

'How wonderful it has been restored,' I said to myself.

There was a great feeling of expectation and a parade of gladiators, soldiers and scantily clad women. Then elephants, lions, rhinoceros, monkeys and giraffes. Food and wine was being distributed to the crowd. There were, in particular, I noticed, large bunches of grapes being handed around. Then there was a great trumpet sound and the centre of the stadium was cleared.

There followed the spectacle of animals being hunted: a deer, a lion and a bear. It was all a bit gruesome but I couldn't take my eyes off it. And then there was something I could not quite believe. There was Cameron... being chased by a bear right across the centre of the arena going as fast as his sandals would carry him.

'No, Cameron,' I shouted. 'I told you we had to leave!'

I was screaming at the top of my voice but no one seemed to be taking any notice. Cameron looked up at me pathetically. Although he was a long way away I could see his face and his expression very clearly. Now he was rooted to the spot and the bear was upon him. I struggled to get out of my seat but somehow I was stuck...

I woke to the sound of my phone and pushed away a cushion from the sofa that had fallen on top of me. It was Laura.

'Any news?'

'Not yet.'

'You sound a bit agitated.'

'It's just... I nodded off for a second and dreamt about Cameron being chased by a bear in the Circus Maximus.'

She laughed.

'That would be quite a sight.'

'Well it was – in my dream - of course - perfectly real.'

'I'm sorry, I shouldn't laugh.'

'No, it's good to share it.'

I went on to tell her what I had done on social media.

'Yes, I have checked it out already. No results I presume?'

'No, afraid not. Not as yet. At least, not last time I checked. Let me check again.'

I picked up my tablet, which had fallen off my knee, to see if there had been any updates.

'No, there doesn't seem to have been anything.'

'I was thinking, I know this guy in the *Carabinieri*, not far from you. He's on duty this evening. Perhaps I could come across and we could go and see him. In the meantime, it would be worth trying to remember any specific details about times and so on.'

'OK, I will have a think. Can you make sure you like me and follow me on Twitter?'

'I'm doing that right now.'

I left a respectful pause while I heard tapping in the background.

'I know we said we would wait until twelve,' she continued, 'but I think that is too long. I should be with you within half an hour, hopefully around eleven.'

When she had gone I rang Rachael to let her know what was happening.

'At least it's something positive,' she said. 'I feel a little useless at this end.'

'Well, I suppose we can keep watching Facebook and Twitter for any news.'

'Yes, there is that.'

'I'm sorry for bothering you and worrying you again.'

'No, it was better that you did. I would rather know.'

I could feel the anxiety in her voice and had the impression that she was struggling to keep her worries and fears from taking over.

I was still not hungry but my stomach rumbled. Once again I wondered if Cameron had eaten.

'Probably good to eat something myself in case it's a long night,' I thought.

I grabbed a banana from the fruit bowl. The fruit was the result of Cameron's shopping the previous day. He was so looking forward to our day at the Forum and the Palatine Hill. It all seemed such a long time ago. I shouldn't have left him to the Japanese tourists, I told myself. Perhaps something happened to him at that time - though I could not think what. Perhaps it was something bizarre like being arrested for conducting unofficial tours of the Palatine, I thought, remembering again how we had been told off for eating in Piazza Navona.

After I had finished my banana and fetched a yoghurt from the fridge, my phone pinged. There was a text from Laura saying that she was waiting outside in her car. I grabbed an apple to make my snack into a three course meal and went down in the lift and out through the courtyard to meet her.

26

Laura appeared younger than I may have guessed from our conversation on the phone, perhaps 35, blonde rather than the stereotypical black haired Italian and, I soon discovered, a nose that easily wrinkled into a smile.

I met her in the courtyard rather than invite her in as she had been in touch with her Carabinieri friend only minutes before and did not want to miss the opportunity of meeting up with him. We exchanged greetings and handshakes and I slipped into the passenger seat beside her.

'You know Cameron from University?' I asked her.

'Yes, I was a year at Manchester at the same time as he was there – and we have always kept in touch.'

'That's nice.'

We were at the police station within minutes. Laura parked in what I considered was rather a cavalier fashion at a rakish angle. Alessandro was waiting at the door as we came in. He shook my hand. We went into a corner and I went through my story again while he made some notes. There was a lot of noise in the background, aggrieved shouting and attempts on the part of two Carabinieri to calm a man down, lowering their hands to try and placate him, which seemed to work for a while until he exploded again.

'A busy evening,' I said.

'It's normal,' said Alessandro.

At that moment Laura's phone rang.

'Do you mind if I get this, it may be about Cameron?'

She went over to one corner and began an intense conversation. There was an uncomfortable moment of quiet so I said to Alessandro:

'Where are you from?'

'The south, Calabria. A lot of us Carabinieri come from the South. Sicily, Calabria, Puglia, Campania.'

I could not hide my thoughts from him.

'I know what you are thinking, where the *Mafia* come from. You're right, of course, but I think it's one of the reasons so many of us come from there. It is you know *un senso di giustizia ristabilire l'equilibrio* – a sense of justice, making the balance right. They choose crime and we choose the law. The only problem is we are far from home. You cannot serve in the region you come from – not for eight years.'

'That must be difficult for your family.'

He smiled.

'It's good for transport system, I think.'

'Ah, yes I see, when you travel home and back.'

Laura had finished her call and returned to us.

'I'm sorry, it was nothing. A friend of mine thought she had come across him but it was another man with the same first name.'

'I suppose that's bound to happen. It's not that uncommon a name.'

'I think the first thing is to check the hospitals,' said Alessandro. You could do it but I think it would be quicker if we did it for you. Try not to worry. We have a lower rate of crime than London and, though we cannot promise anything, things usually work out OK.'

I shook his hand and we left.

'Would you like a coffee?' I said to Laura as we began driving back.

'That's very kind but I have an early start tomorrow. If it is OK I will drop you back and then go on.'

'I don't mind walking or getting a bus.'

'I would be happier if you let me take you. I don't want two of you British men going missing.'

As we drove back I asked her about her job.

'I'm a kind of co-ordinator between libraries. I'm also researching a book.'

I told her about my own job as a bookseller, though Cameron had already filled her in on many of the details, and my experience of meeting Cantalbrini. She seemed interested in our meeting. By this time we had reached the apartment building.

'Maybe I will come in for a quick coffee,' she said and followed me up to the apartment.

While we drank the coffee she returned to the subject of our visit to Cantalbrini. I was keen to receive her opinion.

'To be fair to people like Cantalbrini, the Italian law does not help. It's too strict. You are not allowed to export books over 50 years old without an export licence.'

'Whatever, the value?'

'Whatever the value. And, before you ask, getting an export licence usually takes at least two months.'

'Ah, I see. So when I am being suspicious that there is something funny going on, maybe there is room for a legitimate complaint.'

'I think so. You can understand why someone may be tempted to put something in a suitcase, especially when it is of no great value or loss to the Italian cultural heritage.'

'Perhaps Cantalbrini's and Laura's views were not so far apart after all,' I thought.

As if divining my thoughts, she continued:

'Don't get me wrong, I'm not officially condoning breaking the law. I can just see that the law is a bad one and I do have sympathy for respectable antiquarian booksellers. My advice is to be a little careful. Everybody thinks about the art theft and forgeries in Italy but the theft of books is very common too. It's not all about paintings. You know this has been going on a long time. Have you heard of a guy called Guglielmo Libri Carucci dalla Sommaja?'

'Who, what?'

We can call him Libri for short.'

'Thank goodness.'

'He was a very clever man, a Professor of Mathematical Physics in Pisa when he was only 20. Can you believe that? But he did not like teaching and soon he travelled to Paris and met many of the great French mathematicians of the day. When he came back he became involved with the *Carbonari* - not to be confused with the *Carabinieri*! They were a secret society advocating a liberal constitution.'

'Ah, yes, I think I remember Cameron mentioning that.'

'Anyway, once it became known by the authorities that he was a member of the *Carbonari*, he fled to France. He eventually became a French citizen and professor at the *Collège de France* and Professor of Calculus of Probabilities at the *Sorbonne*. He was elected to the Academy and given the *Légion d'honneur.*

'Quite a distinguished career.'

'Then he wrote *History of the Mathematical Sciences in Italy from the Renaissance of Literature to the 17th Century.*'

'Also quite a mouthful.'

'The work for this was based on a number of manuscripts from famous academics such as Galileo, Descartes, Fermat and so on. He claimed to have collected them but, here's the thing, it turned out that he had stolen them from the Bibliotheca

Medicea Laurenziana in Florence. And it did not end there. He later became Chief inspector of French Libraries and began borrowing rare books and never returning them. The extent of his thefts was extraordinary. He stole a sixth century Latin manuscript from the library of Tours which became known as the *Ashburnum Pentateuch.* The authorities were on to him but he received a tip-off and fled to England taking about 30,000 books and manuscripts with him. He was helped by Antonio Panizzi who was director of the British Museum.'

'Ah, another Antonio...'

She smiled.

'Ah, yes, and another Italian. Libri convinced him that many of the problems he had in France from the authorities were because of a prejudice about him being Italian. In England he was able to live a comfortable life by selling the books he had stolen. He sold over 2,000 manuscripts to Bertram Ashburnham. Many of the manuscripts he'd stolen were from Italy as well as France and were sold in London, only for many of them to be repurchased later by the Italian government.'

'Have they all been recovered?'

'Only some. In fact, the odd thing has turned up very recently. There was a letter dated 1641 from Descartes, written to Father Mersenne which concerns his *Treatise on First Philosophy* where he claims the existence of God and the immortality of the soul. It was discovered by an American undergraduate at a small American College and was returned to France only in 2010.'

'That must be priceless - in terms of its historical value apart from anything else.'

'It may be that all of these thefts by Libri influenced the original law on exporting books, which has not changed all that much and dates back to 1903.'

'Really!'

'The other reason the law was so strict, I'm afraid, is that Italian institutions were not so interested in building their collections through purchase as many foreign libraries were.' She yawned and stretched her arms. 'There's a lot more I could say but I am afraid I will have to try and get some sleep before work tomorrow.'

'Of course, but thank you for coming round.'

'We're not all corrupt in Italy, you know, and sometimes it is difficult to separate what is corrupt from what it bureaucratic.

There is a view that if everybody stuck exactly to the rules nothing would ever get done.'

I accompanied her downstairs to her car.

'We have to stay positive,' she said. 'Alessandro is very good.'

'Yes,' I said, but I could see the frown of worry on her face, which I was certain was reflected in my own.

We shook hands and she gave me a little peck on the cheek.

'Thank you, Laura, for all your help. It's really nice to meet you at last.'

'Let me know the moment you hear,' she said, waving a goodbye and accelerating away in her car in one smooth action. Are Italians born with style or do they work at it, I wondered? I thought of the contrast with Cameron and his ill matching attire. His friendship with Laura was an unlikely one but no doubt it was Cameron's obviously English ways verging on eccentricity that were part of the reason that Laura was attracted to him as a friend.

27

While Laura was there I had felt more like something was happening. Now, once again on my own, my anxiety about Cameron returned. The demons in the back of my mind came to the fore. Rome may be safer than London statistically, as Alessandro had said, but it was still a large city and in any large city, and even rural idylls, bad things could happen. And there was that reckless driving I had witnessed. The more I thought about it the more I thought that the most likely explanation was that he had been knocked down by a car. The trouble with Cameron was that when he was concentrating on his guides he could sometimes become a little absent minded and wander about without being aware of his immediate surroundings. And if he had been knocked down and was not able to contact me or Rachael or Laura that meant that he was probably unconscious, which meant it was probably a bad accident.

Having felt encouraged by Laura's visit I now went into a state of gloomy despondency. After a while I began feeling nauseous. I had still not eaten anything except the banana, yoghurt and apple that evening. I thought that if I ate something more I may feel better. I chewed a piece of a bread roll but could not finish it. Perhaps I needed sleep? I took off my shoes and lay on top of my sofa-bed with my clothes on and the mobile by my side. There was a call from Esther.

'Have you heard anything?'

'No, not yet - but we have spoken to the police.'

I went on to explain about our visit to the Carabinieri.

'I won't keep you,' she said when I had finished, 'I just wanted to know how you are. I don't suppose you're able to sleep much?'

'No, not really. I'll text you as soon as I hear.'

'I don't mind if you need to ring – at any time. Stay strong. I know you will.'

At two in the morning, after only a fitful sleep, I made myself yet another coffee and wandered out onto the balcony. I could not see anything but darkness below and the bright lights of

Rome in the distance. There were no missed calls or messages on my phone, nothing. I had expected, I suppose, a further call from Rachael - but then what good would it do if I had no news? If it was bad for me I could not think what it would be like for her. Part of me wished I had not told her as there could be nothing gained until we knew the real situation.

I heard the sound of cats fighting in the streets. There was a shout and a clanking sound and then the screeching of wheels and the roar of a car accelerating at tremendous speed.

'Reckless driving.' I thought again. I hoped that if Cameron had been knocked down his injury was not life threatening, perhaps a broken arm or leg that would require an anaesthetic, which would explain the fact that he had not been in contact.

I idly googled pedestrian accidents in Rome and found an article headed *Roman roads are becoming like The Wild West for pedestrians.* It reported how the number of pedestrian accidents had increased exponentially in Rome in recent years.

I thought about having a glass of wine but it didn't seem wise. I needed to keep my wits about me – though I wasn't sure what for. I went back into the lounge and checked my Facebook and my phone for the umpteenth time.

Then I heard the sound of the lift parking and, moments later, a rustling of keys. The door burst open and there was Cameron.

'Thank God!' I said.

I embraced him awkwardly.

'Where on earth have you been?'

'My phone ran out of charge.'

'I thought it must be something like that. But why didn't you come back here? Had you forgotten where it was?'

'Well, that's a long story. Any chance of a stiff drink, no better make it a strong cup of tea – with all these drugs inside me a stiff drink might just do for me. '

'Drugs? Just a moment, I'll put the kettle on.'

I was back in a trice. He was shuffling around making strange little punctuated complaining noises rather than being his usual robust self. His face was pallid and he was standing at an odd angle.

'You're not quite right are you? Did you have an accident?'

'Kind of, well, yes. Where were you anyway? I waited for ages.'

'I was at the Palatine exit.'

'Ah, yes. I worked out afterwards that was probably what happened.'

'By the time I had worked it out it was too late. You must have moved on, did you?'

'I waited a good long while.'

'Probably missed you when I went back to the other exit. But why didn't you come back here?'

'Believe me I wish I had. I had every intention of doing so but just as I thought I would try and find my way back – I thought I would have a quick check in my guidebook to confirm the route – you know because my phone was not working – it has a decent map in the back – I found I was near the cat sanctuary.'

'The what?'

'The *Torre Argentina Cat Sanctuary*. It's only five minutes' walk from Piazza Venezia. A fascinating place - though it was actually closed at the time. It was excavated under Mussolini when he was doing all his rebuilding. It contains the remains of four different temples and some of Pompey's Theatre. It's believed that Julius Caesar was assassinated in the portico of the Pompey Theatre in 44 BC. After the site was excavated, Rome's wild cats moved in and the cat ladies, the *gattare*, began feeding them.'

He had only been back five minutes and he was already into one of his history lessons. I sighed.

'I'd love to know where this is going and what it's got to do with you going missing.'

However, inside I was smiling. I was so relieved.

'Well, I knew when I didn't find you you would probably do the sensible thing and go back to the apartment so I thought it wouldn't hurt if I spent a few minutes looking around before I went back. I thought a few more minutes' diversion wouldn't hurt. '

'How could you miss an opportunity like that?' I said with what I thought was heavy sarcasm, but Cameron just took it as confirmation of the reasonableness of his actions.

'Exactly! Though it was closed, there were cats on top of the wall and you can still look down into the sanctuary. You know, there are around 250 cats there? It's a "no kill" shelter which means they only put down the most seriously ill cats. The archaeologists tried to get rid of the cats a few years ago but there was a petition which 30,000 people signed to keep the sanctuary open. I have to say that this is one of the few times when I wouldn't have sided with the archaeologists.'

I raised an eyebrow but I did not say anything. I wanted him to get on with his story.

'Well, it was like this. Unfortunately, there was this little altercation – among the cats on the top of the wall and one of them, a tabby I think it was, began to fall off the wall – poor little thing. Well, I reached up to grab him – or her – I'm not sure which. Anyway, I reached up to save it from falling and it just clung on my finger with its teeth. I don't think I've ever experienced such pain. It shot right up my arm and I'm afraid I swore rather badly.'

I knew any further questioning was futile. I would just have to sit in for the rest of the story.

'I'm sure you'll be forgiven. I hope you swore in your best Italian.'

'Anyway this nice lady was there. She said when it was deep like that I had to see the doctor. She was right. By the time I got to the hospital my hand was like a balloon. The doctor mentioned *pasteurella multocida* and said I could get a serious infection unless I took some antibiotics.

'I did say I needed to get a message to you but they seemed more interested in treating me and pumping me full of these antibiotics and painkillers and, I admit, with all that stuff inside me after a while I forgot about contacting you and drifted off to sleep. I wanted to phone you on a public phone but I couldn't remember your number and everything seemed to happen so quickly once they'd admitted me.

'I must've slept for ages and then, all of a sudden, I woke up in a panic and discharged myself. It was not easy convincing them you know.'

'I was so worried I contacted Rachael. You'd better ring her now to put her mind at rest.'

'You don't think it's too late?'

'Of course not, she'll want to know right away.'

I went to make the tea. When I returned a few minutes later he had already finished his call.

'I'm going to ring her again tomorrow. She says now that she's heard she can sleep. She has work in the morning.'

We drank our tea for a moment in silence. He did look shattered.

'I'll get you something to eat. You must be starving.'

'Not especially, but you're probably right.'

I had not visited the shops to buy any food that day so the cupboard was bare.

'Soup, that's probably the best thing.'

I had seen a packet of minestrone soup among Cameron's things

– emergency rations. I poured over boiling water and heated some bread in the oven. While I waited, I texted Esther who returned the text straight away. 'Marvellous news. Well done. XXX.' Though in truth, I didn't feel I had done anything except worry. Then I texted Laura who also came back immediately. 'So good to hear,'and a flood of hearts.

A few minutes later I returned to Cameron with two bowls of soup and the bread.

Cameron was gently dozing, the half consumed cup of tea about to fall from his hand.

I took the cup from him and woke him. As we ate the soup and bread (and, I have to admit, at that moment it seemed like the best soup I had ever tasted – my appetite had suddenly returned), we chatted some more.

My phone rang.

'That's probably Esther or Laura.'

I answered the phone. In fact it was neither. It was the policeman Alessandro.

'We have found him, Mr Todd.'

'Ah, yes. We're so pleased to have him back.'

'What? But he's in a hospital.'

'He was. Now he's back here. He discharged himself. He's in the apartment right now.'

'That's good but you tell him to be careful. You know he should really be in hospital where they can properly take care of him.'

I thanked him for his trouble and promised that I would take Cameron back to the hospital in the morning to be checked out.

'That was the Carabinieri,' I said to Cameron when I had finished the call.

'You didn't get them involved?'

'What choice had I? Nothing came from our efforts to find you via social media. Besides, it wasn't me, it was Laura. She has this friend in the Carabinieri called Alessandro. That was him just now. He seems like a really nice guy.'

'I'll never live this down. I was thinking of applying for the Royal Geographic Society one day. They will never have me now I can't even find my way out of the Palatine and back to my flat. But why the Carabinieri? I thought they only dealt with serious crime.'

'As I said, Laura knew someone there. And maybe they consider the disappearance of a British National important.'

'I've been feeling bad about that too.'

'She got my number off Rachael and came round and took me to the police station. She's very nice, like you said.'

'See, I told you that you two would get on.'

He was looking increasingly weary. I saw him nod off briefly again after just sitting for a moment but he forced himself awake.

'Are you sure you should be out of hospital at all.'

'I think so. Dreadful places - all those sick people.'

I laughed but I could see that he was far from recovery.

'Perhaps you should get a night's sleep here and then we can go to the hospital in the morning. In fact, you don't actually have a choice. Alessandro insisted on it. I'll text Laura and Esther now.'

28

Laura picked up Cameron at eight in the morning and returned him to the hospital where he was kept back for observation. Eventually he was told that he could go but that he would require looking after. It was decided, after a conversation with Laura, that Cameron would stay with her for a couple of days as she had a few days vacation to take and was in a better position to look after him and seek further treatment if he deteriorated – and, I suspected, she would have better control over him.

A few minutes after Cameron and Laura had left I received another phone call. It was Antonio Cantalbrini.

'Good day Mr Todd, I was wondering if I could invite you and your friend to the opera this evening. There is an outdoor performance of *Tosca* at the Marcellus Theatre that I have complimentary tickets for.'

'Ah, yes, we were looking at a poster for it. But, I'm afraid Cameron's not too well at the moment.'

'Nothing serious I hope?'

I did not feel like going into all the details at that time.

'Just a nasty infection. He'll be all right in a day or two.'

'Well, perhaps you would like to accompany me?'

'The truth is, I don't really know anything about opera. In fact, I've never been to a live performance.'

'Well, in that case there is no better time to start – while you are in the home of opera. You know, it originated here at the end of the sixteenth century.'

'Are you sure the tickets are complimentary? I would be happy to pay something.'

I knew that opera tickets could be very expensive. I read that you could pay over 300 Euros for a ticket for *La Scala* opera house.

'Absolutely, I have some contacts in the opera world and I am usually granted a few complimentary tickets each season.'

'Well, in that case, I would love to try the experience.'

'Well, that's settled. I will pick you up around 6.30.'

I cooked some pasta and then spent the rest of the day catching catching up on some sleep before until Cantalbrini arrived to take me to the venue that evening.

The weather, as it had been all along during our holiday, was dry and hot, perfect for an outdoor event and the setting in the Archaeological Park in front of the building was magical. The scattered remains of pillars, flooring and blocks of stone were utilised to represent the church that was the setting for the first act, and there was a temporary raised stage in the background that I presumed would be used for the later acts.

I was joined on my left by the man whom we had seen visiting Cantalbrini in the restaurant on our first night in Rome. He introduced us.

'This is my friend Giacomo Abruzzio.'

'You probably don't remember but I sat opposite you at the *Fortunato* a few days ago when you were in the company of Antonio,' I said.

He looked confounded for a few moments and then I noticed the light of recognition.

'Ah, yes, you were with another tall English man.'

'Yes, Cameron, though he would be mightily offended if you called him English. He's passionately Scottish. I'm Elliot Todd.' We shook hands.

'I have a translation of the opera into English that you may find useful,' said Cantalbrini.

It was a parallel text with the Italian on one side and the English on the other.

'Thank you.'

He talked across me.

'Mr Todd is new to opera, Mr Abruzzio.'

'I've never quite had the opportunity or, I have to admit, the inclination.'

'I understand,' said Mr Abruzzio. 'The plots can be a bit... what's the word...?'

'I think in English you may say a bit silly,' interjected Cantalbrini.

'Yes, but then the music is beautiful and there is much drama in this opera.'

'There has to be a reason it is so celebrated,' I said.

'Perhaps I can give you a brief summary?' said Cantalbrini.

'Yes, I would like that.'

'Tosca is set during the Napoleonic Wars when there was a lot of political unrest. You may ask: *What has changed*?'

I laughed.

'And it all takes place over one day. There are three main characters. Floria Tosca who is a Roman diva, her lover Mario Cavarodossi (who is a painter and a republican) and Baron Scarpia, a corrupt chief of police who "fancies" (I think you say in English) Tosca.'

'Sounds like a recipe for mayhem.'

'As you will see, Caravadossi is captured by the police for helping a friend, Angelotti, who has escaped from prison. When he is captured Scarpia offers Tosca a terrible choice, to give herself to Scarpia, or her lover, Caravadossi will be executed. I will let you witness what occurs.'

The music began, we ceased our discussions and settled into the opera. A good deal of the first act seemed to be taken up by Tosca exhibiting her jealousy as she thinks Caravadossi may have another woman and that he is using her features to paint a picture of the Madonna in the church. There are multiple references to the woman in the painting having blue eyes while Tosca's are black which brings out protestations from Caravadossi of his love for Tosca. This went on for some time. I began to think that perhaps opera is just a piece of frivolity after all. When Angelotti, the escaped prisoner, enters the church (for the second time) and suggests that he escapes dressed as a woman and is then hastened away by Caravadossi to hide in a well in his garden, I began wondering if I should make my excuses and leave after the first act. I thought about the pleasure of finding a quiet space, reading a book and drinking a cup of coffee. But as we moved into the second half of the first act things began to progress rather quickly and my interest was aroused. Scarpia enters looking for Angelotti and, feeding Tosca's jealousy of Caravadossi, suggests he is interested in another woman. She rushes off to confront Caravadossi and Scarpia has her followed by the police.

At the end of the first act there was a short interval. Cantalbrini insisted on buying us a glass of wine each. While he was gone I talked to Mr Abruzzio.

'When I saw you at the restaurant I noticed that you had brought a book with you. It looked like a nice old edition. Was it something special?'

'I don't remember now, sorry.'

He was looking a little uncomfortable.

'Are you a bookdealer like Mr Cantalbrini?' I continued.

'Ah, no,' he hesitated, 'I work in the library.'

'Oh, which one?'

'I move from place to place.'

'Peripatetic.'

'*Si, peripatetico.*'

'I do so love the culture in Italy. And you have so much of it.'

He seemed to start relaxing a bit.

'And you, Mr Todd, you obviously like books.'

'Yes, I'm a bookseller, new and old.'

'Tell me, Mr Todd, do you like bookselling in the UK?'

'Well, you know, I'm like most people, I complain about online competition but really bookselling is my life. I look across enviously at France and think how well their bookshops are supported. Is it the same in Italy?'

'I am afraid not so. I wonder if sometimes we have so much culture we forget to value it. Over 2,000 bookshops have closed in the last 5 years. And in the last decade, 200 in Rome alone.

'I'm sorry to hear that. A similar thing happened in the UK a few years ago. There seems to be a bit of a recovery in the independent sector now – but it is slow.'

'We would love it if Italy supported its bookshops like they do in France. There is talk of a law on book promotion coming but whether it is too late I do not know.'

He sighed before continuing.

'I sometimes think I would like to live in UK.'

'Why? It can't be for the climate or the food.'

'I think it is a bit more open and honest.'

'We have our problems too. There was a scandal of MPs expenses some years ago.'

'Ah the wooden duck house. We would love to have that level of corruption in Italy. We come number fifty-one in corruption in the world – the same level as Rwanda and behind Grenada.'

'But you are all so stylish - and the food - and the ancient monuments.'

'The trouble it is, how you say, *endemica*?'

'Endemic.'

'Yes, corruption is endemic and it is everywhere. It is difficult sometimes for ordinary people not to get caught up with it. It becomes a *crisi di coscienza*. You know, do you feed your family or do you go along with something you do not agree with?'

'Yes, well if the choice is between feeding your family or stealing a loaf of bread – like Jean Valjean.'

'Ah, yes, *Les Miserables*. A great book I think. You have to remember,' he continued, 'that Italy is a little different from most western European countries. People don't pay their taxes in the same way. Do you know, almost 13 million don't pay personal income tax. 10 million officially earn nothing – of course that is nonsense.'

'I had heard that.'

'And you know the reason that we don't pay taxes? It is because we are Catholic. We are used to committing a sin and gaining absolution.'

I laughed, though I had the feeling he was being serious. Then his phone rang.

'I'm sorry. I thought I had turned it off.'

He patted both his pockets before he found it inside his jacket and in his haste to retrieve it and switch it off, he dropped it on the floor. I picked it up for him. I noticed that on the base of the phone was a sticking plaster – no doubt the result of several such incidents in the past. I sympathised with him as I was often in the same state of panic when my mobile phone rang and I couldn't find it on my person.

Cantalbrini returned with the wine just in time for the beginning of the second act. The raised stage was used to represent the Palazzo Farnese with a large table where Scarpia was drinking wine. I noticed several members of the audience who had bought a drink in the interval raise their glasses to him in a mock greeting. Scarpia has a message sent to Tosca asking her to come to him. In the meantime Cavaradossi has been arrested and is brought in for questioning. Tosca arrives and Scarpia has Caravadossi taken away to be tortured. Cavaradossi has told Tosca not to say anything about the whereabouts of Angelotti but, after initially resisting, she reveals that he is hiding in a well when she hears the screams of Caravadossi being tortured. They bring Cavaradossi before Scarpia. He taunts Scarpia with news that the French are marching on Rome after victory in The Battle of Marengo. As a result he is taken away to be shot. I began appreciating something of the drama of the situation, caught up in the moment rather than thinking of the unreality of the plot. Scarpia proposes that he will fake the execution of Caravadossi if she gives herself to him. She is disgusted with him. She hears the drums roll signalling the execution and then

Tosca sings *Vissi D'Arte* lamenting her situation and asking for the intervention of God. I was overcome with the emotion and joined in with everybody else as they applauded the singer at the end of the piece. It was some of the most beautiful singing I have ever heard. There is then, of course more drama with her unfortunate and tragic demise, but this was the moment that stood out for me above all.

'Why didn't you warn me about that song?' I said to Esther later. I rang her as soon as I had returned from the opera.

'I think they call them *arias* in opera.'

'It caught me completely off guard.'

'I wanted you to discover it.'

'It made me cry.'

'Good, it means she must have sung it well.'

'But I didn't know what the words were until I checked afterwards.'

'Yet you knew it was something really powerful.'

'How does that happen?'

'You've probably had that experience with a pop song – not heard the words properly but known that you liked it.'

'I suppose that's true.'

'Did you join Cantalbrini for a meal afterwards?'

'I didn't want to impose – he was with this friend that we saw at the restaurant, a Mr Abruzzio. And, well, I'm trying not to put on too much weight.'

The line crackled and we both waited for it to clear.

'It was very nice of him to invite me. He really is very kind.'

'It seems so.'

'He wants to show me some libraries in the morning.'

'That sounds interesting.'

'Anyway, I think I may have a little stroll out and see if I can grab a coffee. I'm not feeling sleepy yet.'

'Good plan, I think I'll have a coffee too.'

'I wish...I could share one with you.'

'Yes that would be nice. It won't be too long.'

'No.'

'Well, goodnight then, Elliot. I'm glad things are back on track – and that you enjoyed the opera.'

'Night Esther.'

29

I had arranged with Cantalbrini that I would meet him at his apartment. Originally, he had asked me if I wanted to visit the Vatican with him but I declined the invitation as I wanted to make the visit with Cameron. That was when he came up with the idea of visiting the libraries - something different that he thought I might enjoy. I rang him when I arrived and he asked whether I would mind coming up to the flat for a few minutes while he finished getting ready. He met me at the top of the lift.

'It is good to see you again Mr Todd. I won't be long.'

I suspected it was a ruse to try and get me interested in buying one or more of his books, but if it was, I could think of worse things.

'Would you like a coffee or tea?'

'I'm OK, thank you. I had breakfast not too long ago.'

'As you wish. Perhaps we can have something a bit later.'

'That would be nice.'

'I will be back in a few minutes.'

While he was gone I thumbed through one or two of the volumes, once again marvelling at the quality and breadth of his stock. He was, as he had promised, back within a few minutes.

'You know I had a good feeling when I met you, that we share things in common. I would like to show you something that I do not show to all my clients.'

I was not ready to call myself a client. How he did persist.

He moved across the room to one of the large bays of shelves on the wall furthest away from where I was standing and reached forward, as I supposed until that moment, selecting one of the books on the shelf in front of him. He made a movement with his hand, replaced the book and then pushed on the bay of shelving in front of him. It moved sideways and opened like a door revealing a room behind.

He saw the astonishment on my face and smiled.

'Clever, eh? Please!'

He gestured with his open hand and I made my way through the archway. There was a small room, perhaps 10 ft by 6 ft. In the centre was a small table and chair, a laptop, and a few books piled on top of each other. It was like a miniature version of the room I had just left, lined with books, though there were a few more gaps and some books were in small piles on their sides.

'There are some very interesting volumes here. Go on, take a look.'

I went over to the shelf on the right and picked up a volume, an old prayer book. I read, *Modus Orandi Deum Aliaque Pia et Christiana Exercitia Nec Non Deiparae Virginis Maria Litaniae.* There were books by Galileo and Ariosto.

'Some of these must be priceless?' I conjectured.

'They are my best stock.'

'Someone was telling me that there is a problem exporting books from Italy over 50 years old whatever the value.'

'Yes that is true. You need an export licence and that can take an age.' Then he came up to me and said conspiratorially: 'But if you purchase a book in English and you are returning from a holiday to the UK, who is to say that you did not bring it with you on holiday?'

'I see.'

'For example, I have these volumes of the *Lyrical Ballads.*'

He presented me with the two volumes bound in decorative leather.

'Please.'

I had studied this at University as one of my modules so I knew one or two things about these early editions. The first thing I did was to turn to the beginning.

'Ah, so no *Ancient Mariner*. Is this the second edition?'

'In fact, the third edition of volume one and the second edition of volume two. *The Ancient Mariner* appears near the back.'

'I believe Wordsworth was quite critical of the style of the language Coleridge used for *The Ancient Mariner.*'

'Exactly. Coleridge's poem *The Dungeon* has also been removed as has one of Wordsworth's poems. Also, Wordsworth's famous preface has been expanded.'

'I believe Wordsworth actually thought the *Ancient Mariner* was harmful to the sales of the first edition and asked the publishers to remove it completely.'

'That's right. Only Wordsworth's name was on the title page in the later edition. Of course, everyone would like an edition of the Bristol Cottle first edition but I believe there are only one or two of those in existence.'

'Even so, it is very nice.'

'Again, I could offer you a very attractive price.'

'They are lovely editions and I really appreciate you showing them to me. The truth is, Antonio, I really do scrape by as a bookseller. I'm not in this league. I have, what is known as a cash-flow problem.'

'Ah, *liquidità*.'

'I'm sorry. I don't want to mislead you – you have been so ... accommodating.'

He looked straight into my eyes.

'I do understand. You know, my parents were poor. We grew up in poverty in the south.'

'I don't think of myself as poor and I do enjoy what I do. But I am definitely not rich. We manage ... just manage.'

'I did not go to University. There is a word for it. I think it is almost the same in English, *autodidatta*.'

'Ah, yes, autodidactic. Self taught. You would never know it - and your English is so good. I would have guessed you would have gone to some prestigious Italian university – perhaps topped off with a doctorate.'

'Books have been my saviour in more senses than one. They have educated me and now I make a bit of money out of them. I do have one piece of advice for you, though. You are welcome not to take it but it is based on my years of experience trading as a book dealer.'

'Oh, yes?'

'Sometimes, in order to prosper you have to take a risk. And in Italy, especially, it means not always playing exactly by the rules. You know, bureaucracy can be a large impediment to trade so it is not surprising that it gets circumvented now and again.'

'Well, you know we have quite a bit of bureaucracy in the UK as well.'

'But, of course we have the advantage of you because we have been practicing it since Roman times. Anyway, let us not dwell on it now,' he continued. 'Perhaps now we will visit those libraries I talked about. They are all quite close to each other in the district near the Vatican.'

As we made our way through the Rome traffic he explained his plans for that morning.

'I have four libraries for you to see. I'm not intending that you should spend hours leafing through their volumes. I want to introduce them to you and give you a flavour of their contents. They are all within easy reach so it should not take us more than two or three hours.

'We will go to the Library of Archaeology and Art History first. The library is actually split between two sites. We are lucky. It is not open most days.'

I was not disappointed. Beneath three chandeliers of spherical balls was a long room. Down the centre, filling perhaps three quarters or so of the length of the room, were two continuous rows of neat study desks facing each other, flanked by walls of ancient books on all sides. A balcony and walkway meant that the books were able to continue right up to the ceiling and still be accessible.

'It really does take your breath away,' I said. I took some photos on my phone.

Not far away in Via di S. Agostino was the Biblioteca Angelica. If anything, the space was even more impressive than the archaeology and art history library we had just visited. There were three tiers of shelving on each wall with two balconies running along all the walls. Two windows at the far end allowed a good degree of natural light and the soaring arches above the books gave a feeling of airiness and space.

'I can see why this is called the Biblioteca Angelica – I think I can hear the angels singing,' I said.

'Ah, you would think so would you not? However, it is named after its founder, Angelo Rocca. He was an Augustinian bishop who donated twenty thousand of his own manuscripts and left money for its upkeep. Libraries were private up to that time but he wanted this library to be open to all.'

'If not an angel, it certainly sounds like he was a saint.'

'It would seem so.'

Our next stop was the Bibliotheca Casanatense. It was named after Cardinal Casanatense. A huge statue of Casanatense dominated the reading room. There were two large globes on either side of the room. Though it was impressive, I preferred the atmosphere in the Angelico library. It was impressive in another way, though. Cantalbrini told me that the library contains 400,000 volumes.

'You know, the library contains over 2,000 books printed before 1500. They have Greek codices, Samaritan codices – all sorts of biblical manuscripts. One of my favourites is the

Tacuinum Sanitatis. It is a Latin translation of an eleventh century treatise - a kind of medieval health and well-being treatise. The illustrations are beautiful.'

The final library we visited was the Accademia Nazionale dei Lincei e Corsina at Via del Lungara. We entered through the imposing baroque building that is the Palazzo Corsini.

'The origins go back to 1603,' explained Cantalbrini. 'It was founded by Federico Cesi and attracted young men who were passionate about science. You know what *Lincei* means?'

'No.'

'It's the Lynx. They admired it for its "sharp focus" and thought that this was what science required. Galileo became its intellectual centre. It disappeared when Cesi died but it was revived in the nineteenth century and eventually moved here to the *Corsini Palace*. It has over 500 members. They have included Albert Einstein, Louis Pasteur and your Herbert Spencer.'

'A distinguished list.'

'They have thousands of volumes and they are loaned throughout the world.'

We began to explore the many rooms. The ceilings were rich in gold ornamentation, and, as one would expect, lined with row upon row of ancient volumes.

Cantalbrini began to exchange a few words with an attendant seated on a chair. I detached myself and began wandering into the next room before pulling up mid stride. There, on the far side of the room, leaning against the marble pillar that framed the entrance to the next room was Laura, with her arms folded and talking to none other than Mr Abruzzio. It was doubly unexpected as I had understood that Laura was looking after Cameron. Abruzzio, in turn, was resting his right arm against a shelf of books. There were several other visitors in the room and I was reluctant to shout across - especially as they appeared to be in the middle of a deep conversation. I began to slowly walk across to them.

'I'm sorry about that,' called Cantalbrini from behind just at that moment. 'Someone I know. His wife has not been well.'

I turned back to him.

'That's OK. It's so impressive,' I made an open-handed gesture. 'I have just noticed Mr Abruzzio and...'

But as I turned back towards the far side of the room I could see that Laura had gone. Mr Abruzzio was still there. He had one of the glass covered display cabinets open and was making some adjustment to the books inside.'

'Ah, Mr Abruzzio,' Cantalbrini called from afar and moved towards him. 'Excuse me a moment,' he said as he strode to meet him on the other side of the room.

'*Salve! Come va*?' I heard him say.

I hung back a little as they began to engage in a short and very intense conversation. Cantalbrini pointed his finger. If it had been in England the body language would have suggested an argument but then, this was Italy. Cantalbrini returned, Mr Abruzzio exited the room.

'I am sorry about that. I was going to offer you lunch but something has come up that I need to attend to. Will you forgive me if I make my way? There is a nice café just down the road from here if you would like something. Just turn left out of the entrance.'

Though he still exhibited his customary politeness, I could tell something was playing on his mind.

'Of course, thank you for your kindness in showing me these magnificent libraries.'

'My pleasure. Let us stay in touch. Think about that book and let me know if you change your mind. In any case, there are probably other ways we can help each other. Perhaps we could have a talk about that sometime.'

He shook my hand and said, '*In bocca al lupe.*'

I knew that was a common expression of good luck in Italian – in the mouth of the wolf - but I couldn't remember the response so I just said 'Grazie' tamely.

When he had gone I looked it up on my phone. The response should have been 'Crepi' – May he die!' I promised myself I would remember that next time.

I went to the toilet and lingered a while in the grand old building before deciding I was hungry enough for a meal.

Following the directions I was given, I found the café easily enough and was contemplating going in, already having in mind a crusty baguette filled with something delicious. However, another thought had occurred to me. I had remembered reading in my guide book that Castel Sant'Angelo had a small café and it was not too far away. I particularly wanted to visit now I had seen *Tosca* and knew that the final act of the opera takes place there. It made sense to combine my lunchtime snack with a visit.

*

Some minutes later I was sitting atop the imposing building, squeezed in at a table next to the castle wall eating my salami and pickle baguette. I experienced a pleasant cooling breeze, while I read about its history, over a coffee, and tried to imagine the unfortunate demise of Tosca.

I also wondered about the coincidence of seeing Laura, Mr Abruzzio and Cantalbrini all within the institute library – though Laura had made herself absent by the time Cantalbrini had come upon Abruzzio. On reflection, I rationalised that Laura could not be expected to remain in Cameron's company all the time and it was not unreasonable that she may want to visit the library. But then there was the fact that she was talking to Abruzzio. As far as I had been aware, she did not know him. Did that also mean she knew Cantalbrini? Had she made herself scarce because she had seen me and did not want me to discover her association with both of them? That phrase, 'It's not what you know, it's who you know,' came into my head and I recalled the conversation with Laura when she had defended bookdealers like Cantalbrini and criticised what she considered to be antiquated export laws. Perhaps, if the law or the regulations were not always fit for purpose, it was not surprising if they were bent now and again?

I returned to my guidebook. It told me that the castle had undergone a number of transformations over the centuries. It was originally built as a mausoleum by Emperor Hadrian, it was thought, between 134 and 139 AD, with the name derived from the legend of the vision of the Archangel Michael, seen by St Gregor the Great. The story went that in 590 AD, when he was leading a procession and crossing the Ponte Elio (now known as Ponte Sant'Angelo, the beautiful bridge I had walked across on the way there), he saw the ghost of St Michael take out his sword on the top of the castle to announce the end of the plague.

In the 14th century the building was converted into a castle by the Popes when it was used as a fortress, residence and prison. It became, for a while, the tallest building in Rome. A covered corridor was built to connect it to St Peter's Basilica. One of the stories I particularly liked was that one of the popes, Leo X, was so overweight that he had an elevator installed. Traces of the mechanical elements could still be viewed from the grille of the Hall of Apollo. The Papal Court built scaffolds for public executions and, in 1758, there was a bell installed in the Campana della Misericordia, which was rung to announce them. One such case was the beheading of the aristocrat Beatrice Cenci in 1599. She and other members of her family were convicted of the murder of her abusive and incestuous father. There is a legend that she haunts the Ponte Sant'Angelo with her head tucked underneath her arm. The story of her execution formed the basis of *The Cenci*, a play by Shelley.

When I left the Castel St Angelo I took the opportunity to stroll around and take in the atmosphere, stopping to read my book at a bench on the way. I was enjoying my relaxed style of exploration but felt that I could do with one more thing to see before I headed back to the apartment. I flicked through my copy of the guide to Rome and found what I thought was the perfect place, the Keats-Shelley Memorial House at the Spanish Steps. I had been put in mind of this by the reference to Shelley at the Castel Angelo and his play about Beatrice Cenci. It would also nicely round off the literary flavour of my day.

Before I reached the Spanish steps I stumbled upon a bookshop selling English literature. It was all on one floor, quite small but crammed full of books. I went inside and starting leafing through the shelves. I noticed that the prices had been marked up considerably from the retail prices in the UK – but then, I thought, one had to take into account the carriage costs. Given that I was about to visit the memorial house, I searched for and found a volume on Keats and a volume on Shelley. Flicking through the Shelley volume I found *Adonais*, Shelley's elegy to Keats who died in Rome in 1821 when he was just 25. I began reading.

I weep for Adonais—he is dead!
 Oh, weep for Adonais! though our tears
 Thaw not the frost which binds so dear a head!
 And thou, sad Hour, selected from all years
 To mourn our loss, rouse thy obscure compeers,
 And teach them thine own sorrow, say: "With me
 Died Adonais; till the Future dares
 Forget the Past, his fate and fame shall be
 An echo and a light unto eternity!

I sat down on a sofa in one corner of the shop, finished the whole poem and became further engrossed. I spent some time flicking through and reading several more poems. It is a curious thing about poems, how you often revisit them over the years and how, over time, they change in their meaning and significance. I had always preferred Keats and found some of Shelley's poetry a bit gushing - like his elegy to Keats. But as I sat there I experienced great enjoyment from reading the evocative and mysterious *Ozymandius,* which begins *I met a traveller from an antique land*, the very short *Music, when soft voices die*, and *To a Skylark*, appropriately written while Shelley was on holiday in Livorno in northwest Italy and which begins *Hail to thee, blithe spirit!* Another poem that reflected the mood of the moment and the hot weather we were experiencing was *Stanzas Written in Dejection Near Naples,* which begins *The sun is warm, the sky is clear.* All these years I had known about Shelley and read some as a duty, preferring Keats and now, suddenly, I found myself appreciating his poetry in a way I had failed to do previously. I thought that perhaps there was a similarity with music, where some songs acquired a kind of force and significance with time, while others just faded away or, in later years, appeared frivolous.

Even though I knew I had collections of Shelley and Keats at home and in my own bookshop, I bought the copy of Shelley feeling that I had some sense of obligation to help support a fellow bookseller, especially as I had spent so much time reading it and given what Mr Abruzzio had told me about the plight of Italian bookshops. It also spurred me on to go and visit the memorial house.

I spent some time walking up and down the Spanish Steps, which connect the Piazza de Spagna at the bottom and the Pizza Trinita dei Montei at the top, before walking over to the house where Keats lived for the last three months of his life until his death in February. The Spanish Steps were busy with a constant stream of visitors walking up the stairs to the top and back down again, and taking photos. The first thing I noticed was the quietness and coolness of the house once I had crossed the threshold.

Keats had come here, I learned, with the artist Joseph Severn. It was thought that the warmer climate may be good for his tuberculosis from which he was suffering. Severn nursed him. Despite his illness, it was only three years earlier in 1818 that Keats had had his great year in which there was a prodigious outpouring of poetry. In that one year he wrote *The Eve of St Agnes*, *The Eve of St Mark*, *Ode to Psyche*, *La Belle Dame Sans Merci,*

Ode to a Nightingale, Ode on a Grecian Urn, Ode on Melancholy, Ode on Indolence, Lamia, The Fall of Hyperion, and *To Autumn.*

A doctor who lived in the Piazza de Spagna saw Keats and did not think that the tuberculosis diagnosis was correct, suggesting instead that he had digestive problems. He recommended regular exercise. Keats could often be seen walking out on the Pincio, the hill that overlooks the Piazza del Popolo. However, that ceased when he suffered a serious haemorrhage in December 1820.

I was fascinated by a painting by Severn, of Keats among classical ruins, composing his lyrical drama *Prometheus Unbound* in the Baths of the Caracalla. This was where I missed Cameron. I am sure he would have given me some interesting background about the history of the baths in which Keats posed.

The most moving part, I found, was the letter by Joseph Severn in a glass display cabinet describing Keats last moments. I read:

He is gone. He died with the most perfect ease. He seemed to go to sleep. On the twenty-third about four, the approaches of death came on. "Severn, aye, lift me up. I am dying, I shall die easy. Don't be frightened. Be firm; and thank God it has come." I lifted him up in my arms – the phlegm seemed boiling in his throat and increased until eleven when he gradually sunk into death, so quiet that I still thought he slept.

When Keats died, the walls were scraped and all the things in his room were burned as required by Roman health laws at that time. The fact that the house was purchased as a memorial was due initially to the interest of the American poet Robert Underwood Johnson who noticed its poor condition. He called together a dozen or so of the American Literati and their partners in Rome, and the English diplomat and poet Rennell Rodd. Committees were established in America, England and Italy with the support of President Roosevelt and Edward VII and, as a result, the house was purchased in December 1906 and opened in 1909 as the Keats-Shelley Memorial House Museum.

The area as a whole had for generations been visited by English and American architects, painters, musicians, novelists and poets because of Rome's thrilling classical past – and continued to be after Keats death. George Eliot (Mary Ann Cross, née Evans), Byron, Turner, Walter Scott, Henry James, Nathaniel Hawthorne, William Thackeray and Robert and Elizabeth Barrett Browning had all visited.

30

After I had left the house, I rang Cameron to check how he was.

'I'm much better,' he said. 'I will definitely be ready to come back tomorrow.'

He was pleased with the idea of seeing The Vatican.

'Shame I missed the Castle and the Keats-Shelley house, though. The libraries I'm not so sure about.'

'Well, perhaps you can sneak in a visit at least to the castle after we have visited the Vatican while I wait outside – though make sure your phone is charged. We don't want you going missing again.'

Esther rang me almost as soon as I had finished on the phone to Cameron, looking for an update.

'You're like Jack Lemmon and Walter Matthau,' she said, 'The odd couple.'

'Anyway, tonight, I will have a nice solitary reading evening on the terrace of our apartment,' I countered, 'with a glass of wine.'

'I know you Elliot Todd, make sure it's a glass and not a whole bottle.'

We said our goodbyes as I started to wend my way back along the streets towards the apartment. I prepared myself some pasta and salad and restricted myself to just one glass of wine, as I had promised Esther I would. After my meal I felt a little restless and decided I would take a stroll and maybe find a coffee bar. For a little while I had enjoyed the freedom of touring around by myself without the intense history lecture provided by Cameron. Now, after one whole day without him, I felt I would have enjoyed his company at that moment.

Once I was out in the air, though, it was pleasant enough strolling along in the relative cool of the evening. I found a shop that was still open and sold English newspapers.

Just along from the shop, I spied a café with tables on the pavement, though not too near the road. It was attached to a posh looking hotel. I had the place to myself at that moment save for a woman sitting at the table just along from me, drinking a glass of wine. Now I had become accustomed to the idea of spending the evening alone, I looked forward to a solitary hour reading the newspaper and catching up on the news in the UK after I had studiously avoided it in the few days we had been in Italy.

'I'm so sorry to disturb you but would you mind if I joined you? I am dying for some English conversation.'

I started. I was so absorbed in the newspaper and a review of a new novel that I had not noticed the woman approaching me, glass in hand.

'Sorry, I startled you.'

She had a soft American accent, was dressed elegantly in a silver brocade dress and, I guessed, was in her early fifties.

'You are quite within your rights to say no – I won't be offended.'

She didn't exactly sway or slur her speech but I had the feeling that she may have had one or two drinks.

'Not at all,' I said, 'You just surprised me. I was engrossed in my newspaper. You're very welcome.'

'Would you like a glass of wine? I'm happy to treat you. It's the last day of my holiday and I need to use up some Euros.'

'Actually, I had a glass earlier and I need to keep a clear head. Another coffee would be nice, though. Thank you.'

She called over the waiter who was conveniently waiting by the entrance to the hotel.

'Now let me guess, are you one of those touring professors?'

'Certainly not a professor. I'm on holiday with a friend. Just another tourist I'm afraid.'

'Well, welcome fellow tourist, my name is Sally Harding.'

She extended her hand.

'And I'm Elliot Todd. Pleased to meet you!'

'So what do you do – when you're not being a tourist, I mean?'

'I'm a bookseller.'

'Wonderful, I love books. I could see you were a man of intelligence.'

'I'm not sure about that. I think it similar to what they say about teaching – if you're not good enough to write books, sell them.'

'No, I disagree, I think it's a most noble occupation – especially as I know you're not doing it for the money.'

She looked at me with a sideways look when she said that.

'Well, that's true.'

We both laughed.

'But how about you?' I continued. ' What do you do when you're not travelling around the world?'

'I don't actually do anything really. I'm a gay divorcee. My husband left me enough in the settlement. I don't really need to work anymore.'

'Ginger Rogers and Fred Astaire wasn't it? *The Gay Divorcee*, I mean.'

'You've got it. I thought you'd be too young to know that.'

'The *Continental* was in it I believe?'

'You know your films.'

'I'm not a great one for musicals I must admit but Ginger Rogers and Fred Astaire were fabulous. What was that other famous song in that film?'

'Oh! I know.' She held her head a moment. And she began singing, rather well, the first lines of *Night and Day*.

'Yes, that's it! You hold a note pretty well.'

'They were both so talented,' she said. 'And Rogers was his equal in many ways. Astaire was a perfectionist and yet he thought he was not that good, that he always got something wrong. He claimed he couldn't sing but he was a great interpreter of songs and then there was his piano playing skills. He was brilliant in *I won't dance*.'

'You've made me really want to go back and watch some of those films now. '

'You should. His choreography changed everything. Before him there used to be these big Busby Berkeley set pieces. He used dance to move the plot along and be part of the film. It was very revolutionary in its way. '

There was a pause after this sudden rush of conversation.

'It seems almost quaint that term: *Gay Divorcee*,' she said.

'Yes, gay has a different meaning now.'

'Yes, there's that but I really meant the divorcee part.'

'Oh, yes, well at one time you would have been looked down on as "that sort of woman."'

'You're right. Now the thing that surprises most people is that we were ever married at all.' She slapped the table lightly. 'But thank God we were, otherwise it would be much more difficult getting the money out of him.'

'Sounds like it didn't end amicably?'

'Well, you know, we still see each other, really for the sake of the children and we're quite civil to each other. But it was my decision. I don't regret it. It's funny how you can be so in love one minute and then in later years...'

'You're not.'

'Yes, sorry, I'm rambling on. I have to admit I've had a bit too much. I hope I'm not being too embarrassing.'

'You're not.'

My coffee arrived and I thanked the waiter. She whispered something in his ear. Another glass of wine no doubt.

'I think, you know, in a way I prefer it,' she went on, 'I have plenty of money. I can do my own thing. This was just a short trip. My girlfriend had to go back a couple of days ago.'

'Well, I have been abandoned too, by my friend – but in this case it was entirely unintentional.'

I told her the story, embellishing it a little. She lapped it up and intervened several times. She explained that she had visited the Forum and the Palatine too and how impressed she was by it. She had a face younger than her years and her eyes were alive when she spoke. She was good company.

She laughed heartily when I explained to her about Cameron's finger getting bitten by the cat.

'I'm so sorry, I didn't mean to be rude.'

'You're not being rude. It's very funny – and so typical of my friend Cameron.'

The waiter returned with another glass of wine and a brandy.

'I hope you don't mind, to go with your coffee. It's only a small VSOP. I don't feel right drinking on my own.'

'You American ladies are so forward. Well, thank you.' I took a sip. 'It's very nice.' As indeed it was.

'Your friend. Are you and he?'

'Oh, no, we are just friends. The oldest of friends.'

I wondered what I had said about Cameron that made her think that we were a couple and couldn't help thinking back to Esther's remark.

'It's funny, though,' she said after a few moments. ' I still hold on to the idea of marriage even though I can't see that I'll ever get married again.'

I smiled.

'Do you have anyone?' she said.

'Is this a marriage proposal?'

'No, I'm just curious – no, more than curious, nosy.'

'There is someone I am close to but not actually hooked up with.'

I observed how I suddenly had started introducing American slang into my conversation.

'What do you think – about marriage? Would you like to marry this person you're fond of – what's her name?'

'Esther.'

'Esther, that's a nice name.'

Her question was a tricky one to answer given that I had co-opted Esther as my partner without asking her.

'I'm not sure.' I thought was the safest thing to say.

'You mean you haven't made up your mind. Or is it that Esther hasn't made up her mind?'

'Well, I think if Esther really wanted to, I would. I can see advantages and disadvantages. I don't think it matters in itself, the ceremony and all that, except that it's a good excuse to have a party.'

We chatted some more – about her husband's ranch, about her two grown up children whom she obviously adored, how she had nearly become an actress and singer, might have done, it seemed if her husband had not held her back.

We had finished our drinks. It was after eleven. I thought I should get back.

'I'm so pleased that I joined you. You have made what could have been a very boring evening a very pleasant one.'

'That's kind of you – but the same applies on my side.'

Her eyes shone again and she looked at me for a moment.

'I'm staying at the *Marriott*. You could come and join me if you wish.'

'I'm not sure if...'

'I understand. I hope I haven't offended you?'

'No not at all. Another time, another universe...'

'Well goodnight, I've enjoyed our chat.'

She put out her hand. I gave it a little kiss. I thought it was somehow appropriate.

She in turn gave me a little bow as she left. For a moment I had a slight regret. She was very charming and it seemed was just looking for some comfort. I realised that what was really holding me back was an invisible tie to Esther – which I had expressed to Sally Harding in more real terms than I had previously articulated to anyone else, perhaps including myself.

31

I walked back to the apartments, pleased that I had not given in to drinking more alcohol than the one brandy. I wanted to be fresh and clear headed for the return of Cameron and the inevitable demands of his touring schedule.

In the foyer I was once again presented with the situation I had had a few days before. The lift said *occupie* but there seemed no sign of it operating. No doubt the same person, probably a tourist like ourselves staying in one of the apartments, did not yet understand the necessity of shutting the inner door. I did wish they would learn though as it was certainly becoming irritating and energy sapping in the heat. I trudged sleepily and truculently up the stairs before I was suddenly brought wide awake as I was passed by a man running quickly past me down the stairs. He was so intent, I moved back against the wall to prevent myself from being flattened.

I continued upwards. Again, it seemed it was on the third floor that the lift was stuck. I saw that the door was partially open.

Likely, the same culprit as before, then, I thought.

I pushed at the door but there was some resistance and it would not close even though I pushed quite hard. I pulled the door back to check what was obstructing it. A hand flopped out towards me, followed by the body of a man...

I took a moment to take it all in. At first I thought he must have fainted in the heat but as I attempted to put the body in the recovery position on its side, remembering my first aid course, I saw blood oozing from a wound in his chest. I also realised that I knew the man. It was Mr Abruzzio...

He was in a bad way, barely conscious. His eyes flickered open. I was not sure whether he recognised me or not. He clutched a piece of paper in his hand and tried to speak.

I knocked on the nearest door - the apartment next to the lift. I dragged up the few Italian words I knew that were relevant.

'*Emergenza, medico.*'

'I'm fetching help,' I said to Mr Abruzzio, not knowing whether he could hear me.

The door to the flat was opened by an elderly woman in a turban style headgear. I repeated my call for help. She looked at the prostrate figure, crossed herself and disappeared. I heard her punching in numbers on her landline.'

At that moment Abruzzio's body slumped and he lost consciousness. The piece of paper dropped to the floor and I slipped it into my pocket. I felt for his pulse and found a very weak intermittent one.

I tapped his face.

'Mr Abruzzio!' I shouted.

I could not see the rise and fall of his chest and only felt a faint exhalation of breath from his mouth. I found his breastbone and placed the palm of my right hand over it and then linked the fingers of my left hand and began pushing down and then releasing continuously. A few moments later an older man with a moustache appeared on the stairs. The woman had returned from her phone call and said, '*A, Paulo, emergenzio!*'

'I help,' he said and took over from me. He had obviously been well trained in CPR and continued with an easy rhythm.

I decided to ring Laura. Being first on the scene would mean I would have to remain here to tell the police what happened and I only had a few words of Italian. Luckily, I was able to get straight through to her. I had barely begun explaining when the ambulance arrived with a stretcher.

'I'll come right away,' Laura said.

The woman pointed to me when they began asking about Abruzzio. '*Io sono inglese*' I said. In broken English the female paramedic said 'How happen?' I explained as best I could the circumstances of my finding the body. They did a number of checks while continuing with the CPR. A policeman arrived and said, 'Come with me this way.' We walked down the stairs to the foyer and some seats in the corner. There were several people being turned away from the entrance and a taped barrier had been put in place. Then I saw Laura had arrived. She spoke to another policeman in urgent tones. He let her through.

'I'm so pleased to see you,' I said. 'How did you get here so quickly?'

'I was nearby already, on my way back to my apartment. I came straight here. I told them I have come to act as your interpreter.' Over her shoulder I saw the body of Mr Abruzzio being carried through the door on a stretcher.

'Poor Mr Abruzzio!' I said.

*

The policeman had a little English but, in the main, Laura translated his questions and spoke for me.

I explained how I had come upon the scene. I told him how Mr Abruzzio had tried to say something but could only get out a couple of words, which we thought in translation could have been 'my responsibility'. I then explained about the person rushing past me, the meeting at the opera with Antonio Cantalbrini and Mr Abruzzio and that I had also seen them eating together at the restaurant on our first night in Rome. I also explained our recent meeting with him in the library.

'Yes, Mr Cantalbrini,' the policeman said. 'I think I know this man.'

I expected Laura to jump in at that point and add the details of her own meeting with Mr Abruzzio but, at that moment, the policeman was called away.

'I'm worried that they think I did it.' I said to Laura.

'They will want to exclude you so they may want to search your apartment, but if you think about it, if you were guilty, why would you hang around at the scene of the crime?'

The policeman returned.

'It's now a murder enquiry,' he said dramatically.

He went off to one side to instruct one of his officers. I turned to Laura.

'I saw you at the Accademia dei Linci this morning. I'm sorry I didn't get a chance to speak to you.'

She looked at me curiously for a moment, as though taken off-guard. Had she not noticed me there at the library? I guessed if she had, she would have stayed to talk to me at the time. Unless she was trying to avoid me - or my questions?

'I thought I should go and see him – after you told me about him. Obviously, I had no idea this was going to happen.'

'After you left, he had an intense discussion with Cantalbrini.'

The policeman began walking back towards us.

'I'm sorry, I need to check a few things before I give my side of the story. I will let Cameron know what has happened here.'

*

Soon after Laura had left, the policeman said that I could return to my apartment but that they may want to speak to me again and that I may have to extend my visit to Rome. I rang Esther. She was predictably shocked at the turn of events. After she had taken it all in and sympathised with the predicament I found myself in, she began trying to rationalise what had happened.

'Perhaps he was coming to see you.'

'And he was murdered before he could get to me. It feels so dark and sinister.'

'If it is true that he was coming to see you, how did he know how to find you?'

'Cantalbrini has my address. In fact, I remember, Mr Abruzzio wrote it down for him in the restaurant as he did not have a pen.'

'You think that Cantalbrini's a suspect.'

'It just seems too much of a coincidence that he had been talking to him earlier.'

'Maybe it was nothing to do with you – maybe he was just visiting a friend who happened to live in the same building.'

'Whether he was visiting me or a friend, he still got murdered.'

'Perhaps it was just someone off the street?'

'There was the guy who came running past me. I suppose he's the obvious suspect. I had very little description to give the police as it all happened so quickly. All I know is that he was young – maybe early twenties, with a dark mop of hair, no beard or any obvious distinguishing features. He was wearing dark trousers and I think a dark jumper or hoodie. But, to be honest it all happened so quickly it was a bit of a blur. I don't think I'm a very reliable witness.'

'I think you need some sleep. We can discuss it again later.'

Despite the late hour I made myself another coffee. I wanted to take my mind off things and sat down with the last two chapters of *Pereira Maintains*. But then, Esther rang again. She could not sleep because she had a new theory.

'What if it wasn't him? What if he was running away just because he witnessed it and he wanted to escape?'

'You mean he may have been murdered by someone else who'd already left the scene? But nobody else was around.'

'What about before you entered the apartments? Did you notice anyone in the street before you came into the courtyard?'

'Can't say I did.'

'The other possibility is that the other person, if there was one, didn't go back down the stairs...'

'He couldn't have taken the lift (assuming it's a "he") because the lift was blocked with Abruzzio's body.'

'Unless he didn't try to go down the stairs or into the lift but went up the stairs,'

'What, you mean he (or she) lives in one of the apartments?'

'I was thinking more there could be a fire escape somewhere near the top of the building – but what you said is not impossible.'

'All very interesting speculation but, whether it was the person rushing past me on the stairs or someone else, it's the motive for his murder that's important - and whether there is any connection to Cantalbrini - or anyone else for that matter.'

I had been pacing up and down on the balcony since she had phoned, as was my way, speaking with one hand in my pocket. There was something there, a ten euro note? Then I remembered the piece of paper that Abruzzio had in his hand.

'I've just remembered there was a piece of paper. To tell the truth I had forgotten all about it.'

'What?'

'He was holding it in his hand just before he died. How could I be so stupid not to remember? The police seemed more concerned about whether he had a mobile phone.'

'What does it say?'

I smoothed it out on the table in front of me.

'Let me see. A book title by *Boccaccio*. Perhaps the *Decameron*, I can't read it very well.'

'I suppose it's not such an unusual thing for a librarian, I imagine they are always jotting down notes.'

'Not unusual, maybe, but why was he clutching it in his hand? And he tried to say something but I couldn't understand him. I wonder if it was something to do with the piece of paper and the book?'

'Is there anything on the back?'

'Ah, yes, my address. Well, just the number and the building. It may be the note he made for Cantalbrini in the restaurant.'

'Ah, then he was visiting you!'

'I wonder if we may have Mr Abruzzio wrong,' she continued. 'We assume that he was in collusion with Cantalbrini but what if he was a good guy? Perhaps he started off thinking he was giving a bit of innocent help and then he realised what he was getting into.'

'So, why would he come to see me? How did he think I could possibly help?'

'Perhaps he wanted to tell you his intentions or even he may have wanted to discuss it with you so that you could expose Cantalbrini.'

'Or possibly, just to warn me not to deal with him. I suppose it's feasible - but it's all so bizarre. We only came to Rome for sightseeing. I should never have gone along with Cameron and his accepting Cantalbrini's invitation to his apartment.'

'Too late to worry about that now!'

'I know.'

'You'd better let the police know about this piece of paper. I'm sure they'll want it as evidence anyway.'

'I've already handled Abruzzio's phone. Looks like I'm building up quite a list of things with my fingerprints on. There is something else.'

I told her about seeing Abruzzio and Laura talking in the library and how uncomfortable she was when I mentioned it.

'It does seem a little strange but I wonder if she thinks that it is important to tell the police about this and not discuss it with you. After all, it sounds like she may not have seen you.'

'You don't suppose...?'

'What?'

'I don't really want to go there but I can't help but consider it. You don't suppose Laura could be in some way in collusion with Cantalbrini? Some of the things she said about the regulations about exporting books from Italy – it was as if she was defending those who broke the law.'

'You don't trust her?'

'She's a good friend of Cameron's - but you know, it is all a bit strange.'

'So you think she might be somehow involved with his murder?'

'No, I can't believe that. But you know, it's odd that she appeared on the scene within minutes of the assault taking place. I expected she would be at her apartment with Cameron.'

'Perhaps she was trying to give him some space. Or give herself a bit of space from Cameron.'

'I suppose that could be it.'

'Well, perhaps you should mention the library meeting, next time you have an opportunity – to the police – to make sure you have told them everything you know. If she hasn't told them already they'll have to question her and it will come out one way or another.'

'Perhaps you're right. Don't stay up too late. You have work in the morning.'

'Don't I know it?'

'Everything all right?'

'Absolutely fine.'

'And Aggie?'

'Fit as a flea.'

'Good.'

'I know it's difficult but try to get some sleep.'

'I will – and I'll have Cameron back tomorrow – as long as he is well enough.'

'That's good. Night Elliot. Take care.'

'I will. Night Esther.'

32

I had a restless night going over and over the evening in my head. It was after four by the time I slept.

I was woken in the morning by my phone. I usually kept it by my bed but on this occasion had left it in the kitchen. I forced myself up quickly so I would get to it in time. I expected it was Cameron who was due to return (I hoped refreshed) from Laura's, so that we would be ready for our visit to the Vatican the following day. I wondered if this was the right moment to express my possible fears over her involvement with Cantalbrini.

As I picked the phone up I saw that it had just turned eight o'clock.

But it was not Cameron. It was Antonio Cantalbrini.

'Mr Todd, I have just heard the sad news about Mr Abruzzio.'

It took me a few moments to get the fuzziness out of my head and to get my brain in gear.

'Oh, yes,' I agreed, 'very tragic.'

'I've had the police here asking questions. As I mentioned to you before, the authorities in Rome can be very suspicious. But luckily I have some friends…'

There was silence at my end as I tried to take in what he was saying

'I'm sorry,' I said, 'I was sleeping when you rang. I had a late night. I just need to get my head straight.'

'Oh, I'm so sorry to wake you. Shall I call again later?'

'No, it's fine. Go ahead.'

He continued in his elegant English.

'I hope you don't mind me asking but am I correct in thinking you found the body of poor Mr Abruzzio?'

'Yes, that's right. I'm not sure if I'm supposed to discuss it with anyone except the police, though.'

'I understand. We all have to be so careful. I just wanted to ask you if he perhaps mentioned anything to you before he passed away?'

'He tried to mouth something but I couldn't hear him.'

'Was there anything found on the body?'

'Not that I'm aware of. They were hoping to find a mobile phone but it wasn't on him.'

I decided not to mention the piece of paper – especially as I had not informed the police yet.

'Ah, probably left it behind somewhere.'

'Is there anything else I can help you with?'

'I was wondering if you would do me the favour of another brief visit. There are one or two things I would like to explain to you that would be better done face to face. And I would like to offer you a memento of your time here.'

'I'm sure that's not necessary.'

'But I do insist.'

'I am a bit busy – you know with everything going on.'

'I understand but if you could come here at around eleven-thirty today, just for a few minutes, I would be very grateful.'

'I'll have to get back to you. My friend is due to return here later this morning.'

'Perhaps I can come and see you?'

'Let me get back to you.'

I put the phone down.

To be truthful, I had no desire to visit Antonio Cantalbrini at all, especially as I felt he might be involved in some way with Mr Abruzzio's demise. I just wanted to go back to enjoying sightseeing with Cameron, though, as usual, Cantalbrini was being very persuasive. In fact, it was more like a summons than an invitation.

I rang Esther and told her about the call.

'That's a very odd conversation.'

'You think I should go?'

'It's difficult. I wonder what this gift is?'

'I'm sure I could live without it. In any case, I might refuse it.'

'What's the advantage of going otherwise?'

'I'm not really sure.'

'I suppose the advantage of not going is that you'll avoid a possible difficult conversation. From the way you described it, it sounded like he was not giving you an option about whether you should see him or not.'

'Perhaps the advantage of going is that I might discover something about his possible involvement. But then, we'll be gone in a few days – unless the police delay us.'

'I suppose it can't hurt. After all, what can happen between two bookdealers? Why don't you ask Laura what she thinks?'

'Yes, that makes sense. I'm worried about Cameron. I was going to phone him but this may be a better way – as he is her friend and everything. I can't believe that Cameron is really in danger but if she is involved in some way on the margins... The more I read about corruption in Italy the more common it appears to be and seems accepted as a way of lubricating the wheels of commerce.'

'You may have your suspicions about Laura but you may be able to gauge something from the conversation – you know, the validity of her story and how Cameron is.'

'I need to ring her about the piece of paper anyway. I thought it would be best to get her to explain for me. I don't want to get done for withholding evidence. It's kind of funny ringing someone you think may be involved themselves for advice on doing the right thing by the police.'

I rang Laura and told her first about the piece of paper.

'Well, that's intriguing – especially the fact that it had your name and address on it.'

'Not my name but my address.'

'Well, I suppose it amounts to the same thing. I think you should definitely hand it over to the police.'

She put her phone on speaker and I spoke to Cameron.

'Awful business,' he said. 'I'm sorry I wasn't there to help you take the strain of it all - but I'll see you later - just a couple of chapters to finish in this book on the Vatican. And don't worry about hurrying. I have my own key and I definitely won't be visiting the cat sanctuary on the way this time.'

I asked Laura her opinion about whether I should visit Cantalbrini. As Esther had pointed out, if she was involved in some way it would be good to gauge how she reacted.

'Do you think I should go?' I said.

'I think if you don't feel too uncomfortable about it, it would be interesting to see what he has to say. Are you worried you may be in danger?'

I was not going to pretend otherwise.

'Yes, a little.'

'Well, if you do decide to go, we can make sure Alessandro is aware of the situation.'

*

I was in a state of confusion about Laura's possible involvement and I contemplated the unthinkable. What if Laura and Cantalbrini and Abruzzio were all in it together – maybe even the policeman Alessandro – and something had gone horribly wrong? Perhaps a rival group had been involved. Laura may be trying to re-assure me that Alessandro would be aware of my visit - but would that help me if they were all involved?

Another phrase that Laura had used came into my head: 'Some people say that nothing would ever get done if everyone played by the rules.' But, then, why was Abruzzio killed? Was he perhaps trying to come clean and that was why he was visiting me – to warn me? And then, a chilling thought occurred to me. Was the reason that Laura was so quickly on the scene due to the fact that she *was* somehow implicated in Abruzzio's murder? At that moment I thought I did not know who to trust.

Though I was wary of visiting Cantalbrini and his reason for seeing me, there was a part of me that was curious to know what he wanted to say to me and what that gift was. If I did not visit him, I may never know - and that bothered me also. After much agonising, I decided I would meet him at the time he had suggested and texted him to say so. I received an instant reply saying that he was looking forward to seeing me. If things got at all tricky with Cantalbrini, I was going to make it clear to him that the police had been informed – hoping that it would be to my advantage.

Another voice in my head was telling me that we may be jumping to an awful lot of wrong conclusions and denigrating an innocent man. Cantalbrini was one of those people who at the time you were talking to them seemed perfectly charming. It was only after, when I had recalled what he said that I reassessed the conversation and it appeared to take on a more sinister aspect. Wasn't it possible that Abruzzio was visiting me for a perfectly innocent reason but just had the misfortune to be attacked by someone off the street?

I texted Laura and Esther to say that I had decided to make the visit. However, before I left the house Laura rang me.

'They have asked if you would drop it into the station next to Piazza Venezia. They may want to take your finger prints as well to eliminate you from any enquiries. I suggest that you take a photo of the piece of paper, both sides, just in case. Once they get into the system sometimes these things have a habit of disappearing.'

'It seems as though you are talking from bitter personal experience.'

'There are one or two instances I could mention but I don't want to bore you with them.'

'I can assure you this sort of thing is not just confined to Italian bureaucracy.'

What she said was entirely logical, though another part of me was saying: *what if they want to take my fingerprints to incriminate me? What if you want to incriminate me to deflect from your own involvement?*

I made the journey to the police station in good time, on foot as had become my habit. I left the envelope and had my fingerprints taken.

33

When I reached the apartment buildings where Cantalbrini lived, I had a feeling of trepidation. But he welcomed me warmly and shook my hand.

'It's good to see you Mr Todd. Can I get you a drink?'

'No, thank you, I had something before I came out.'

'Do you mind if I do?'

'No not at all.'

He went over to a table in the corner where there were a couple of glasses and a decanter. He poured himself a generous glass of whisky, despite the early hour.

'You know Mr Todd, life can be a strange business at the best of times but especially, I think, here in Italy.' He took a sip of his drink. 'It's a *Glemorangie*. I do like your Scottish whisky. I know you are English not Scottish, but it's very good stuff.'

'I know, saying British whisky doesn't sound right.'

'You're sure you don't want one?'

'I'm sure, thanks.'

'You know, I didn't know poor Mr Abruzzio very well, really – just an acquaintance. Well enough to suggest that he was our companion to the opera, but that's about it. It was just strange that we bumped into each other again only yesterday. But then, he is a librarian and we were in a library.'

He laughed, as if to make light of it.

You knew him well enough to have a meal with him and were excited to see the book he had brought you at the restaurant. And the conversation you had at the library was rather intense and did not seem like a casual affair.

'I guess it was just some crazy person off the street,' I said.

He shook his head.

'Yes, or someone who had a grudge against him. Even librarians can have enemies.'

'There was a man who ran past me when I was climbing the stairs. I'm afraid I didn't get a very good look at him.'

'There we are then. I'm sorry to say there have been quite a few of these unfortunate incidents over the years in Rome.'

I nodded. He continued.

'I have to warn you that Italy is not like the UK. You have to be a bit more careful about who you associate with, especially in certain circles. There are unwritten rules but they are just as important as anything written down – and if you fall foul of them – well, it has its consequences. So much...' He searched for the appropriate English phrase, 'is a matter of interpretation and... association.'

'Association?'

'Yes, who you choose to associate with. Sometimes this occurs almost as if by accident. You English have a good word for it I think. Serendipity.'

'Ah, yes.'

'I think it was popularised as a word by your Horace Walpole.'

'Ah, I didn't know that.'

'You don't know the story, *The Three Princes of Serendip*?'

'No. You're making me feel very ignorant.'

'It comes from the Italian story: *Peregrinaggio di tre giovani figliuoli del re di Serendippo* published by Michele Tramezzino in the sixteenth century. I wish I owned an original copy of that! It would be worth quite a lot I think. But he, Tramezzino that is, got the story from Cristoforo Armeno who translated the fairy tale from the Persian. You see, we all borrow from each other.'

This was, I supposed, a kind of coded warning to me. While I may have been on my guard, there was no doubt about his erudition and knowledge. I wondered if this was leading to a conclusion or whether I was expected to take what he said away and interpret it.

'Well, yes, our own Mr Shakespeare, of course, was well known for borrowing stories from Italy.'

Then I noticed something out of the corner of my eye and it made my pulse race. On the ledge of the window where there was a corner seat, next to the small trolley table where he had poured his whisky, there was, partially concealed by a newspaper, a mobile phone – covered over on one edge with a small piece of sticking plaster. Abruzzio's phone, surely, that I had noticed when he had dropped it at the Opera. Unless it was a common Italian trait to decorate your phone with a plaster?

'And he did not always get it right,' I blurted out, not wanting Cantalbrini to notice my being distracted by the phone. 'There's the famous case in Julius Caesar where he talks about the clock striking.'

I was pleased I had not told him about the piece of paper I had found, which could possibly be incriminating.

'Ah, yes.' He drank the rest of the whisky and put his glass on the table. As he had his back slightly turned away from me I could not help looking again at the phone just beyond him. He turned back towards me and I looked away from the phone. I was certain it was the same one.

'But going back to our earlier conversation...' said Cantalbrini, 'I take it you understand the meaning behind my remarks?'

I met his gaze, nodding my head and adopted a placatory tone.

'I believe so,' I said. 'Though I have enjoyed being in Rome I realise that I have a lot to learn about its customs and people.'

He shrugged in a rather Gallic way.

'This is the way things are here. There is a code of honour that is widespread in Italy and, indeed in many Latin countries.'

Omertà, I thought.

'Of course, when you found Mr Abruzzio you had no choice but to call the police.'

Why would I ever think otherwise? And why would Cantalbrini connect the code of silence with this incident. As I suspected, I was about to find out.

'The poor man was dying. I was sorry I could not save him. I'm afraid I was too late.'

'Of course, that's right. We must all do our best to save the life of a dying man.'

There was the sound of a siren in the streets outside. An ambulance or police car, I was not sure which. He walked to the window and looked out. For a moment, I thought, he was going to pick up the mobile phone that I believed belonged to Abruzzio. After a few moments, though, apparently satisfied, he turned back towards me and continued.

'But, you know, the police and the prosecutor often get the wrong idea. It is sometimes in their eagerness to make a conviction that they poke and prod around and ask questions and make spurious connections – and often come to erroneous conclusions. We must not aid them in their desire to travel down this unnecessary path. And if we do, well it will just have negative consequences and innocent people might get hurt.'

Which innocent people were we talking about, him or me?

'Don't look so worried my dear friend.'

I couldn't deny that I probably was looking concerned at that moment.

'I just wanted to make you aware of the practicalities of the situation. As I have told you, Mr Abruzzio and myself were just passing acquaintances, who happened to meet at the opera. I think I may have heard you mention a meeting at the restaurant and a book that Mr Abruzzio had brought there. My recollection is rather different. I think you may not be remembering quite correctly or confusing the incident with another time and place. And when we visited the library, all I did was pass a few words of recognition in the manner I would to someone who I did not know well.'

'You want me to lie,' I thought. But I did not express my thoughts aloud.

'All I am saying Mr Todd, is that we do not need to bring these other supposed meetings up at all when they may only complicate the issue. It may be simpler just to leave these things unsaid. I know you British put a lot of store on the truth. No one is asking anyone to lie, just not to mention things that will not help anyone. You know, if the facts are not absolutely clear and evidence is anecdotal, that evidence may be proved inadmissible.'

How to react? Should I tell him that I had already mentioned some of these things to the police? Yet, I had not gone into all the details, and in particular, the details of the book that Mr Abruzzio had brought to the restaurant, as no doubt I may have the opportunity to do so later.

Just tell him what he wants to hear. That was what came to the forefront of my mind.

'Of course, I have no wish to incriminate an innocent party.'

'That is very refreshing to hear.' He smiled, as though satisfied with my answer.

'And now, before you go let me give you your gift.'

'There's no need, really'

'No you must have it, you deserve it.'

Deserve it? What had I done? What had I agreed to? Silence, I guessed and, in particular about the book. It had seemed such an innocent moment at the time it was witnessed by myself and Cameron. But, perhaps it was stolen from the library? Probably, almost certainly. I wished I had seen the title of the book. Perhaps Cantalbrini thought I had?

He disappeared around the corner behind an alcove for a moment.

What was the significance of that phone in Cantalbrini's

apartment? It had to be Abruzzio's hadn't it? It was too much of a coincidence for there to be another phone with a plaster on it. Then I had it, or thought I did. The man who had rushed past me on the stairs and nearly bumped into me? What if he was carrying that phone, the phone with a piece of plaster on? Could he be the murderer and working on behalf of Cantalbrini who wanted the phone in case it contained evidence that implicated him? Abruzzio had not left it behind at all. It was on him and that man who was undoubtedly the murderer took it so the records could not be retrieved by the police. The enormity of that fact hit me as Cantalbrini returned with the gift. Books, of course.

'Here, I would like you to have these.'

It was the edition of *Lyrical Ballads*, in two small volumes.

'I can't possibly accept these.'

'Nonsense, please take it in the spirit it is intended - between two fellow book dealers,' and again he held my eyes.

I could have, maybe should have, said no, but if I did I was afraid of what the consequences might be. If I said yes, I had the opportunity of leaving at that moment rather than extending my visit and any complications that may arise. I took the book from him.

'Oh, well, thank you, but *it is* too generous.'

'Good. I think we understand each other.'

'Before I go,' I made myself cough. 'I feel a little dehydrated and have a bit of a headache. Could I possibly have a glass of water?'

'The Rome heat. You English are not used to it. Of course, just one moment.'

He left the room. This was my chance. I moved swiftly on tiptoe, as noiselessly as I could to the other side of the room and grabbed the phone. The newspaper dropped to the floor. I put it back as I heard the door open. I slipped the phone into my pocket and moved back to where I had been when Cantalbrini left the room and hastily opened the front cover of *The Lyrical Ballads*, exclaiming as he returned, 'This is, indeed, a very nice edition. Just as I remembered.'

'Yes, and such interesting men, Coleridge and Wordsworth, don't you think?'

'Yes, while very different from each other.'

Part of me at that moment wanted to believe in the charming Antonio Cantalbrini. Perhaps it was all a misunderstanding.

Perhaps Abruzzio had made another visit and left the phone behind and even now Cantalbrini was not aware of it?

'Here I have brought you a bottle of cold mineral water so you can take it with you.'

I smiled playing the part that was expected of me while feeling something completely different inside.

'Thank you Antonio, that's most kind.' I took the water and shook his hand. He nearly crushed mine with his firm shake.

'I'm glad we were able to meet again and have our little discussion.'

I turned and made towards the door.

My heart was pounding away uncontrollably. He strode in front of me and for a moment I thought he was blocking my path. He grabbed the door handle.

'Allow me.' He opened the door. 'Have a safe journey back to the UK. And remember: *Amor Librorium nos unit.*'

'What's that?'

'The love of books unites us.'

I walked down the stairs rather than wait for the lift. I did not look back. There were just two flights of stairs. I tried not to walk too quickly. I felt his eyes on my back.

How long I wondered, before he noticed the phone was gone? As soon as I was past the entrance to the gateway I began jogging. I needed to put as much distance between myself and Cantalbrini as I could. I took a side street onto another main street, then another side street, losing myself and, I hoped, evading anyone following me.

I thought of ringing Laura, but if she was implicated I might be making things worse for myself and Cameron. My first thought was that Cameron and I should get away from the apartment.

I rang him. He had been due to return later that morning. Midday had just passed. I had to believe he was there and nothing had prevented his return - but I knew this was not guaranteed. Frustratingly there was no reply. I left a message for him telling him to ring me back urgently. Ideally, I would have asked him to meet me away from the apartment. If he did not ring me back I would have to make my way there.

A little part of me thought –and wanted to think – that I may be worrying unnecessarily. I ran over in my mind a scenario of how it may have been that Abruzzio visited Cantalbrini's apartment, especially if he was doing some work for him, which could be perfectly innocent on a consultancy basis (perhaps bringing him back a book he had been asked to identify), and left it behind. Perhaps it wasn't Abruzzio's phone and the plaster was just a coincidence? If I had taken Cantalbrini's phone this could be very embarrassing – though I was pretty sure I had seen him using a newer slicker type than the one I had in my pocket.

I went in to the middle of a nearby square, sat down on a bench and switched the phone on. Luckily there was no password to negotiate. I flicked through the contacts. I could see at least two or three mentions of *biblioteca* so was confident that it was Abruzzio's. There it was, the last time the phone had been used was on the day of the attack. Approximately thirty minutes before. It was possible he could have been coming straight back from Cantalbrini's after leaving his flat – though that would have meant him travelling very quickly given the distance.

Just at that moment, Abruzzio's phone rang. It was flashing Cantabrini. I ignored it. Then my own phone rang. Again it was him. I ignored that too. I was keeping to the code of silence but I guessed that was not quite what Cantalbrini had in mind.

I made my way hastily down the side streets towards the apartment. I felt a tightness in my chest every time a vehicle slowed. I did not like the thought of being assassinated from a passing car. As soon as I reached the apartment building I ran up the flight of steps not trusting to wait for the lift, even though it may have been a quicker option.

I fumbled my keys as I tried to find the correct one that fitted the lock. There was no one in the lounge or the kitchen. Perhaps Cameron had decided to go on a short tour somewhere in Rome on his way to the apartment. That would have been typical of him – and very inconvenient. Or perhaps Cantalbrini had already sent someone there?

Then I detected a droning noise from the bathroom. It sounded like some kind of Italian opera.

I did not have time for niceties.

'Cameron,' I banged on the bathroom door. It was unlocked. I opened it.

He gave a shriek.

'Can't a fellow have a bit of peace and quiet while he's having a bath?'

34

We were out of the apartment in minutes with Cameron's hair still dripping wet.

I had explained briefly about my visit to Cantalbrini and my suspicions about his possible part in Abruzzio's death - and that I had taken the phone. Thankfully, he accepted what I said without argument and went along with my instruction to leave the apartment immediately. We packed as fast we could: a rucksack each, passport, money and phones. Rather than take the main street we cut down the first side street and zigzagged until we were a mile or so away.

As we went along the streets I filled him in on more details.

'This is the really difficult bit,' I said. 'I am not sure if Laura may be involved in some way.'

'What?' He stopped dead in the middle of a zebra crossing.

'Come on,' I said, urging him forward. 'You'll get run over.'

'You must be joking,' he said. He stopped and leaned against a shop window once we had made the other side of the road.

I explained about her not revealing to me her connection with Abruzzio – and possibly, by extension, that she may know Cantalbrini.

'Look, I grant you it's a little odd but...'

Then Cameron's phone rang.

'It's Laura. What shall I say?'

'You'd better tell her about my visit to Cantalbrini. See what she says.'

'Laura, we're in a bit of a spot,' I heard him say. I didn't hear him say much more as he turned away and walked a few steps.

He finished his call and turned back towards me.

'She says she'll meet us at the Victor Emmanuel Monument. What do you think?'

'We'll just have to go along with it.'

It took us a while to find our way down the maze of streets but after ten minutes or so we had negotiated our way and rounded a corner to the Piazza Venezia and the familiar white monument. I did not raise the subject of Laura's possible complicity again but my doubts about her hung in the air between us as we hurried along.

Once we had reached the steps at the front, we thought we would sit for a few minutes to get our breath back - but the officials were out in force and had other ideas. It was not just a case of not being able to sit down and eat but not being able to sit down at all. Standing was allowed and the taking of photos – but sitting was definitely out.

As we knew Laura was likely to be a few minutes before she got to us, we strolled up towards the top of the steps to look at the view. Not as good as going right to the top but even from here we could get a feeling of the panorama of buildings and monuments of the Colosseum and the Forum and the surrounding area, and, of course, of Piazza Venezia itself.

Cameron was sombre. I knew that he, like me, was plagued with anxiety about the situation in which we had found ourselves, and now my suspicions about Laura, and, no doubt, the residual effects of his illness.

'Amazing panorama,' I said, trying to lighten the mood.

'Yeah, shall we go back down?'

We slowly made our way down the steps avoiding the wrath of the officials doing an effective job in not allowing anyone to occupy the steps for more time than was, in their view, strictly necessary. We negotiated a string of people of varying nationalities having their photos taken. As we did, so I peered intently into the piazza looking for a sign of Laura striding, as I hoped, purposefully across the square towards us. My eyes began to hurt after a while with the strain of looking. A couple of Laura look-a-likes appeared who turned in the wrong direction. I continued my gaze. An Asian couple requested we take a photo. Cameron held my rucksack while I did the honours.

They were, of course, very grateful. I took one of Cameron while at the same time keeping my eye on the area beyond the bottom of the steps and the piazza. Then I did notice someone striding purposefully across the piazza in the far distance coming in our direction - but it was not Laura. It was Cantalbrini, accompanied by two men.

'Cameron, look. How on earth?'

'I don't understand. How would he possibly know we are here?'

'Laura, Laura was the only one who knew we were coming here.'

'But she wouldn't.'

'How well do we know her really?'

'I've known her for years. I just don't believe...'

'People change. You don't suppose she is working with him? She was saying that she understood the problems there were with export licences and how sometimes there were grey areas between legality and illegality.'

'I know, you said, but I can't believe she would do anything like that.' He hesitated. 'No, I trust her implicitly.'

'All right. But what should we do?'

Cameron's phone rang.

'It's Laura.'

I went right up to him so I could hear the conversation. He touched the speaker button.

'I'm just approaching the square. Are you there?'

'Unfortunately, Cantalbrini has found us first and he has someone with him. They're only a minute away.'

'They must have set up tracking on Abruzzio's phone – it's probably how they knew he was going to your apartment in the first place before the killer took it.'

'Of course,' said Cameron.

Any doubts I had about Laura were beginning to evaporate.

'What should we do?'

'No time for heroics. The people with him may be armed - now he knows that you are on the wrong side of him. You have to get moving before they get too close to you. Listen to me carefully. Look to the right of the square. Opposite the green circle in the centre is the approach to the Carabinieri Station. If you can make it there I will meet you. If you don't think you can make it, dump the phone and run as fast and as far away as possible.'

Cameron cut Laura off without saying goodbye. Cantalbrini and his henchmen were by now approaching the bottom of the steps of the monument from the left hand side. My heart was thumping and I felt nauseous.

I propelled Cameron forward.

'Run like the clappers!'

We reached the bottom of the steps of the monument, taking two or three steps at a time, just as Cantalbrini and his accomplices approached.

We ran through streaming traffic. A car and a bus braked sharply, another car refused to give way and passed millimetres in front of us despite our outstretched hands. Horns blared at us, fists were shaken. Then something dropped from my pocket and went shooting back towards the road. It was Abruzzio's phone. I started to go back for it as Cantalbrini's accomplices closed in on it.

But Cameron pulled me back.

'No,' he said. 'It's too dangerous.'

At last we gained the centre of the green circle and were free of traffic for a moment. We ran across the walkway towards the entrance of the Carabinierri building once more risking life and limb as we dodged past traffic in front and behind us. Laura was waiting on the edge of the kerb and propelled us through the entrance. I glanced back. Cantalbrini and his accomplices had disappeared.

35

Once in the station, I told the story of my visit to Cantalbrini and the later consequences to Alessandro, with some help from Laura.

'It's a shame about the phone,' said Alessandro.

'Isn't there a way of tracking the calls without the phone?' I said.

'Yes, possibly, if we can establish the phone was Abruzzio's and trace the number. But it may not be easy.'

'What about the fact that I'm a witness?'

'I'm not sure if the Pubblico Minstero will think there is enough evidence to justify a conviction. If Cantalbrini is responsible for Abruzzio's murder it is almost certain that he was not the one who carried out the act. Let us say it is the man who ran past you. We have to find him and prove it, and then establish a link to Cantalbrini. While our suspicions may be well-founded, proving it is another matter. That's where the mobile phone may have been useful. It can sometimes provide us with all kinds of other information. '

'I hope I won't have to stay and testify. I would like to make my flight home in a couple of days.'

'I can't promise anything but it may not be necessary. What we may have, with your evidence and this piece of paper is enough to enter his apartment and find those stolen volumes. We may not be able to convict him for murder – at least not immediately - but stolen books can carry a heavy sentence in Italy.'

I felt a slight uncomfortableness in Laura's presence even though she had not been a witness to my doubts about her.

'The secret room, you must find the secret room.' I explained again about the way he seemed to enter it but I was not sure of what the exact mechanism was.

'Don't worry, we will find our way in. But we have to act quickly, I think.'

'What do you suggest Cameron and I do?'

'Well, here is the difficulty, of course. Even though we think we have grounds to secure a conviction of some kind, we think you may be in possible danger if you go back to your apartment. We could look into putting a permanent guard on the apartments but with budget cuts I am not sure if we have the resources...'

'That's OK. They can stay with me,' said Laura.

Cameron, though, had a pained expression on his face.

'What is it Cameron, are you ill?' said Laura. 'Was it the mention of blood?'

'No, not ill. In fact I feel much better. It's just that, does this mean that we won't be able to visit the Vatican tomorrow?'

Alessandro considered it for a moment.

'I don't see that you should be locked up in a flat all day, just that you should not be located too easily until it is resolved. It is probably a good idea to be out and about in the crowds where you won't be easily found. There's probably nowhere better to lose yourself than the Vatican during the tourist season.'

Cameron was visibly cheered up.

Laura had given us the spare key to her flat, which Cameron had used while he was there. Laura went with Alessandro and another policeman to fetch the rest our things from our apartment. Her flat was in an unfussy terrace but inside, it was to my eyes very welcoming as the sitting room was lined with bookshelves and filled with books new and old.

'Must remind you of being at home, Elliot,' Cameron said. 'Bit too much of the made up stuff for me.'

He meant fiction.

I rang Esther while I had a moment.

'How's it going? Cameron OK now?'

I thought of Cameron racing across Piazza Venezia like an Olympic athlete, albeit in long socks and a cheese-cloth shirt. That surely was the proof that he had recovered. What a relief he wasn't wearing those open-toed sandals, I thought. He might not have made it.

'Yes, almost fully recovered I would say.'

'I have a few moments as Aggie is here and it's quiet.'

'Oh.'

'But, it has been quite busy overall you will be pleased to hear.'

'Oh, good.'

'How was your meeting with Cantalbrini?'

'There have been further developments.'

'Oh, Elliot, why does this happen to us?' she said once I had finished describing our close escape from Cantalbrini and his accomplices.

Esther had been attacked the previous year over the theft of the Shakespeare Folio, and still sported a small scar on her face. She wanted to come straight over to help.

'I think you need looking after.'

'But we are flying home the day after tomorrow.'

'They don't want to keep you there?'

'They haven't said so.'

'I couldn't bear it if anything happened to you.'

'It won't.'

But I was touched. That is what I wanted her to say.

'We are being very sensible and taking the advice of the police.'

I explained that we were safer among all the tourists at the Vatican rather than in our apartment.

'In fact, we're staying at Laura's.'

'Lucky that you have Laura.'

'Yes. I feel bad about suspecting her.'

'How are you going to get the rest of your things?'

'There's not much to get but Laura and a couple of policemen are fetching the rest of our things for us.'

Later that evening, Laura made us *Carbonara* and a large bowl of mixed salad, accompanied by fresh crusty bread.

The plan had been to retire to bed soon after we had eaten, as we wanted to make an early start the next morning. But somehow, it did not happen that way. It may have been the excitement and danger we had been in that day, but none of us felt sleepy.

There was something I had to get off my chest. I chose the moment when Cameron went to use the toilet.

'Laura, I have to make an apology. I'm afraid when you were evasive about your meeting in the library with Mr Abruzzio...'

'Yes.'

'Well, I'm afraid I suspected you of being complicit in some way.'

'Well, I'm sorry that I was not entirely truthful. My job with libraries does involve quite a lot of investigation of stolen books. Thefts from libraries in Rome have been all too common in recent years. And there has been widespread corruption in local authorities around Rome. Some of them have been infiltrated by local Mafia style organisations. A few authorities have been taken into state control when things have got really bad. There is also a suspicion that some of the police are in the pay of organised crime.'

She sipped a glass of wine and then continued.

'When you told me about Mr Abruzzio I felt I had a duty to talk to him but I needed to tread carefully and give my evidence at the appropriate time and in the appropriate way. I did not want my testimony to be compromised. When Mr Abruzzio was killed it confirmed my worst fears. It is possible that when you asked him about the book he brought to dinner with Cantalbrini you may have inadvertently pricked his conscience.'

'And led to his death.'

'You cannot think of it like that.'

Cameron returned but she continued.

'In Italy, the prosecutor is often influenced by the local police chief. If he feels strongly about the evidence being put forward, the prosecutor will often recommend it being taken before a judge. Of course, it can work the other way...'

'That's why you were reluctant to talk about your meeting with Abruzzio.'

'I needed to pick my moment and the right person to give my testimony to. I absolutely trust Alessandro but he was not the one investigating the crime that night.'

In order to lighten the mood, I asked Cameron and Laura about their time in Manchester.

'We had some fun times,' Laura said. 'Do you remember the three legged pub crawl, Cameron?'

'Of course, how could I forget?'

'Unfortunately, he already had a girlfriend.'

'Who later became my wife.'

'But we became good friends.'

'I can see that.'

I could not imagine Laura and Cameron together so I guessed she said it in jest – though stranger things have happened. There was obviously a warm and close friendship between them. I tried to compare it with my friendship with Esther but I had to accept it was a little different.

Having had one or two drinks I was maybe a little indiscreet when I said:

'Now that I presume you have got over the heartbreak of losing Cameron, is there anyone else?'

'Well, as you can see, this apartment is a bit of a single person's set-up. I was in a long term relationship but, in the end, it failed. I'm quite happy on my own at present, but I suppose that might change one day.'

'You just have to find the right one,' said Cameron. 'The trouble is, I don't think I've come across anyone that's good enough for you.'

'You flatterer.'

'Though of course, Elliot's free.'

I coloured.

'I don't think I'm anywhere near good enough.'

'I can think of worse choices I might make.'

She gave me a warm smile.

'Besides,' I said, 'I'm in a relationship already.'

'Oh?'

Cameron gave me a questioning look.

'I'm married to my bookshop.'

'Yes, I can see that can be a full time commitment.'

I couldn't help returning to the subject of recent events.

'I think the thing that really disappoints me about this business is that I quite liked Cantalbrini - and you can't deny he is an intelligent man.'

'I know, it's difficult to accept that intelligence and honesty don't always go together,' said Laura.

'You would think that with his brains he wouldn't need to take part in a life of crime,' said Cameron.

'You were saying about more recent thefts in Italy,' I said to Laura. 'I remember there was a big one from a warehouse in the UK not so long ago. It was like *Mission Impossible* – they abseiled from the roof to get at the books.'

'Yes, I know about that – it was extraordinary. They were really valuable books including one by Copernicus worth 250 thousand Euros. I know the Carabinieri Special Unit for the Protection of Cultural Heritage was involved in the operation to catch them. I have quite close and regular contact with them.'

'Two of the bookdealers were Italian, I believe,' I said.

'The odd thing is that they are so rare it will be impossible to get rid of them. This is what a lot of these thieves don't think through. Stealing is often the easy part. It's when you try to get rid of them that the problem arises. There was one man in the USA who stole for years. He was quite clever at first because he didn't steal the most expensive books. It was when he began to get ambitious and steal more famous works that he got caught.'

'Wasn't there a big theft from a library in Naples a few years ago?' I said.

'Yes, the Girolamini Library. That was extraordinary too. A university professor turned up at the library and found it in a dreadful state – rubbish everywhere and piles of books on the floor. He wrote an article about it and criticised the director - and then started a petition for him to be removed from his post. It seemed he had gained the position at the library without being properly qualified. A lot of the books were being passed through auction houses in Germany where the law is more lax - the opposite of Italy. The trouble is, the director had access to many other libraries. We may never know how many books were really stolen.'

'I suppose it can be a great temptation.'

'For dishonest people. The problem, as I was saying before, is when the person stealing the book wants to sell it on. That is often when the theft is discovered. But it does rely on the integrity of the bookdealer. Many of them trade on their integrity but it only takes one bent dealer.'

'And you suspect Mr Cantalbrini is one of those?'

'You have to remember that nothing is yet proven – but yes, it could be someone like Cantalbrini. If you have an archivist and a bookdealer collaborating it makes it so much easier. The bookdealer pays the archivist a fee, not necessarily anywhere near the value of the book but if it is, say, a thousand Euros and the book is worth ten thousand, it is still easy money at this stage. Then the bookdealer perhaps takes it to a bookfair and sells it on at a higher price, though perhaps relatively cheaply. Maybe, a reputable dealer may pick it up thinking, perhaps unwittingly, that he or she, has got a bargain.'

'When you say "perhaps unwittingly", I get the feeling that's not always the case.'

'Well, you know, in that sort of world sometimes there are grey areas. You want to think that you are being especially clever and knowledgeable but there may be something in the back of your mind and you may be thinking this is a little too good to be true. But the further you are away from the original theft the easier it is to accept it as a legitimate sale.'

We had already downed a bottle of Prosecco and now we started on Cameron's bottle of Pecorino. We had enjoyed our bottle in the restaurant so much at the start of the holiday it had seemed like a good choice when we found some in the local supermarket.

We then talked about literature. Laura was interested in the popularity of Elizabeth Ferranti and Andre Camilleri in the UK and I told her how much I enjoyed the Italian television version of the Camilleri novels (which had been an occasional Saturday evening treat for Esther and myself). She told me about two contemporary Italian novels I should try, which she believed were available in English, *A Day in the Life of Rome* by Alberto Angela and *Timeskipper* by Stefano Benni.

We then somehow got onto Italian politics and the length of service of prime ministers and governments since the Second World War. Cameron reckoned there were only fourteen British prime ministers, one less than the number of US presidents and managed to name them all. He then went on to name all the US presidents since the war. He reckoned there were about thirty Italian prime ministers. Laura tried to name them but could only manage ten – though the wine was by now probably taking its toll on her memory faculties, as I knew it was on mine.

'In case you want to scoff, we once had a prime minister who was in power for over twenty years,' said Laura.

'Mussolini!' we both shouted.

'But, of course, he was a dictator.'

We were now on our third bottle of wine. Cameron rather unwisely drained the bottle by filling up our three glasses.

'Might as well finish it now we have opened it,' he said.

'The Holy Trinity,' I said, 'like in that Graham Greene book, *Monsieur Quixote*. Except there were only two of *them*. The communist mayor and the priest shared three bottles, so I suppose it could be worse.'

'I shouldn't have invited you guys around. I might have known you would be trouble.'

'When are you going to come and visit us in the UK, Laura?' said Cameron.

'Soon, I hope. It's ages since I've seen Rachael.'

'You have to find time to visit the bookshop.' I chipped in.

'Yes, I certainly will.'

'You can all come and stay. I have one spare bedroom and Esther or Aggie, I am sure, would be delighted to put you up.'

'I've heard you talk about Esther but who is this Aggie?'

I explained how Aggie had been at the bookshop right from the start and about the Lambretta and how it had been a part of the window competition that had led to our holiday in Italy. We chatted some more before eventually getting to sleep in the early hours of the next morning.

We woke around eight and shared coffee and fresh croissants, which Laura had picked up from the bakery at the end of her street. In fact, we were all in terrific form considering the fact that we had over-indulged the night before and the gravity of the situation: the murder in the apartment buildings, the degree of Cantalbrini's involvement and what we think may have been an attempt, if not on our lives, certainly an attempt at the very least to scare us – in addition to Cameron's self-inflicted stay in a hospital.

It was an enjoyable breakfast. While Cameron examined his maps and guides, Laura gave us some examples of what she thought it would be good to see at the Vatican. She warned us, though.

'Don't worry about all the propaganda for getting fast access and avoiding the queue. They are just trying to get more money out of you. If you get to the Vatican in good time you should be OK. And, any bit of trouble, get straight on the phone.'

36

Arriving early, as Laura had suggested, we did not have too long to wait to get into the Vatican City. We would leave the Basilica of Saint Peters, we decided, to the last.

Finally, it seemed, we had managed to pick up from where we had left off on the first two days of our holiday when we had visited the Colosseum and then, the following day, the Forum and the Palatine.

'Something tells me that a long wide street like this has to have Mussolini's hand on it somewhere,' I said to Cameron as we approached Basilica Sancti Petri along the Via della Conciliazone.

'Well, you're kind of right. It was Mussolini who started things off. A lot of this route was covered by buildings of various sorts but there had been plans since the fifteenth century to have a link between the Vatican and the city. Some of the buildings were moved. Others, including churches were destroyed, even after Mussolini died and Fascism was eradicated.'

'It sounds like you disapprove less about this than some of Mussolini's other attempts at altering things,' I said.

'Well, it does mean that more people can access the area, such as they were able to for the funeral of John Paul II, so I suppose it can't all be bad. It wasn't completed until 1950 when Mussolini had been long gone. '

'I wonder what the popes thought of it all?'

'You know, for most of the time the popes didn't live in the Vatican. They were in the Lateran Palace on the opposite side of Rome. Of course they were in Avignon for much of the fourteenth century. They came back to the Vatican and then went to the Quirinal Palace, and then in 1870, when Rome was captured, they moved back to the Vatican again. The popes were left to their own devices but much of the Church property outside was confiscated. It was not sorted until the *Lateran Treaty* in 1929 when the Vatican City Independent State was established.

'And in recent years, apart from all the recent sexual abuse scandals, the Vatican had a big problem with corruption as well. The Vatican Bank has been at the centre of scandal and corruption since it was formed in 1942. Even the Sistine Chapel Choir, the world's oldest choir is believed to be involved in a money laundering scandal.'

'Looks like Boccaccio was right all those years ago about the corruption of the Church,' I said.

When our turn came to see the Sistine Chapel, it was so busy we only had a limited time to view before being encouraged onwards. We craned our necks to see the outstretched fingers of Adam touched by God.

'He had to build his own scaffolding, you know?'

'Who did?'

'Michelangelo. Donato Bramanto was supposed to build it for him but it wasn't any good – or, at least, he didn't complete it. So the Pope told him to build it himself. He built these high wooden platforms suspended from brackets near the top of the windows.'

'I don't know how he did it – lying on his back like that.'

'Ah, well, that's a myth. There was room for him to stand and paint.'

'Oh. I'm sure I saw Charlton Heston on his back in *The Agony and the Esctasy*.'

Cameron ignored my comment.

'You know he was four years painting that ceiling. Vasari thought that Pope Julius II was encouraged to give the contract to Michelangelo by his rivals Raphael, and Bramante the architect, so that he would fail. Michelangelo was known for his sculptures of David and the *Pieta* – not as a painter. If they hoped to see him fail, though, of course they were spectacularly wrong.'

We spent a good long time looking upwards, like everyone else.

'Don't just look at the ceiling, though,' said Cameron. 'The walls are amazing too.'

We made our way over towards the altar wall to look at *The Last Judgment* showing the dead rising up to face the judgment of God. It was considered to be the masterpiece of Michelangelo's later years, Next to it was *Moses Journey into Egypt* by Perugino and Botticelli's *Punishment of the Rebels*.

'It was twenty years later that he was invited back to do the *Last Judgment*,' said Cameron.

The fresco depicts the second coming and shows Christ as a

naked, youthful, beardless, muscular figure and the Virgin Mary naked.

'That was considered by some to be sacrilegious and there was a campaign to have the fresco removed or altered,' Cameron continued. 'Michelangelo got his own back, though. Can you see Minos the God of the Underworld to the right there. It is in the likeness of Biagio da Cesana, his severest critic.'

'What are those, horse's ears?'

'I think they are meant to be donkey ears. And look what's happening below.'

'A snake biting his genitals. Very unflattering!'

'After Michelangelo's death, it was decided at the *Council of Trent* to have all the genitals covered over and Danielle de Volterra was given the task. He became known as "Il Braghettone" – the breeches maker...but the picture of da Cesana remained.'

As we were looking at the portrait, quite a crowd had gathered so that we could not get as close as we would have liked. Just then I froze, as I observed just in front of me the straight back of a well dressed man of familiar appearance. It couldn't possibly be...

'It's quite something isn't it? ' Cameron was saying.

I grabbed Cameron's arm, ready to run through the crowds of the chapel.

The man turned and looked past me. His face sported a moustache and his features were very different. I let out a sigh of relief.

'What is it?' said Cameron looking perturbed.

'Nothing,' I said. 'I thought I recognised someone. What were you saying?'

'We must give ourselves enough time to see the Raphael Rooms. People often forget that Raphael was working at the Vatican at the same time as Michelangelo – though a lot of the painting is by his assistants.'

In the Hall of Constantine we found the fresco of the *Battle of the Milvan Bridge,* depicting when Constantine triumphed over Maxentius during the civil wars of the Tetrachy. There was a dispute over the *Holy Sacrament,* representing the triumph of religion and spiritual truth. It was designed by Raphael but finished after his death in 1520 by Giulo Romano and other of Raphael's assistants. It was a striking fresco but I preferred the one opposite, *The School of Athens* which centred on the debate for truth between Plato and Aristotle. I felt I could more easily identify with this. In the painting were many of Raphael's contemporary artists, Michelangelo, da Vinci, and Pope Julius II.

In the music room were more frescoes, the most interesting being *The Fire in the Borgio* based on a supposed miracle that took place in 847 when Pope Leo IV extinguished a fire there, a part of Rome where the first pilgrims of St Peter's were housed in hostels and hospices. Greek heroes appeared again, this time Aeneas, the Trojan hero, with his father on his back fleeing from the fire.

'You know the significance of that, of course?' said Cameron.

'It may just have eluded me for a moment.'

'Aeneas is seen as an ancestor of Romulus and Remus. In the Aeneid, he survived the Trojan War and travelled to the area where Rome was later built.'

There was so much to take in and I realised that when I had visited many years before, I had only seen a fraction of what was there.

Some of the most interesting pieces for me were the Egyptian and the Greek and Roman art. There were statues lining the corridors and main courtyards. In the Chiaramonti Museum was a colossal head of the goddess Athena. I was also really impressed by the Vase Rooms. I found particularly fascinating the black figure vases from Corinth. There is one that shows Achilles and Ajax playing a game that looks like draughts.

We stayed until the very last moment, when the museum closed at six. This time, though, unlike our visit to the Palatine, we had not strayed from each other's side for a moment - except when one of us had to go to the WC. Even then, we each stayed outside the toilets on guard.

We had to decide what to do for an evening meal, our last before we returned to the UK. Should we go out somewhere or would it be better to eat at Laura's? As we could not decide I rang Laura to discuss it with her.

'I'm easy,' was her answer.

'Of course, if we go out we would like you to come along too if you have time.'

'I don't want to put you to expense on your last night.'

'Don't worry. We haven't spent too much. We have been quite frugal really due to Cameron's enforced absence.'

'In that case, why don't we go to local café just round the corner

from me. It's nothing special, just good honest plain food.'
'Sounds perfect!'

The Cafe was buzzing when we arrived and the lady who served at our table was friendly. We had a sample menu of various types of pasta, a bottle of wine and a pitcher of table water and sat outside in the evening warmth.

Not far away there was the drift of music from an open air classical music concert. It was Verdi, and I recognised what is known colloquially as the drinking song.

Here was Alfredo:

Libiamo, libiamo ne'lieti calici
che la bellezza infiora;
e la fuggevol, fuggevol ora
s'inebrii a voluttà.

'I love the sound but what does it all mean, Laura?'

'It's not easy but I will try and translate a little.'

'Alfredo has finished his opening verse. There is a short chorus and then Violetta is singing, it is quite appropriate I think: *With you I will be able to share my happy times, everything is foolish in the world that is not pleasure, let's enjoy ourselves*...then it gets a bit difficult...but this chorus bit is good: *Ah, let's enjoy the cup and the chants, the embellished nights and the laughter...*'

'The embellished nights and the laughter indeed,' said Cameron. We all clinked glasses.

The samples of pasta were so good we decided to have exactly the same again followed, by ice cream and coffee.

Laura told us that she had made a decision. She would like to come to the UK soon, to visit us but also to do some touring, perhaps over two or three weeks. She knew Manchester, of course, and had been to the Lake District and London but nowhere else in the UK.

'Where are the best places to go?' she asked.

'I love the West Country. Exmoor, Dartmoor, Somerset, Devon, Dorset and Cornwall,' I said.

'Fortunately you don't have to travel that far, said Cameron. If you go east you have Norwich, Cambridge and the glorious east coast resorts of Sheringham and Cromer.

'Sounds like you are in competition,' she said. 'Perhaps I shall do both.'

*

This time we did manage to have a relatively early night and Laura woke us at seven with coffee and rolls from the bakery.

After breakfast we packed and Cameron struggled to find room for all his books. I found room for some of them in my luggage.

And then we realised we had let the time slip by. If we did not leave in the next few moments we were in danger of missing our bus to the airport. Having had plenty of time, we now rushed around checking everything and made a hasty exit with just time for some quick hugs from Laura.

As we made our away along the concourse adjacent to the apartment we heard a shout. Up above us from a window in the flat, Laura was waving.

'Missing you already guys!'

While we were waiting for our flight there was a phone call for me from Laura.

'Alessandro spoke to Mr Abruzzio's wife. It seems that Mr Abruzzio was trying to raise some money and may well have been tempted to sell some books from the library. His daughter has been very ill. Some rare form of cancer. Apparently he was trying to pay for a new experimental treatment in the US. It's not certain whether his wife knew about it or not. Alessandro says she was in tears a lot and it was difficult to make sense of everything she said.'

'It must be difficult having lost a husband and perhaps being about to lose a daughter.'

'So it seems that Mr Abruzzio may have stolen books from the library to sell to Cantalbrini - though that is yet to be proved.'

'Poor Mr Abruzzio. He did have a haggard look about him.'

'I checked him out. He has given years of service and I can't find anything in his records to say that he was anything but hard working and respected by his colleagues.'

'What about Cantalbrini?'

'It is still too early to say but if I were to guess, I think he will play down his association with Mr Abruzzio.'

I thought of our conversation the last time I had visited Cantalbrini. He had done exactly that.

'Why *do you* think he came to see me?'

'I'm not sure. It could be he wanted you to not deal with Cantalbrini or perhaps he wanted to make a confession. He may even have wanted to sell some books on to you – but somehow I think that's unlikely. Whatever it was, it was seen as a threat by Cantalbrini or whoever was responsible. We may never know.'

As I sat on the plane in the skies above Rome, at the beginning of our return journey, I reflected on how differently things had turned out from what I had expected when I was sitting on the runway waiting to take off from the tarmac in the UK. I had been looking forward to an innocent holiday of good food, wine and historic sightseeing. I could never have guessed the fatal consequences of that meeting in the restaurant on our first evening.

As usual, I reached for a book in my rucksack to accompany me on my journey. I had just started a new book by Elena Ferrante. Despite the trials and tribulations of our vacation this time around, I knew that I wanted to return before too long and was keen to extend my knowledge of Italian literature with some more modern Italian writers.

Just as I was about to start my book, Cameron tapped me on the shoulder across the aisle.

'Sure you don't want to read these? I packed them in my bag when we were rushing to get away to the airport. They should have been in your bag really.'

They were the two volumes of *Lyrical Ballads*, given to me by Cantalbrini.

'I meant to leave them with Laura.' I took them from him. 'I don't think, in conscience, I can keep them. I was hoping they could be a donation to the library.'

They must have been in the bag with Cameron's other books which Alessandro had collected - and remained unnoticed until now.

I opened the first one and read the title page and the inscription *Quam nihil ad genium, Papiniane, tuum. (Something not at all to your taste).*

I would have to decide what to do when I got back to the UK. I wondered whether I should even send the two volumes back to Cantalbrini. Perhaps by doing so I would be making a statement that I was relieved from my vow of silence. But there was a good chance that they had been stolen. When I got back to the UK I would consult with Laura and Alessandro to see if they were on a list of missing books and, if so, I could make arrangements to return them to their rightful place.

Just before departure, I had rung Esther to tell her I was on my way. She said how much she had missed me in the shop. Next time, she said, she would have to go on holiday with me as she could not trust me and Cameron together. I am not sure how firm a commitment this was, but I liked the sentiments...

Acknowledgements

Acknowledgements are due to Jo, my wife and my first port of call when I have finished my first draft. She sets me straight on all my plot inconsistencies. Thanks also to my sister Vivienne with all her proof reading skills and other helpful suggestions. My daughter, Lucy, designed the cover. I have been lucky enough to travel to Rome in recent years and had the book in mind on my most recent visit. I found the Eyewitness Guide to Rome valuable back-up as well as the numerous histories on the subject, especially those of Mary Beard. It is, of course, though, mostly made-up and I may have taken a few liberties with location.